FALLEN LEGEND

EMMANUELLE

USA TODAY BESTSELLING AUTHOR

SNOW

Smart Lily
Publishing

#1
Dad
SAM STEVENS >>>>
ECHOES WORLD TOUR
FEBRUARY 16
THURSDAY
8:00PM
SEATTLE, WA
SAM STEVE

Fallen Legend
Emmanuelle Snow

First edition - January 2023 (V_1) - 2025 update

ISBN eBook: 978-1-990429-77-4

ISBN paperback: 978-1-990429-78-1

This book is part one of the Lonesome Heart duet.

Editors: Shalini G. and SLE

Cover: SMART Lily publishing inc.

Published by SMART Lily Publishing inc.

————

Emmanuelle Snow
emmanuellesnow.com

CARTER HILLS BAND UNIVERSE
(SUGGESTED READING ORDER)

Carter Hills Band series
False Promises

HEART SONG DUET
Blindsided
Forevermore

Whiskey Melody series
Sweet Agony

SECOND TEAR DUET
Cruel Destiny
Beautiful Salvation

BREATHLESS DUET
Wild Encounter
Brittle Scars

Upon A Star series
Last Hope

Midnight Sparks

Love Song For Two series
LONESOME HEART DUET
Fallen Legend
Rising Star

TWO OF US DUET
Snowbound

Wicked Love

All titles available at
emmanuellesnow.com

For the best experience, read in the order as shown above

TRIGGER WARNINGS

Disclaimer

My books are realistic and emotional love stories.

I'm an advocate for mental health, and some topics could be sensitive for certain readers since they are portrayed as close to real life as possible.

I've listed the potential trigger warnings for each title on my website.

Be advised that those trigger warnings could potentially be spoiler alerts for the storylines.

Those sensitive topics have been written with the utmost care and respect. Please reach out if you have questions or comments.

All books contain sexuality, mature content, and language
not intended for people under 18 years of age.
For other readers' sake, please avoid spoilers in your
reviews.

Thank you and have a wonderful day!

Emmanuelle

emmanuellesnow.com

To life
A few times you've given me a
shitty hand to deal with.
But now that the sun shines brighter,
I can thank you,
Because I wouldn't be here today
if you hadn't shown me,
How strong and resilient I could be.
I'm sorry it took me a long time
to understand the lesson.
But now I'm finally happy to be
where I'm supposed to be,
And I'm grateful for the bumps
you put in my road.

BECOME A VIP
TO NEVER MISS A THING

Snow's VIP

Join **Emmanuelle Snow's VIP newsletter**

Be the first to know about new releases, giveaways, sales, and special events. And step into a space where big emotions are celebrated, love is messy and beautiful, and stories linger long after the last page.

emmanuellesnow.com

Snow's Soulmates

Join Emmanuelle Snow's Facebook VIP group, **Snow's Soulmates**, to chat with her and other readers, get updates, and more bonus content.

facebook.com/groups/snowvip

KISSED BY AN ANGEL
THE SONG

I've been turned to stone long ago
I can't feel the sun warming my skin
I can't feel the raindrops on my face
I'm numb. So numb.
My heart is locked up in a cage
No one is allowed inside
I've been hurting bad. So bad
It still haunts my dreams
I don't know days from nights
    anymore
I am just being alive right now
I have forgotten how to live

[CHORUS]

The sight of you jolts my heart back
    to life
Your smile thaws every layer of ice I
    hide behind
Your touch soothes my sorrows

It heals my pain
Your lips taste like freedom
Your skin feels like passion
Let me love you, girl
Let me shine in your light
Let me breathe in your air
With you, I'm living again
With you, I'm myself again

Hope has made its way to my heart
Now I can see the colors around me
Now I can smell the lilac flowers
And hear the birds chirping in the
    trees
I'm a mere country boy
And you're an angel from the sky
Please shower me with your light
Please let me love you tonight

[CHORUS]
I've been broken and sad
Until there was no place to hide
I bled until I died
A million times

I stepped back
Not ready to open my heart to you
There were too many things
Pushing us apart
Too many winters
Icing our hearts
But spring came this year
And shattered the ice around my
    frozen heart

Now summer is here, melting the
    last restraints
Leaving my heart raw and exposed
Filling it with renewed hope
Ready for you to make it yours
Ready for you to love and kiss me

[CHORUS]
I'm ready to fight for you
Ready to fight for us
There're no more clouds shadowing
    us from above
Nothing stands in our way anymore
I'm a country boy
And you're an angel
Please shower me with your light
Please let me love you tonight

And kiss me
I crave the kiss of an angel
Of an angel
A kiss from my angel

Music and lyrics by Sam Stevens

Chapter 1
Sam

Fisting my hands at my sides, I paced the room, a ball of lightning bouncing around in my chest. This was a nightmare. A disaster about to happen. How had I not seen this one coming? How could I have been so blind?

My nails dug trenches into my palms, drawing pinpricks of blood, but I would keep my composure. I had to.

The lump in my larynx rubbed against the chaffed walls of my throat.

I reeled in some of my wrath and tried another approach. My voice came out a ragged whisper, but calmer this time, as I put my pride to rest and urged my sanity to stay in the game. "Lisa, you can't be serious. Listen, there must be something *I* can do. Can we talk about it first? And what about the kids? How am I going to explain any of this to them? We'll get help... You can't just leave like this."

No emotions—rather not the ones I wished to see—crossed her hardened features. No *I'm having second thoughts.* Or *you might be right, we'll get help.*

My wife had turned to stone, unmoving and unreadable.

Hoping the pain would numb the one ripping my chest in two, I tugged at the roots of my hair. How could I have been so clueless about the woman I'd been married to for the last four years?

She pushed another shirt into her bag, ignoring my words.

Maybe I could reach out to the mother inside her. "Lisa, your leaving will fuck them up for the rest of their lives. Abandoning your own children, really? That's not what motherhood is all about." I halted and turned around to face the woman, who I thought I knew so well, zipping up her royal-blue suitcase. The one that had traveled around the world with us for years. Yeah, what a joke.

She finally raised her gaze, and I saw determination pass through her eyes this time. She wasn't doubting her decision to walk away from us, her family.

I studied her for a long minute, wishing I could see tears glistening somewhere in them, or regret marring her features. But there were none.

She was done.

When did my wife harbor a rock in place of her heart?

"Is it about the miscarriages?" I asked, praying she'd say yes and that I could call her doctor and set up an appointment to discuss her psychological distress. "I know how difficult it's been on you, but it's been hard on me too. We can get through this. Together. We're a good team. We love each other."

She sighed and shook her head, her eyes still showing no sign of hurt or sadness. Or anything. "That's the thing, Sam. I don't love you. I did. Once. But both miscarriages were eye-opening. I need to find myself. I'm twenty-eight. For the last six years, I've followed you around the globe. I liked that. For the last four, I've played wife and mommy. And I enjoyed it…at some point. Being a parent is your thing. We had babies because you wanted to be a daddy… I never asked to be a mother. In all honesty, I thought it'd grow on me…" She shrugged. "But it didn't. I crave fresh air. To be free to do whatever I want. Whenever I want it. And being a parent isn't just what I hoped it would be. I'm sorry, but I'm over it."

I blinked. What? Was she serious right now? *She's over it?*

I was having one of those crippling nightmares that felt too much like reality. This was it. No woman in her right mind would say such horrible things about her own children. About her family.

Her flesh.

Her blood.

My Adam's apple bobbed, and bile rose in my throat, tinted with disgust and disdain.

My wife was delusional.

Who should I call to get her some help?

Could her state of mind be ruled a mental breakdown? Did she need to see a psychiatrist? Or go on a vacation? No matter what I told myself, she looked sane.

Lisa smiled at me as if quitting on us was just a daily occurrence and not something about to wreck our entire world.

My shoulders fell, and so did my heart. I inched closer when she moved to her feet. "Can we talk about this? Please. You at least owe me that. We've been through so much together. Did you forget everything?" I asked, forcing my voice to sound even and trying my best to keep my anger under wraps.

She offered me another twist of her lips. This time, she looked diabolical. Who was this woman? Where did my wife go? "I owe you nothing, Sammy. The ride has been fun, but I'm not playing this family game anymore. I'm out. Oh, and I'll send you the divorce papers in a week or two."

My eyes sprang wider.

What the actual fuck?

"Divorce papers? Don't you think it's a little early to talk about divorce? We haven't even fought about anything serious in the past, and now you're talking about dissolving our marriage. Tell me you're kidding. Where are the cameras? The crew? Is it for a celebrity prank TV show?"

My wife—or soon-to-be ex-wife if she had her way—huffed, as if anything I said sounded childish. Asking her to stay seemed to get on her nerves.

"C'mon, Sammy. I'm moving to the other side of the world. I won't return. Ever. Come to terms with it. Nothing you do or say will change anything." She sighed again and shook her head, looking desperate. "I. Am. Not. Coming. Back. Ever. This"—she pointed around the room with her finger—"is over. You and I, we're done." A car honked outside. "Now move, my cab is waiting." She pushed past me, rolling her suitcase behind her.

I stood there, frozen. None of this made sense. The dream had lasted long enough. I could wake up now. *Please, someone, make this nightmare go away.*

My heart stuttered, and the sound of little feet padding near our bedroom snapped me back to the present. I spun around and watched Lisa as she stood in the doorway, a mask of annoyance painting her frigid face.

My heart froze. Ice frosted the blood inside my veins, and I held my breath.

Mikaella, our four-year-old, ran our way in her one-piece unicorn white PJs, her wild, curly light-brown hair looking like a bird's nest, a fluffy baby-pink blanket hanging from her tiny hand.

She stopped before Lisa, her round golden eyes traveling from her mama to the suitcase beside her. "Going on a trip, Mama?" Sparks shone in our daughter's eyes, and she lifted a finger. "I love going on the plane. *Nneeeaowww,*" she said, her hand imitating the aircraft. "The ladies always gimme chocolate. Justine *lovvvves* chocolate too. She always eats mine. Can I bring Miss Froggy with me? She's never been on a plane. She wanna come. You said she could come next time. You promised."

Lisa looked at our daughter, her gaze empty and back held taut. I prayed to see an emotion crossing her flat gaze. None made an appearance.

Mikaella tugged at her hand. "Mama, can I pack by myself? I'm a big girl. Can I bring my purple dress? And my ballet shoes? Can Boa the raccoon come too? And Holly? She always misses me when I'm gone. She hates being a doll. She wants to be a real baby…or a lady. And drink tea."

Lisa finally said something. My ears scorched the moment the words left her mouth. "Mama is going on a trip by herself, Mika. To Thailand. You can't come, I wanna be alone."

Tears pooled in our baby's eyes. She tugged at her mother's hand once again. "But I wanna come. Justine wants to come too. She'll be sad if you leave without her. Mama, we'll be good, good girls. And be silent if your head hurts."

Lisa ruffled her hair. "Sorry. You're not coming. I gotta

go. Be nice to your daddy. And take care of Justine. Can you be a big girl, Mika?"

Our daughter nodded, a wide smile now brightening her sweet face. Lisa ignored her and stalked away when the cab honked a second time. My heart sank deeper in my chest at the sight of my wife walking away from our baby girl.

Once at the top of the staircase, she pivoted to face me. "Bye, Sammy. Have a good life." She removed her wedding ring and placed it on the banister.

My heart tumbled down my chest until it hit the hardwood floor. Smashed and bleeding.

I stood there, acid filling my throat and dissolving the words I wanted to speak.

Mikaella's sobs brought me back to her. "She didn't kiss me goodbye. Mama. *Mammma*. Come back. I'll be a good girl."

I rushed to my daughter and lifted her in my arms, both of us needing each other's love and affection now more than ever.

I brushed her hair with my fingers, dried her tears, and hugged her closer so my heart could soothe hers. Because I had no clue how to heal her pain with words.

I followed Lisa down the stairs. My eyes zoomed in on the front door. My head pounded, and my chest cavity filled with piling rocks as the sound of the revving engine outside faded away. What had just happened?

Two hours ago, everything was fine. Or I thought it was. We bathed the girls, read stories in bed... Where did it go wrong?

My stomach heaved. Lisa left. She fucking left.

"Shhh, sweet pea. It'll be okay. We'll be okay... I'm here..."

In that instant, I didn't even believe my own words.

I fished my phone out of my back pocket to call my wife. We needed to talk—before she left for good. Before she regretted any of it. Before it was too late to fix that rift keeping us apart.

Beep. Beep. Beep.

The last thread of hope holding me together burned to ashes.

Chills lined my back.

Lisa had disconnected her number.

Reality hit me. It wasn't a prank or a spur-of-the-moment decision. It was premeditated.

How long had she been planning her escape?

How long ago had she decided the girls and I were inconveniences in her life?

Oxygen could barely make the journey from my lungs to my brain anymore.

My wife had vanished in the night without giving me any kind of explanation. Or a way to reach her.

I buried my face in the crook of Mikaella's neck, hiding my numbing emotions from her.

My head spun. A weight I'd never carried before grew in my chest, crushing my organs. How would I ever be able to tell my baby girls their mama had ditched them for a reason I still didn't get?

The last fragment of my heart broke free as my baby's sobs doubled, now heart-wrenching, coming from some place deep down her little body, her sadness drenching my shirt. "I want Mama. I love the plane. She didn't kiss me. I want a hug…from her."

My eyes glazed over.

My little girl tilted her head back and stared at me, her lower lip trembling and her face a map of confusion and sorrow.

She cupped my cheeks with her hands and blinked.

"Daddy, why are you crying? Do you miss Mama too? Did she forget to kiss you goodnight?" She wrapped her baby arms around my neck and fastened her hug around me. "Don't cry, Daddy. I'm here. I love you. Don't cry, okay?"

I pulled my daughter against my heart. "I love you too, sweet pea. I'm not going away. Ever. You hear me, Mika? I'll never leave you. I promise."

We held onto each other until she relaxed in my embrace, and sleep claimed her.

I tucked my daughter in, doing my best to avoid waking up Justine, my two-year-old, sleeping in the adjacent bed. In one corner of their bedroom, sitting in a rocking chair, I watched my children fast asleep, their steady breathing acting like a bandage around my hemorrhaging heart.

With a slow look around, I took in the pastel-pink walls, the glittery matching unicorn bedspreads, the dolls sitting around a small wooden white table with tiny porcelain teacups in front of them, the net with over twenty stuffed-animals hanging across the ceiling, the fairy lights casting a golden glow wrapped around the princess-inspired headboards.

Would we ever be okay again?

My eyes landed on the family picture framed on the wall we had taken last Christmas.

Our smiles looked so genuine.

I studied Lisa. Was she faking being happy the entire time?

I slouched forward, my face landing in my hands, my shoulders heaving as sobs rocked my body.

The fresh wound ripping my chest in two widened. How did I go from having a picture-perfect family at dinner time to being a single dad mere hours later?

How did I not see my world crumbling? There must

have been signs leading to this moment. How did I miss all of them? How could I have been so blind?

That's the thing, Sam. I don't love you. I did. Once.

My life was built on a lie. It was a fucking illusion.

Lisa had faded into the night like she had never existed.

That was when the truth hit me, like a ton of bricks weighing on my fractured heart. I was on my own and had no one to connect to on this journey.

My daughters had become motherless. Not because their mama had died, but because she chose to leave them behind.

Not because she was incapacitated, but because she couldn't love them the way they deserved to be loved.

I cupped my thundering organ with both hands. Every cell in me hurt as the truth of my new reality, *our* new realities, crashed on me and settled in my soul.

My girls' lives would never be the same.

My life would never be the same.

Tonight, I'd lost not only the mother of my children, but also the woman I loved. The one I'd been sharing the last few years of my life with. The one I had traveled the world with, went through great moments of joy and hardships with. The one I had promised forever to. The one who'd said in front of our dearest friends and family I was her only true love.

I perused the bedroom for the final time, my eyes locking on my babies fast asleep.

They had no idea that by the morning, nothing would ever be the same.

That the light of a new day would carry a truckload of sorrow in its wake.

How would I ever be able to do this on my own? Be a single dad.

How would I ever be able to explain the harsh truth to my girls without shattering their hearts in the process?

Closing my eyes, I let darkness descend upon me because right now, I had no clue how to do this by myself and survive the heartbreak at the same time.

Chapter 2
Sam

Two years later

"I'm not wearing this." Mikaella folded her arms over her chest, giving me some not-so-welcome morning attitude. "Daddy, you have a horrible taste in clothes. I'm too old to wear pink and ribbons." She huffed, and I oscillated between laughing at my life and wanting to kill myself.

Raising two daughters on my own had proven to be a greater challenge than I'd ever expected.

Two years later and we were still dealing with the aftermath of Lisa's departure. The weight of anger I'd nursed for the longest time had receded, but I still found it hard to juggle all the responsibilities on my own.

For a full year, I never had time to heal my own heart, too busy trying to patch every hole in Justine and Mikaella's lives, wishing every night before falling asleep that their mother's abandonment wouldn't screw them up in the long run.

Playing mommy and daddy had been hard, and it had taken its toll on me. Both physically and psychologically.

I never hit the gym anymore and barely ever took an evening off or hung out with grown-ups.

For the first few months after Lisa had walked away, I even forgot to shave or shower most days. I lived in a state of detachment. Going through the motions, staring at the front door, expecting her to walk in, smile, and say it was all a big misunderstanding and that she was back. For good. Something that never occurred.

Then things got a bit better. We found our rhythm. After I had gone through every stage of grief until I fostered no more hatred for the woman I had been married to. Until I was kinda content with my life. And my kids were thriving…for the most part.

These days, I often went to bed in stained clothes or dozed off while watching the credits of yet another princess movie rolling across the screen. But it was a small price to pay after what we had endured.

My kids had become my anchor, my reason to live. The reason I woke up every morning and refused to give up.

Not wanting them to suffer because of their mother's absence, I refused to be away from them—except when they were at school. I had the conviction that if I were around, they wouldn't fear I would leave them and never return.

During weekdays, I did grocery shopping and laundry, cooked and cleaned the house so my weekends were free of chores or any distractions, and I could be just a father, fully involved in my kids' lives. I also squeezed in about thirty hours of work per week at the hardware store belonging to my uncle not far from here.

It kept me sane. A real job. Forcing me to focus on something other than my ruined career and lack of personal life. Faking I'd turned into some sort of social creature. If I believed it strongly enough, perhaps one day it would become true.

After Lisa had left, my parents had come over every weekend to help me out—and to pick up the scattered pieces of me. But since they moved to Florida eighteen months ago, trying to enjoy their new semi-retired lives, I'd been doing everything on my own. Working a full-time job while raising kids all by myself was exhausting.

Rewarding, but tiring.

In the process, I had ditched my own career. At first, it was supposed to be a six-month hiatus until I wrapped my head around being a single dad. But six months became a year that bled into two. Anyway, working at the hardware store provided regular hours and stability that a career in the limelight never would. Not that I needed the money so bad, but the store had become my little sanctuary over the years. Nothing there reminded me of Lisa. Her ghost didn't haunt me with painful memories of a previous life while I was there. A more-than-vital reprieve since everything at home brought back recollections of the life we once shared, the four of us together.

Over the last year, I had removed most signs of her from the walls and replaced them with new memories we were creating along the way.

Lisa had left with not only a piece of my heart that night, but also my dreams. She disappeared, taking the husband in me and leaving behind nothing but a father—and some hollow shell of who I used to be. Sure, I loved being a daddy. These little girls were parts of my soul and owned every chunk of my battered heart. But I missed being a man too.

Some days, I missed my wife. I missed the idea of her. Of us. Of what we had been for years—companionship, and maybe love. I wasn't even clear on the specifics yet... I just missed being a family.

How many times did I have to drill into myself that Lisa fucking abandoned us to believe it?

I sighed. Too many to recount.

Until every part of me gave up those slivers of hope and finally came to terms with the fact a year ago. One day, the weight pressing on my shoulders dissolved and set me free.

Returning my focus to my daughter, I lifted my hands in surrender. "Fine. You know what, sweet pea? Wear the black skirt and a black top if it makes you happy. I'm sorry I forgot you were six, and old enough to pick up your own outfit."

Mikaella tipped her hip and frowned, her arms still folded over her chest, before sighing and storming to her room.

My sweet girl had turned sixteen the day she realized her mother wouldn't be coming back.

She had transformed into an opinionated six-year-old teenager who only dressed in dark colors. Only laughed on rare occasions. Enjoyed confrontations. And some days, preferred shade to shiny lights around her.

Lisa had stolen her smile the night she bailed out on us —along with her innocence.

I missed my daughter. I missed her bubbly side. Her *it will be okay Daddy* enthusiasm and her hugs.

Two years later and she still cried herself to sleep sometimes and kept high hopes Lisa would return.

Her therapist told me not to worry, but clouds regularly invaded my little girl's eyes, and darkness swirled around her more often than not. I lacked ideas on how to bring the sunshine back into her days. God knew I'd been trying. Hard. So far, I'd been hitting a wall. Every single time.

On the worst days, her temper could erode every string of patience I still possessed. On the best days, she'd battle with me for everything. From the food on her plate to the color of her nightgown or the music I played in the car.

Overwhelmed, I could barely hold it together myself. How was I supposed to deal with a moody child always at war with anything I said or did? One who challenged every decision I made? She treated me as her enemy most days, and I couldn't help but wonder if she blamed me for Lisa abandoning her.

Justine, now four, was the antipode of her sister. She sparkled and brightened every corner of my dark existence. Nothing seemed to bother her, as if her role in life was to bring peace and calm to those around her.

My baby girl had only scarce memories of her mother, which I was sure helped her neither resent me nor be swallowed by the pain of what used to be. Sure, Lisa's absence wasn't easy on her, but her wounds weren't as visible as her older sister's. She rarely talked about her mama anymore. Justine seemed content to have a daddy wrapped around her little finger. I knew one day she'd ask questions, and I already dreaded the moment we'd have a heart-to-heart that might unearth the scars she had no idea were there, carefully tucked away for now.

Just thinking about all this sent my heart into a frenzied mess.

"Come on, girls, we must go. You don't wanna be late for school."

Justine traipsed my way, her contagious grin lighting up the few slices of my heart still alive.

I lifted her into my arms and kissed the tip of her nose.

"Baby, you look pretty today," I said as I carried her to my white SUV.

Her smile widened. Her blonde pigtails—the ones I had to learn to make—bounced at her sides as she made some sort of dance move with her head.

"Mika is mad at you, Daddy." I leaned forward, studying her to learn more. "She said it's stupid you don't want her to dye her hair black."

I pinched my lips together to avoid smiling. This was a debate Mikaella and I had been having for three weeks now. "I know, Justine. But little girls aren't allowed to dye their hair. It's a grown-up thing. We'll talk about it when Mika is much, much older."

"Like an *adulst?*"

"Adult, baby. But yes. Don't worry, she'll get over it."

Justine shrugged. "She also says she'll *slave* her head to prove her point." She snickered, and I rolled my eyes. Great. Damn perfect. My six-year-old teen now wanted a bald head.

I swore I'd aged twenty years in the last two.

"It's shave. Not slave. Shave her head. And no, Mika won't do anything to her hair."

I buckled my youngest daughter in her car seat just in time to witness Mikaella walking toward us, now dressed in all-black, her hair tied into a ponytail, and wait—? What the hell had she put on her eyes? Makeup? No, there was none in the house. She stopped inches away from me, her chin tipped up, daring me to object, a frown darkening her visage. Resting her fists on her waist, she tapped her foot with growing impatience. "What?"

For a second, I closed my eyes and inhaled, trying to calm the raging storm building inside me.

Swallowing my imminent burst of anger, I squatted in front of my daughter, doing my best to keep calm.

I reached for her hands, but she jerked them away, so I rested my palms on my knees instead. "Honey, tell me. What did you do to your eyelids?"

Mikaella muttered something I didn't quite catch and cocked her head to the side with a pout.

"Sweet pea, I need to know what you used to draw those black lines. It looks…huh…interesting. I'm not mad, okay?" *No, I'm fucking dumbfounded. And tired. And I have no clue what I'm doing.* "You should never use whatever you used on your face without checking with me first. It could be harmful."

I inched closer and grabbed her upper arms. She flinched under my touch but didn't step back. Another fragment of my heart crashed and burned. My baby was hurting.

"Mika, tell me. Is it a marker? Paint? Or something else?"

She bit her lower lip, and her eyes glistened, but she remained silent.

"Look at me, sweet pea. I'm not angry. I'm concerned. Because I love you."

Could she give me a break? Just one morning of reprieve?

After a long minute, she relaxed and met my gaze before dropping her eyes to the ground. "It-it's the marker you use to label boxes. I…I saw a girl doing it in a video the other day at Stella's. I just wanted…I just wanted to try. I know I'm not allowed to wear makeup, but Stella's mama lets her borrow hers. I-I don't have anyone to try it with—" Her lip quivered, and her eyes filled with fat tears.

My chest cracked in two. "Oh, Mika. It's okay, sweet pea. I'm here. I'm so sorry about your mama. I wish she were here too. I know it's been hard on you, but I *am* not going anywhere. You can talk to me. Always. Maybe we could buy some makeup and try it together. You could paint my face, and we'd be rock stars. Or maybe we could ask Stella's mama to show you how to apply it. No, you can't wear makeup every day, but it doesn't mean we can't put it on for fun or on special days. What do you think?"

Her eyes flared, and a hint of a smile graced her lips. "You sure?"

I nodded.

"I…I'd like that."

I blanketed my daughter in my arms, the visceral need to protect and infuse her with infinite love running deep. "I love you, sweet pea. Now let's try to remove this marker from your eyelids, okay?"

She nodded. "I love you too, Daddy." Her little arms closed around my neck, and for a moment, I felt like we were back to being the father-daughter duo we used to be. Before the earthquake that had shattered our lives. Before the heartbreaks. Before everything had gone to shit that night.

I rose to my feet and held out my hand for her to take. "Come on, Justine. Let's get you out of your seat. We're on a mission to help your sister."

With both my girls at my sides, we made our way inside, not a care in the world if they'd miss school today or that I would have to call in sick.

We needed this. To connect. The three of us.

Our makeup removal session didn't go as well as planned, and the marker on Mikaella's eyelids was still apparent, even after a few attempts to remove it with a warm cloth and some soap.

We all changed back into pajamas, built a castle with blankets in the den, and spent the day binge-watching TV and eating nothing but pizza and ice cream, not caring about food groups and nap time.

I loved our home. Maple hardwood floors, off-white walls, nine-foot-tall ceilings, black trims and doors. It was a Scandinavian-inspired farmhouse. A mix of light and dark decor accents, sleek lines, and soft-colored wood.

The exterior, made of steel-blue clapboard siding, gave the place a rustic and cozy charm. While the front and two carriage-house garage doors were made of natural wood and had been handcrafted by a local artisan.

These days, the den had become our favorite room. The place where the girls could let their imaginations run wild. An arts and crafts station was set in one corner next to a tan leather couch buried under fluffy colorful blankets and half a dozen pillows. An oversized rectangular black rug occupied most of the flooring area, and a comfy armchair facing the stone fireplace completed the decor.

We had redecorated the space last year—erasing all traces of Lisa and making the room fully ours—and I felt at peace here. When we spent time here, the ghosts of the past had no hold over us.

Around seven, both girls were fast asleep in our castle, passed out from a junk food coma.

My phone went off, and I tiptoed out of the room to avoid waking them up.

For the first time in months, my daughters and I had fun together—for more than just a few hours. The three of us, without any drama or interruption. We laughed. We cried when the dog in the movie ran away from home. We sang along with the princess when she swept the floor with her animal friends. We cuddled on the couch.

Yeah, it was a great day. A perfect day.

The face of Riley Burns, country music manager extraordinaire and mogul in his own right, flashed on my phone screen.

"Hey, Stevens. How is it going? Still holding the fort by yourself?"

"Hey, man. It's been a while. Yeah. Trying hard at least. Not sure if the fort is sturdy, though. Some days, I think it could fall apart with just one blow our way. Anyway, it's not like I have a choice. What's going on? You miss me already? How was the tour?" I said, trying to put some spirit into my words.

The truth was that I missed him even more than Riley could miss me. We'd been friends for years, both of us running in the same circles.

When everyone had deserted me because I preferred loneliness to their look of pity, he'd stayed by my side. Even though, for a while, I tried to keep him at arm's length like everyone else, he just persevered. Now I was grateful that he did.

After the first year, when I showed no sign of going back onstage or booking studio time for the album I was set to record, my label had dropped me. The awards I'd won, the double-platinum albums I'd sold, the stadiums I'd filled didn't seem to matter to them anymore.

At first, I didn't care. My days were full, and I couldn't envision embarking on a world tour ever again or living my life the same way I had in the past.

Now, every day, I missed it a little more. The crowd. The adrenaline of singing in front of tens of thousands of fans. Writing songs. Playing music. It all seemed like they belonged to a previous life. To another version of me that I'd lost touch with.

My country music career didn't work with my full-time daddy lifestyle, and I had chosen my daughters over my own dreams. No regrets.

Dwelling on the past would do me no good. Anyway, I was happy—or at least getting there.

Far down in my chest, a spark refused to die. Maybe one day I'd go back there again. Once the girls were old enough. A stubborn part of me refused to give up hope in the future.

"I'm like ten minutes away from your place. Can I come over?"

My eyes traveled all over the space around me. Stuffed animals, toys, princess costumes, empty pizza boxes. It looked like someone had thrown a rager here and had forgotten to clean up after themselves. Well, we sorta did to be honest.

"I…hmm…" Why not? I missed the company. Having a friend over would get me out of my head for a couple of hours. It was about time I started socializing with more grown-ups again. My mental health begged for this too. We were both struggling. With my phone squeezed between my ear and shoulder, I put away the remnants of our day. "Sure. Can I ask you something, though?"

"Anything."

"Can you bring beer over? I have none here, and I'm dying for a cold brew tonight."

"Don't say another word. I have you covered. I'll see you in a bit." He exhaled a huge breath as if he'd been waiting anxiously for my answer. "Stevens, I'm glad we're doing this. Spending time together."

"Me too."

The last time we saw each other was about five months ago. Riley had been busy with Aisha Jones's tour, his latest protégée, and gone to Europe and Asia on and off, following her around for months, making sure everything ran smoothly. He only came to town for days at a time to deal with stuff at the office and be with his ladylove. With our busy schedules, we never found time to meet.

We hung up, and I rushed to my room to change into a

pair of dark jeans and a simple black T-shirt. In the mirror of the en-suite bathroom, I combed my dark hair with my fingers and ran a hand over my stubble. In the last two years, I had slackened on my shaving routine. Lisa loved me clean-shaven. In a way, wearing a scruffy jaw was my way of enjoying the freedom to do things my way, without compromise. A big "fuck you" to her preferences about my look. A reality it took me a while to realize. I attempted to tame my mane one last time and gave up. This would have to do. Not that I had to impress my friend, but greeting him in pajama pants was a big no-no. Even for me. At least, now I looked decent.

Downstairs, I filled the dishwasher and carried the girls to their bedroom, praying they would stay asleep for the rest of the night.

The doorbell rang as I closed their door after turning a night-light on.

I couldn't remember the last time I had friends over. We usually met at barbecues or the park whenever they were in town.

Nowadays, most of my guests were under ten and either lived down the street or came from Mikaella's class or Justine's dance lessons.

———

Riley handed me a bottle of beer once we sat in loungers on the back deck. The night was warm, the sky painted in pink and orange stripes. Summer was a month away, and already I could feel it in the warm breeze sweeping across our faces and the moisture thickening the air.

I sighed as I enjoyed the calm and peace surrounding me.

From the corner of my eye, I scanned the yard. We had

no back neighbors, only acres of woods the kids loved to explore. Last year, with a little help from my father, I had built a castle treehouse for them to play in, that we had painted a vibrant hue of bubble-gum pink. It was the girls' corner in this world that only belonged to them, where they could be children and forget about everything else for a moment as they transformed into princesses.

Riley and I clinked our bottles, and I enjoyed the coldness of the brew as it slid down my throat. It'd been so long since the last time I had a drink—an adult drink.

"So, Ry? Are you going to tell me what brings you here? It's been months since you parked your ass in one of those chairs," I said with an arched brow.

"The tour had been consuming but overall amazing, but I'm glad to be home. Back at the office. I'll miss the adventure in no time, but for now, it's good to sleep in my own bed and see my woman every day." He shook his head, a tiny smile tugging at the corner of his lips. "Let's just say I'm not sure you're ready to hear what I have to tell you."

"Try me. Hurry before I start talking about dolls or playdates. Man, if only you had kids. We could schedule daddy-and-me afternoons together. Learn new ways to braid hair or apply French manicures. Such a shame."

Riley laughed, and I joined in.

More steel coils relaxed around my heart.

I felt better today than I'd felt in a long time. As if the ripples of everything that happened in the last two years were wearing off, and for once, I could just enjoy the ride without worrying about everything else. Or the future.

My friend set his bottle down on the wooden table between us and turned around to face me, his elbows propped on his knees and his hands joined together. "Listen, man. I know Lisa walking away fractured your world.

And I know how hard it's been. I've witnessed the change in you from day one. I also know being a father is your top priority and the most important job you'll ever have…but there's more to life than playing daddy twenty-four-seven, all year-round. You must thrive in life. And I know you're miserable, Sam. I—"

"She fucking quit on us. Without a warning. What was I supposed to do? Tour the world one stadium at a time with toddlers as if nothing happened? With no one to watch over them or tuck them in bed? Fuck their lives by taking them to a different hotel every night, by removing them from their home, the only stability they had left?"

"Tell me. Did becoming a boring version of yourself really solve all your problems?"

"Whatever you wanna think. I'm happy just being a regular father to my girls, Ry. They never asked for their dad to be chased by groupies or splashed across every gossip magazine because he got caught in fame when all he ever wanted was to get on a stage and play music for a living. Why can't you see that? You were the kid with the famous-as-hell dad growing up. You told me multiple times it wasn't easy when he left on tour, whether you and your mother followed him around or not. If there's one person who should get it, it's you."

Riley raised his hands. "Let me finish. I know it wasn't what you had planned. Those little girls will never be able to accuse you of not taking over when their mama walked out on them. But wouldn't you all be happier if you were happy too?"

I shrugged. "I'm not unhappy."

"But are you happy?"

"Yes. No. That's not the point. How should I know? I've forgotten what my life before this"—I motioned to my house with a wave of my hand—"felt like. Now I'm exhausted all the time. And Mika is giving me a hard time. She struggles. It's bad, man. It breaks my heart. I have no clue how to help her. This is so fucked-up." I dragged a hand over my face, trying to control the emotions swirling inside me, overshadowing the progress I'd made. "I can't get through to her. Every time we take two steps forward, she retreats into herself, and we end up back four steps."

"She'll get better. Allow her more time. Kids are resilient."

"I guess."

The old me, the guy from two years ago, would have thrown a fit, broken in tears, kicked something, or screamed at the world that all of this was unfair. For a long time, I had resented Lisa for what she'd done, holding her responsible for everything that didn't go my way.

But last year, after a particularly bad day, I'd chosen to forgive her. I couldn't keep living in a permanent state of anger. It exhausted me and wasn't good for me or the girls. We deserved to be set free.

"What do you have in mind? You wouldn't be here if you didn't have something planned."

Riley let out a heartfelt chuckle. "Am I that obvious?"

I shrugged. "That woman of yours is turning you into a softie. It suits you. You've lost some of your legendary grit. Your *nothing will stop me* drive. But you look happier. Calmer."

"I won't tell Devon you said that because I'll never hear the end of it." He chugged the rest of his beer and fished another one out of the crate. "Listen to me, Stevens. It's time for you to get back out there. I have waited long enough and bided my time. By the way, I'm not taking no for an answer. It will do you good. A change of air. To live like a man again. It'll be better than any therapy. Even if it's just for a couple of months."

My arm froze halfway between my chest and my mouth, the bottle hanging from my fingers. I blinked. One. Twice. Three times.

"You can't be serious. I don't even have a label anymore. I'm the guy who refused big money to take care of two motherless children. I can't leave my kids, Ry. You know I can't. They count on me. I'm all they have left." I slouched in my seat, my shoulders slumping forward. "We already had this discussion…a few months back. Before you left. My answer is still no."

"Who said you'd have to leave them? This time, it's different. Hear me out. I wouldn't be here if I hadn't hatched some plan for your big comeback. And by the way, fuck your old label. Like I told you the last time, I'll be the one in charge. I'll take care of everything. You won't have to worry about a single thing. The girls will be in good hands. I swear." A smile spread across Riley's face. "My cousin owns a nanny agency. She interviewed this woman who also has a teaching degree. I talked to her over the phone. She could go on tour with you and take care of the girls whenever you're not available, teaching them at the same time. This woman, Madison, comes with an impressive number of references. Last year, she was on a yacht, crossing the Atlantic Ocean, with a family of four kids. She even did some voluntary work a summer in Africa, teaching kids when she was eighteen. I'm supposed to meet up with her next week. This could be a great opportunity. This woman is a rare gem. If we don't get her on board, someone else will snatch her up, and it could take months to find another candidate as qualified."

"Fuck. You thought of everything. It even sounds good when you say it out loud… Almost perfect. It can't work, though. It's not that I don't trust you, but the girls need a stable environment." I sipped my beer, thinking about how to explain the situation to him. How to refuse his generous and enticing offer. "It'd be selfish of me to ask them to change their newfound daily routine because their daddy's gotta fulfill his dreams. I'm sorry, Ry. For a moment, you got me thinking it'd be possible. I'm not saying never, but right now, the time isn't right."

My friend gave me a lopsided smile. "Told you, I'm not taking no for an answer. Not yet at least. I want you to think about this. For real. I'll meet with this Madison girl, and if she's as great as she sounds, we can have a talk with her. Grill her. Both of us. Together. Then, and only then, you'll give me your final answer."

I snickered. "You're wasting your time, but I love how persistent you are. Do your homework first and we'll see. But you know what? Thanks for making me believe for a moment I wasn't dead inside. For making me see I still have it in me. The fire to do what I love. I haven't dreamed in a very long time, and I like how it makes me feel."

I clinked my bottle with his.

We sat there, side by side, enjoying the sunset in silence. Every word my friend had said twirled around in my head. Sending frenzied *what-if* jitters to my heart. If only it could be that easy. If only I could go back out there and have the certitude it wouldn't affect my children, then I'd do it without hesitation.

If only.

Chapter 3

"**I** want the blue glass. Not the red one. The blue. I want the *bluuue*," Justine yelled at the top of her lungs. "Gimme the blue, Mika. You had it *yesthursday*. Now it's *my* turn. I want the blue glass. Blue. Blue. Blue."

"Justine, you had it twice last week. Don't be a baby. Now it's my turn to have it twice. Stop whining. Daddy, tell her to shut up."

My eyes rounded.

Did I hear her right?

"Mika, when did you learn to use those words? It's not fine. You can't talk to your sister like this," I barked. "Or anyone else for that matter. I don't want you to use grown-up words." I scratched the side of my face and dialed down my sudden burst of anger. "Use nice words. *Please, I'm sorry, thank you*…huh…whatever."

"Whatever."

I blinked again. My insides were tied in a series of knots. If Mikaella had this much attitude now, how on Earth would I survive her teenage years? She'd be the end of me.

"Mika, language. Talking like that isn't allowed in *this* house. Now say you're sorry to your sister."

"Sorry," she mumbled so low I barely heard her myself.

"Louder. You can do better than that."

"No. I already said it once. I'm not saying it again."

"Mika," I warned, my tone harsher this time.

"Okay. Fine. Sorry, Justine." My eldest daughter turned her head my way. "Happy, now?"

I fisted my hands at my sides, doing my best to disintegrate the fresh wave of wrath bubbling inside me. *Don't say anything,* I told myself, repeating the words Mikaella's therapist advised me to. *She's just trying to get a reaction out of you. Ignore her attitude.* Yeah, well, I'd like to see the therapist dealing with her this morning. And every other morning.

I breathed in and finished packing their lunch when my eyes landed on the empty beer bottles Riley and I had drunk last night. Our conversation replayed in my head. If only I could make this work. If only it could be that easy.

I was tired of being a household fixture.

My eyes traveled around our home. I used to adore this place. Our little family nest…

We'd built it when Lisa found out she was pregnant with Mikaella.

Over the years, I had framed some of the girls' artworks on the walls, next to the staircase, bringing a touch of color to the room. This morning, though, the entire house seemed dull. Faded. Boring and sad.

Same as me.

I'd become all those things too.

I used to be fun. Happy. Joking around. Having barbecues with friends every other weekend. Having date nights with my ex-wife once a week to keep the flame burning strong, as we liked to call our little alone time. Yeah, that one failed. Miserably.

I craved a change. Perhaps selling the house would do it for me. But the girls weren't ready for something so drastic. They had lost too much already. They needed their safe haven.

Could a few months on the road do us some good, though?

Why was I letting Riley's words take a front seat in my mind? Damn it. He'd planted a seed, and now it was begging to grow into a tree. A cherry blossom. Tall, fierce, and beautiful. Fucking, Ry.

My heart throbbed in my chest.

With my back resting against the kitchen counter, I sucked in a breath.

"Girls, can we talk?" I asked, my tone so serious they both stopped bickering over that stupid blue glass. The one about to live its final days in a trash can. "Remember when I told you daddy used to sing songs for a living?" They both nodded, their fight long forgotten. "It's just an idea, but would you like to someday…live on a big bus and travel around the country with me? It would be like going camping, but for longer periods of time."

My emotions clogged my throat. I couldn't breathe. Why was I opening that door?

My head spun, and I gripped the edge of the counter to keep my balance.

"I like *clamping*," Justine exclaimed, jumping to her feet and squeezing her doll against her heart. "Can I sleep in a tent?"

The tension in me lessened—a tad.

My youngest daughter neared me, and I lifted her in

my arms, relishing the scent of strawberry shampoo lingering in her hair. It acted like a calming balm.

"Justine, it's camping, not *clamping*. You two would have a bedroom. Maybe a bunk room to share."

"With pink walls? And a giant unicorn?"

I shrugged. "Why not? We could do whatever we want. It would be like a big vacation. Except that, some nights, Daddy would have to work."

"Work?"

"Yeah, baby, work. Like parents usually do. You know when I spend my days at the hardware store Uncle Jim owns?"

They both nodded.

"It would be like that, but a different kind of work."

"But who's gonna kiss me goodnight? Or hold me when I have *nightlemares*? Or tuck me in? Mika and I are going to be alone when you go to work."

I fastened my grip around her tiny body. "Nightmares, baby. Not *nightlemares*." A smile stretched my lips. "No one would be alone, baby. You would have a nanny. Someone super nice to take care of you and tuck you in the nights I wouldn't be available."

Mikaella walked toward me and raised her arms, asking me silently to pick her up too. With both my daughters nestled against my chest, I answered all their questions.

"When?" Mikaella asked. "Because no way am I missing school."

"You'd be doing schoolwork during the day. The nice lady would teach you everything you have to know. Don't worry about it."

"What's the name of the lady?" Justine asked.

"I don't know yet."

"Where is she going to live?" Mikaella inquired.

"Again, I don't know. We'll have to figure this one out. I'm sure we can find a solution we all agree on."

"Will the lady be our new mama?" Justine asked with big expectant eyes. "I want a new mama."

A lump, hard as a rock, settled in my throat. I swallowed around it and shook my head.

"No, baby. The lady would only take care of you. Make sure you're safe and sound. And play with you when I'm onstage."

"But who will take care of you, Daddy?" Justine asked, her blue eyes drawing me in, in a way only she could.

"Know what? I'm sure I can take care of myself. Anyway, I have you girls. I'm the luckiest man on Earth because I'm surrounded by so much love. Don't worry about me, okay?"

They both bobbed their heads, and Justine kissed my cheek.

My grin widened.

"What do you think, girls?" I knew I shouldn't put them in the middle of this, but now that I'd realized it could be a possibility, the idea of going back on the road started to grow on me. And no way would I ever consider Riley's offer if the girls weren't on board—one hundred percent.

"I wanna go *clamping* with you, Daddy." Justine squirmed until I lowered her to her feet. "Now can I go play?"

"Sure, baby." Once she exited the kitchen, I turned to face my eldest daughter. "What do you think, sweet pea?"

She shrugged and avoided my eyes. "I don't know. Will Mama be able to find us if she comes back and we're gone?"

My heart plummeted down, pooling at my feet. Mikaella, always worrying about Lisa and her antics. My ex-wife didn't deserve her concern. I sat my daughter on the counter and framed her face with both hands. I inhaled through my mouth to keep my emotions on a leash.

"Honey, I'm not sure Mama will be back before long. She's not keeping me updated very often." The truth was, she never did—but Mikaella didn't need to know that I hadn't spoken to Lisa since the day she left, and that the only exchange we'd had since was through our lawyers, when she voluntarily gave up all her parental rights. No, my babies didn't have to learn the ugly truth of our divorce, or their motherless status. "If she ever visits, I'm sure she'll give us a call beforehand."

"Will you still play with us? Or will you be too busy working?"

"Sweet pea, you'll always be my priority. You and Justine are what matters the most in my life. If you girls don't wanna go, then we won't. It was just something I was wondering about. That's all. Anyway, if we do this, it wouldn't be so soon. I would have to get an album out first."

Mikaella jumped off the counter. "It could be fun. Can I tell Stella?"

"Not right now. Let's think about this for a little longer before we give it a go, okay?"

"Okay." She looped her arms around me and squeezed me tight. "I love you, Daddy."

I returned her hug, kissing the top of her head. "I love you too, sweet pea."

And just like that, for a moment, my little girl tossed her rebellious mask aside and became a child again.

Hot tears welled up in my eyes, and I blinked them away.

For the first time in so long, I could envision a future doing what I loved and being a daddy, all at the same time.

A dormant energy woke up inside me and shook my foundations. Excitement and apprehension tangled inside me. How hard would it be to juggle both?

————

With one arm folded under my head, I lay on my back and stared at the dark ceiling of my bedroom. With a wooden king-sized bed, a matching dresser and two nightstands, and an armchair in the corner by the window, my bedroom was decorated simply. Like the rest of the house, it missed a little spark these days. It felt blah. Perhaps I should've accepted my mother's offer to update it last fall. To inject it with a touch of vibrant colors and spice up the decor. I'd been up since five this morning, unable to fall back asleep. My brain was overexcited with all the possibilities Riley's visit had planted inside my head. It'd been a week since he came over, and I'd turned restless since, unable to stay still, my mind hyperactive, and my heart galloping.

Every day, the girls asked me at least once if we would go camping next fall. I still had no answer to give them. I had made countless pros and cons lists in the last few days, the recycling bin in my music studio slash office that I barely used nowadays, overflowing with crumpled pieces of paper.

It used to be one of my favorite rooms in the house. With a wooden ceiling, a dark carpeted floor, and steel-blue walls, it had an industrial yet country chic vibe. Enlarged album covers and framed photos of concerts I had given in the past lined the walls on one side. A cream leather sofa, a desk, and a wooden arched floor lamp offering a soft glow tied the decor together. A glass partition divided the small recording booth, its walls lined with sound-absorbing panels. In the center stood a microphone, a headset, and a stool—waiting to see if I'd ever be ready to record a song again.

Even if I tried, I couldn't remember the last time they had been of any use.

In an attempt to busy myself in the last couple of days, I had even updated the decor. Unlike my bedroom, my music studio inspired the creative side of me. New picture frames, drawings on the walls, and a plant I hadn't killed so far. The additions had transformed a stagnant office into a living space—where I prayed I could get inspired.

The most amazing thing to come out of this new possibility was that I had started writing again. I wrote about love. About loss. New beginnings. And hope. I wrote about my babies. About my life. And my broken heart.

The words flew on the paper so easily that I wondered why I hadn't written a single song in the last two years. No therapy could equal the profound sense of peace that swirled inside me as the lyrics spilled over the pages. My guitar, thick with dust, seemed almost happy to see me again. Long-lost friends reuniting after circumstances tore us apart. The instrument had never failed or wronged me. It had always been my most loyal companion.

Every night, I'd sing the girls the songs I wrote during the day, and they would learn some of the lyrics to sing along with me.

Music brought joy back into our lives.

Mikaella hadn't argued about dyeing her hair black or shaving her head in five days.

Justine hadn't tiptoed to my room or woken up screaming in three nights, which was unusual. She had been having nightmares almost every day for the last two years and bed wetting episodes for the first ten months following Lisa's departure.

Could Riley be right? Could his crazy idea be the salvation we'd all waiting for to start living again?

Even the air in our house seemed lighter these days. Filled with excitement and fervor. With sparks and laughter.

As if Lisa's ghost had finally left us. For good.

Everything looked better and brighter now, optimistic and possible.

Jitters rolled in my stomach, and I rose to my feet to get dressed. Every now and then, I eyed my phone as if it could catch fire any second. Riley had called yesterday before he went to meet up with that Madison woman. He'd even asked Devon, the love of his life, to join him so she could use her woman's instincts, as he had said. Since then, no news. Nothing. Radio silence. My patience ran thin nowadays, and I was desperate to know how their meeting went. What to expect.

Half of me hoped Madison was the gem Riley had described. That she had agreed to this scheme of his.

The other half wanted her to be found crazy and unfit to care for my children, forcing me to put this silly idea of going back on tour to rest.

With a coffee mug in my hand, I paced the living room, relishing the scorching heat burning the walls of my throat. The girls were still asleep. I fought the desire to wake them up so my brain could keep busy instead of anticipating and making up scenarios.

Unable to wait any longer and lacking distractions, I shot a message to the man who could become my manager and change my journey.

ME

Hey, it's me. How did it go last night? Keep me updated.

He took an eternity—well, five minutes—to reply, and I spent the whole time pacing the kitchen, rubbing my nape raw.

RILEY

Good. Why?

I squeezed the device in my hand. How much fun was he having, messing with me like this?

RILEY

How's your blood pressure, Stevens?

I typed. And erased. And typed again. Only to delete it.

I groaned and bit my tongue to avoid cursing out loud.

RILEY

You like the idea?

Was he kidding right now? Was he playing with my patience on purpose?

I blew out a puff of air. My blood fired in my veins.

My fingers itched to ask about the meeting, but I wouldn't play his childish game. If I did, Riley would see that I was hooked on the idea. Right now, I wasn't ready to let him know just how much it had me worked up.

Proud of myself for resisting the temptation to question my friend, I put my phone away and went to wake up my daughters, ready to jumpstart our day and feel useful. And escape the madness of Riley dodging the silent questions calcifying in my bones.

On our way to school, I played the song I'd written last night on my phone, and the girls and I practiced the chorus together until they both nailed it. I'd titled it "Summer Nights," and it was about our lives, the three of us, and the freedom we were aiming for. The girls applauded, and peace rooted under my skin, spreading through me. Once again, my friend's idea didn't appear so insane in the morning light.

On my way back, I pulled into my driveway and noticed him leaning against his red sports car, arms folded over his chest, a smug grin splitting his face.

"What are you doing here?" I asked as I neared him, scowling to mask my reaction to the devilish tilt of his lips.

Riley ran a hand through his dark hair and flashed me another smile, a glint in his eye.

Jerk.

He was well aware I loved the idea of going on tour. He had me all tangled up inside, playing with me and trying to get me to admit it out loud. Still, it seemed too good to be true.

"Stevens, you think I don't know you?" he asked with a quirked brow. "If you think I'm obvious, then you haven't looked at yourself in the mirror in a long time. I saw it in your eyes the other night. You like the idea of going back out there. No. Scratch that. You love it. You crave it. Since I came over, you haven't been the same man. I hear it in your voice each time we talk on the phone. And right now, I can tell you're dying to know how it went with Madison so we can talk real business, you and I. Don't even try to deny it. You know I'm right."

I offered him a pointed look, but my lips curled up, unable to hide the excitement pouring out of me any longer. Yeah, I loved the idea. Who could blame me?

With a sigh, I waved a hand between us. "Okay. Fine. You got me. I wanna know. Spill it already. Doesn't mean I'm on board, though." I paused. "Can't you see I'm too old to extract the information out of you?"

"We're the same age. Find a better excuse," he bantered, the smirk on his face definitely not a good look.

Nah. In that instant, it drove me nuts.

"Stop smiling like that and just get to the point. You know what? Forget it. I've changed my mind. Don't tell me. Your loss." I was heading for the house when he spoke again, forcing me to turn around.

"How many songs have you written in the last week?" His grin stretched wider—as if it were possible. Fucker.

"Ok, fine. Seven. I've written seven songs. Are you happy now? You can hide your stupid smile now. I've seen enough of it, and it's"—I fished my phone out of my back pocket—"not even nine o'clock. You wanna come in, or do you want to have this conversation on my front lawn?"

"I'm not staying. Just came here to see your face." He shrugged, and for a moment, I felt like punching that smug look off his face. "Tonight, I'm picking you up at six. We're meeting with Madison in my cousin's office."

"But I—"

He waggled a finger. "Before you find a million excuses to refuse, Devon will watch over the girls while we're gone. She loves your children and can't wait to spend time with them. Do you mind if she"—he lifted a finger—"just a sec." He unlocked his phone and read something. "Oh, yeah. Do you mind if she paints their nails and bakes chocolate chip cookies with them? She wanted me to ask you that."

I chuckled.

Riley was so deep into his relationship with the woman who stole his heart the first time they met. It took him over a year to meet her again, but since that day, they hadn't left each other's side, except when he went on Aisha's tour. Even I, with my heart filled with grudges, had to admit they made a perfect pair. They complemented each other in every possible way.

"Once again, you hatched a plan behind my back. Should I be afraid?"

"You can thank me later. Be ready. We'll be here at five. I wanna spend time with the girls too before the big meeting. Then you and I we'll have dinner afterward. Carter is in town."

"Fine, I'll be there, man." I gave a shake of my head. "Carter Hills is visiting? I haven't seen him in a long while. Count me in. For what it's worth, thanks for getting me out of my cave. And tell Devon I'll owe her one."

"I will. See you later, Stevens."

Riley hauled himself behind his wheel and drove away as I stood in my driveway, speechless, my heart doing a million weird flips in my chest and my head dizzy from all the crazy ideas swimming in it.

Chapter 4
Sam

I rummaged through my closet. What should I wear to this meeting? A suit seemed too formal, but a pair of jeans and a cotton T-shirt seemed a bit too casual. Nowadays, I mostly owned a daddy's wardrobe. Comfy and versatile options: jeans, T-shirts, and hoodies.

After changing for the third time, I put on dark jeans and a cobalt shirt and pushed my hair, the same shade as Mikaella's, away from my forehead. That would do.

Justine jumped on my bed—dressed in a long, glittery purple skirt with a faux-fur yellow sweater, and a neon-pink boa draped around her neck—and I caught her mid-flight.

"Come here, you," I said, nuzzling her neck and sniffing her like a puppy would do. My youngest daughter giggled while I carried her downstairs. "Uncle Riley will be here soon, baby. Devon will watch over you and your sister tonight."

Justine flashed me an adorable grin, highlighting the

dimples on each side of her mouth. The doorbell rang at the same moment. "*Debon, Debon, Debon,*" she chanted as she hurried to let our guests in.

"Devon, baby. Her name is Devon."

"*Debon,*" I heard my baby girl repeat as she opened the door.

My shoulders slouched and I sighed. Devon would have the entire night to teach Justine how to pronounce her name correctly.

"Hey, guys. Come on in," I greeted them, Mikaella in tow, curious about the commotion. I grabbed the bags from Devon's arms. "What's all this?"

"Ammunition," she said, flipping her blonde curls over her shoulder. "I brought everything required for a perfect girls' night. Don't worry, we won't miss you guys. The girls and I will have so much fun." She lifted Justine in her arms before leaning forward to drop a kiss on Mikaella's cheek.

My eldest daughter's eyes filled with sparks. "Did you bring makeup?" she asked, glancing at me sideways, as some silent approval traveled between us.

"No, but I brought something better. Nail polish. I have at least ten different shades we can try on. I'll do your nails, and you'll do mine. Then we'll vote on who has the coolest mani-pedi."

"Yay," Mikaella said, her face lighting up with a smile.

Nothing was more amazing than seeing my girls beam.

"Nobody is glad to see me? I thought I'd get a full red-carpet greeting, trumpets and all," Riley teased with a pout, stepping beside his woman in the doorway.

Justine chuckled, and Mikaella rolled her eyes dramatically.

"You're silly," my baby said, holding out her arms so he could pick her up from Devon's arms.

"You didn't bring girly stuff. Sorry," Mikaella told him as she started running, and Riley chased after her.

My gaze followed them until they turned the corner and disappeared into the living room, their laughter making its way to my heart.

Devon grabbed my elbow. We hadn't seen each other in months—the last time being Justine's birthday—but I still could read the worry in her eyes. "How is it going? For real, okay? Not the bullshit you serve Riley every time he calls you." Oh yes, her woman's instincts as her man called it.

I inhaled a shaky breath and dropped the bags at my feet on the entryway floor after kicking the front door shut, resting my shoulder against the wall. I stuffed my hands into my pockets—a habit I'd picked up after Lisa left, whenever I felt uncomfortable.

"Last week has been good. Really. Before that, it was on and off."

"Mika still giving you a hard time?" Compassion filled Devon's gray-blue irises. She'd been through a lot herself. If someone could understand family trauma, it was her. She went through hell for years before Riley appeared in her life.

"Most days, she's hurting, Dev. She misses her…or the memory of her… She puts up a strong front, but behind all this crappy attitude, I know her heart is in pieces. She still believes Lisa will come back someday and play mommy again as if nothing happened. It crushes me." I blinked, doing my best to calm the emotions simmering inside me. "I don't wanna feed her beliefs that she'll come back, but at the same time, I don't want to smother her hope even more by telling her she will never come back, you know?"

"It's an impossible situation. Imagine how confusing it

must be for her." She gave my arm a reassuring squeeze. "We're here, Sam. Whenever you need us. Or when you need a break. Riley is a big fan of yours, and all he wants is to help you out. The only way he knows how. I think his grand idea isn't as crazy as it sounds. The change of scenery could do you guys some good. All three of you. Like a new adventure. Something to put the past behind for good. The beginning of a new chapter. A new life."

I hung my head low. "Maybe."

"By the way, Madison is great. The girls will love her. I have no doubt. She's sweet and smart. She'll fit right in with you guys. I can already tell."

I breathed out. "Perhaps you're right. The girls are excited about it. We'll see."

"Trust me. I'm around if the girls need a woman's presence in their lives. Don't be afraid to ask. It's always been my pleasure to be there for you three."

———

"You ready?"

I swallowed the bitter taste sitting in my throat, firmed my back, and nodded. "Yep. Let's do this." I blew out a breath. "I can't believe you convinced me to go through with it."

Riley clapped my shoulder. "You'll see, man. Madison knows her shit. You'll want her on board, I promise. It's a match made in heaven. All the puzzle pieces are now coming together. Trust me."

I rubbed my jaw, trying to dissipate the tenseness in my chest. Coils of steel crushed my organs in tight grips.

"You're lucky I do. I wouldn't do this for anyone else, man. I can't believe we're actually going through with it."

"I know. And I'm thankful you put your trust in me. It

means a lot. Have faith. It's a good call to make. You'll see. C'mon, follow me," Riley said as he opened the door of his cousin's nanny agency to let me in.

I sucked in some much-needed air. I could do this. He was right. This could work. This could be the beginning of something new as Devon had said.

A petite woman in her early forties greeted us. "You must be Mr. Stevens. I'm Janice," she said, offering me her hand to shake. "Riley told me a lot about you. I'm glad you agreed to meet with us."

"It's nice to meet you too. Thanks for having us."

Through a hallway painted in vibrant shades of blue and green and a purple carpet, we followed Janice to her office. Dozens of pictures of smiling kids were framed along the ten-foot-high walls.

The whole place looked cheerful and inviting for families.

I clenched and unclenched my fists at my sides. The room felt ten degrees warmer since I'd come in. Sweat beaded on my nape. "You have a lovely office." Could Riley and Janice sense how nervous I was? I wiped my clammy hands on my denim-clad thighs, forced another breath in, and relaxed my shoulders.

My eyes wandered, trying to distract my mind from overthinking the decision to be here.

A large window, overlooking a park, let the fading daylight filter through. The walls were painted in the same shade as the hallway. A tall plant sat in one corner, beside a children's powder-blue table with a stack of coloring books and a bucket of pencils.

The girls would love it here.

We all turned around to face the door when we heard a soft knock.

Janice let the woman in, smiling. "Hi, Maddie. Come meet Mr. Stevens."

Madison entered the room. I inhaled a sharp breath, her arrival stealing every bit of air from the room, leaving me breathless. I took a step back, solidifying my stance. If I'd been sitting, I would've fallen off my chair.

A surge of misplaced heat washed through me.

A sense of annoyance spiraled in my core, intertwined with an inexplicable fascination whose source I couldn't trace.

I blinked. Once. Twice. A million times. The woman before me had nothing to do with all the nanny images I'd constructed in my head. She looked nothing like the middle-aged women starring in children's movies or the ones we often heard about.

At about five feet eight inches, with dark hair braided over her shoulder and wearing a knee-length red wrap dress, she looked too young to be the girl with all the credentials Riley had praised about.

It was a mistake.

Her smile directed at me warmed my insides when I extended my arm to shake her hand. It overcast my under-lying irritation. A tingling sensation raced up my spine when our palms met. We stared at each other for what felt like forever, both sizing each other up, the weird tension between us thickening with every passing second.

Her lips trembled, and for a short instant, I wished I could tug the bottom one with my teeth. I shook myself out of the daze that had held us both captive. What the hell was wrong with me? Where were these thoughts even coming from? My lack of a social life had clearly messed with my head more than I'd realized. I had become a sick fucker.

I cleared my throat, my vocal cords feeling heavier, her

sea-green irises locking onto mine. I couldn't look away. "You must be Madison. It's nice to meet you. I…I've heard great things about you." Did my voice quiver? *You must be Madison.* Oh geez. Like it wasn't a given already. Great, I must have looked like a complete dork and sounded like an airhead. In my career, and even at the hardware store, I was used to meeting new people all the time, but it had been so long since I'd had one-on-one meaningful interactions that I felt rusty.

This woman, by her proximity alone, threw me off my game—for a reason I couldn't decipher. Except that she didn't fit the profile of a live-in nanny, and the green pools of her eyes hypnotized me. So did the curve of her lips.

"It's nice to meet you too. Mr. Burns…huh…Riley"—her gaze traveled to my friend before returning to mine—"couldn't stop bragging about you yesterday. It's nice to finally put a face to the name. He said amazing things about you and your family." She blushed a little, and I found it fucking adorable.

Yeah, adorable, because Madison wasn't the grown-ass woman I'd pictured in my head, but a kid. Not the severe yet caring woman I'd imagined when I had agreed to this meeting. Or the years-of-experience-candidate Riley had sworn she'd be. She didn't look a year older than eighteen.

How could she have any work experience?

Did she even graduate college? Or even have a high school diploma?

I blinked again, my eyes unable to flicker away, her hand still locked in mine, fumbling with my sanity. And my whole body.

I took in the straight line of her nose, the heart-shaped lips, the angle of her chin, the slender neck.

Yeah, to make things worse, she looked beautiful. No, stunning—for a young woman. One I shouldn't have these kinds of thoughts about. One I was here to interview, not crush on.

My two-year-long dry spell was now making me all hot for a college girl. One with delicate shoulders and a body sinful enough to drive any man wild, even underneath that demure dress.

It wasn't sexy or short or anything like that, but it still had an effect on me. A big one. One I had no control over and that filled my pants. That spiked my heart. And that fucked with my brain.

An invisible vise closed around my heart.

Steel bands tightened around my stomach.

I wasn't here to get my dick back in the game, but to hire a nanny. Someone to watch over my kids.

This Madison girl wouldn't do. She looked too naive to be qualified enough for the job. Too young to be in charge of small children. Too sweet to… Why bother? It wouldn't work anyway. It couldn't.

She eyed me, and I felt as if she could read my soul and every word that didn't cross the rim of my lips. My dirty inner reflections. I broke eye contact, praying the discomfort in my lower self wasn't too obvious and that it would subside quickly.

Another breath in and the pressure rising in me decreased. Once I regained some of my composure, I risked another glance at her.

My stance hadn't changed. No way could Madison be experienced enough to care for my little ones. I bet she still lived with her parents. Or that she shared an apartment with half-a-dozen roommates because none of them had a job steady enough to pay the full rent by themselves, too busy hitting bars every night and working shitty hours for little-to-no money while juggling college classes during the day.

Anger rose inside me. My features hardened, despite myself.

I closed my eyes and balled my free hand at my side.

Was Riley shitting me right now? How could a college kid be the one whom I'd rely on to care for my daughters? This girl wasn't even old enough to run a household in my absence and follow my kids' school curriculum next fall. How could he and Devon have vouched for her? They must have known she didn't fit the requirements. What were they thinking? Clearing my throat, I removed my hand from Madison's grasp. This whole thing was a lost cause. A clump of false hopes.

The moment her palm slid out of mine, something deflated inside my chest, and I missed the warmth of her touch and the prickles raiding my body. Not willing to let her notice my uneasiness and misplaced attraction, because yes, I was feeling things that were not allowed in a business meeting, I shoved my hands into my pockets.

The air in the room stiffened, and I withdrew into myself.

Riley and Janice exchanged a glance, and when my eyes drifted back to the woman fucking with my head again, she busied herself picking the nail of her thumb, a faint blush still tinting her cheeks. I flexed my jaw, grinding my teeth. Inside me, every one of my organs spasmed with foreign awareness. I had no recollection of my heart trying to flee my ribcage before in my life.

With an exhale, I tipped my chin up. All eyes were on me. Expectant. Inquisitive. Apprehensive. I found my voice, deciding not to release my position on the subject. "This meeting was a mistake. I'm sorry if I made you all waste your time. You can bill me for an entire hour." I fished a business card out of my wallet and placed it in Janice's hand.

She watched me with wide eyes, probably thinking I was a rude jerk for walking out on her and her teenage recruit.

"Now, if you'll excuse me, I have little girls I must go back to." I whirled around and hurried out of the office.

Oxygen made its way back to my brain once the door slammed behind me and the distance between Madison and me increased.

My pulse calmed down, and I could breathe again.

My entire body loosened up.

With long strides, I reached the front door in no time. Just when I was about to exit the agency, Riley caught up with me, and his hand connected with my shoulder from behind, stopping my retreat.

"Where do you think you're going, Stevens?"

I unleashed the ball of fury bouncing around in my chest, jumbling together all my mixed feelings. With a roll of my shoulders, I freed myself from his grip, readying myself for a fight. "Are you kidding me right now? How could you even think I'd agree to this? You set me up with a kid, man. You made me believe I could do this whole career-tour-children thing and that you had my back. I believed you. Trusted you even. I fucking put my confidence in you. And it was hard for me to do so, but I had faith you wouldn't let me down and that you understood where I was coming from."

I tightened my fists.

Anger sliced my words.

I shouldn't be angry with Riley. After all, he'd only tried to help me out, but I couldn't help it. I felt tricked.

All the remnants of the bottled-up anger I thought I'd already dealt with over Lisa abandoning us surged all at once. Everything I wished I could have told her, and never did, spewed out of my mouth.

"You have any idea how hard it is for me to trust someone? Mostly around my kids? Do you know how I struggled for the longest time, trying to make sense of the life that was forced on me without my consent? It imploded, and I was alone to pick up the pieces—and I still am doing so. Every fucking day. This single-dad thing is hard enough as it is. I thought you said Madison has a teaching degree and lots of experience. How could another kid be the right fit? Tell me, please. Enlighten me. Because, right now, I can't see your big plan unfolding perfectly. I thought we were meeting a mature woman with years of experience caring for children. I thought you had it all figured out. I thought… I don't know what I thought, but it wasn't this." I pointed to where the office was located down the hall. "It wasn't fucking this… Another kid? Really? As if I'm not already drowning under everything on my plate. I. Can't. Do. This. Nope. It's asking too much of me. Maybe I'm not meant to follow this road anymore… It was a mistake." I sighed. "I feel stupid for wasting every one's time. Forget the idea of a tour, Ry. I'm out. For good this time. I don't even know why I agreed to this in the first place. Deep down, I always knew it wasn't meant to be. God, how could I have been so clueless? I'm done." My words sat in my throat, heavy as a ton of bricks. "For life."

How could I ever let myself imagine this would work out? I was the butt of my own joke.

I spun around in a hurry to leave when he squeezed my forearm. "Stevens, where do you think you're going?"

I swallowed my rage before facing him. "Home. To my children. Those tiny human beings who are my whole world and who expect everything from me."

"Did you forget I drove us here?"

I shrugged. "Who cares? I'll take a cab. Or I…I'll walk. Yeah, it could help to diffuse my anger. I'm furious, man.

If I were you, I'd step back because I'm about to explode. You don't wanna stand in the crossfire."

"Sam, you're not going anywhere. Listen to me before doing something foolish you may regret later. Grant me five minutes. If I haven't convinced you to give Madison a chance by then, I'll call the meeting off myself, and we'll leave."

I blew out a breath, fighting the pros and cons in my head.

I came out short of reasons why I shouldn't trust my friend, and finally agreed. "Okay. Fine. Five minutes. You'd better do exceptional, or I'm out of here, and we'll never talk about my going back on tour ever again. Am I clear?"

Riley nodded and motioned for me to follow him through a door leading to a small conference room. A long white table filled most of the space, surrounded by a dozen teal chairs.

We sat next to each other, and I leaned back in my seat and folded my arms across my chest, waiting for my friend to explain himself. Tension rippled through me. I hadn't felt this much anger in a long time. In a crazy way, the overbearing sentiment reminded me I was alive. That I still could feel passion—whether positive or negative. That I hadn't turned into a rock. A small part of me rejoiced at the thought. I wouldn't dare show it in front of him, but I couldn't deny the fire blazing in my veins.

Riley muttered something I didn't catch, caught up in my own internal battle, and shot a text—probably to Janice. He turned off his phone—something I didn't remember him ever doing—then tossed it on the table and swiveled to face me. "Now just listen. Don't interrupt me. I want to make the most of the five minutes you're allowing me."

I nodded, my posture stoic.

"I didn't tell you Madison's age beforehand because I knew you'd freak out. Sure, she looks young, but she's twenty-one. She graduated early with honors, one year ago. She was homeschooled most of her life and is very smart. Anyway, she owns a degree. And it's legit. She also passed the background check. Hands down. Not even a single speeding ticket in her life. Right now, she's not teaching a regular twenty-five-student class because she loves adventure. She told me so herself. I'd never lie to you, man. You have to believe me. We've been friends a long time, you and I.

"Since Carter has decided to stop going on extensive world tours and is mostly doing low-key concert stretches here and there, and Aisha just came back from a tour, I have a lot of free time on my hands. I have one other group I'm managing, but they aren't as big a deal as you, Aisha, and Carter are… Not yet at least. I'm not doing you a favor or doing it for the money because you know I don't need it. Sam, you gotta get back out there. You're dying a slow death. You're miserable. I'm doing it for your kids, man. Ever since I came to your house the other night with my not-so-wild idea, you've been looking ten years younger. The smiles I saw on your kids' faces tonight were genuine. It was about time those girls started thriving again. It's like ever since I planted that idea in your head, you've decided to enjoy life. You've been rising from your ashes. You guys looked happier tonight than I've seen you in the last two years. Gone was the tension that has been choking all three of you. You were at peace. It wasn't a front…or the mask you usually hide behind."

I closed my eyes to prevent the emotional storm building inside me from erupting. The one about to transform my ire into tears.

Was every word Riley said accurate? Even if I wanted

to deny it, they rang true, shook me to my core, and spoke to my soul.

Did my girls need this as much as I did? Could he have been right all along?

A calmness spread through me. The kind that comes when it's paired with a sense of belonging.

A treacherous smile threatened to slip out, but I pressed my lips together, not ready to let him see how much his words had affected me.

As silly as it sounded, my friend's idea had lodged itself in my heart ever since he drilled it in.

A door I'd kept locked inside me swung open. Air filled my lungs more easily. How could Riley know what was best for my family better than I did? Was I really struggling as much as he suggested? Yet, I couldn't deny it.

"You all right, man?" he asked, forcing me to snap back to the present.

"Yeah….huh…was just thinking. All your words sound great, Ry, but don't you think I'm too old to take care of a college student? I'll be turning thirty soon. I'm not looking for another kid to raise."

My friend burst into laughter. "Stevens, I'm pretty sure Madison can take care of herself. Stop calling her a kid."

"She looks like one."

"She's not. She's an adult, independent, and reliable. Meet with her. For real this time. Trust me, for fuck's sake. I'm telling you, she's the real deal, okay? You two will get along just fine. I swear."

I shook my head. "Why do I feel like I'm gonna regret this?"

"Because you'll tell me I was right to insist, and you'll realize you've been acting like a big baby since we got here. Who's acting like a kid now?"

My warning glare had no effect on him.

"Now let's go. Madison and Janice must be worried we'll never come back."

I released my smile. "*Touché.* Lead the way. I hate it when you're right."

He snickered. "It's love, man. You and I, we fight, then we make up." He pushed me forward, his hands splayed across my back. "Not my fault I was born to be right all the time."

I bowed my head and shook it. "I won't buy you flowers." I joined in on the humor as laughter exploded between us.

Seconds later, he knocked on Janice's door, and I followed him inside the office, closing the door behind me, a grimace forming on my face as shame wrapped around me.

Both women's eyes shot in my direction. Janice offered me a shy smile, and Madison stared at me with glossy eyes. Did I make her cry when I stormed out of here earlier? I scrunched up my nose, feeling responsible for her distress. Did I mess things up already? No wonder Lisa left if I was that bad at reading her emotions all these years. Did I convince myself we were in love instead of seeing the signs that proved she didn't love me back? I raked my fingers through my hair. I shouldn't let Lisa inside my head. It never did any good. I had done nothing wrong in my marriage except love her. She was the one who had run away. I shouldn't doubt myself—now wasn't the place or the time.

I brought my hands in front of me, my palms open before anyone could say anything. "Hey, I'm sorry for leaving like I did. I panicked, and it's nobody's fault but mine. Thinking of going back on tour is a huge deal for me. It-it's something I thought I'd never do again. It doesn't excuse my behavior, but that's the truth... Now I'm ready to listen to everything you tell me. This won't happen again, I swear."

My gaze returned to Madison, and we exchanged a nod as I stuffed my hands into my pockets to quiet the brewing agitation I felt deep in my bones. Our eyes connected. For longer than required. She swept her lip with her tongue, appearing nervous.

This time, I kept my dirty observations to myself and switched to a business mindset.

Janice clasped her hands in front of her, breaking the spell. "Great. Let's all take a seat then." The four of us sat in the colorful chairs surrounding her desk.

She led the meeting, good and persuasive at why I needed to hire Madison as my children's nanny and teacher.

When Madison started talking, she avoided my eyes. She looked between Janice and Riley, but barely at me. I hated myself for making her feel uncomfortable.

But then her eyes, glistening and alluring in the light, found mine, and I lost myself in their depths.

I sucked in a breath, afraid I would drown in her irises if I weren't being careful.

"What are Justine and Mikaella like?" she asked me.

Wow, she knew my daughters' names already. Impressive. My jaw went slack, and I had to force it shut. This small detail was important enough in my heart that my professional interest in Madison grew.

"They are lively little girls. Justine is four, and she thinks she's a princess and can't wear enough glittery stuff or sparkling dresses. She loves to ask questions and can't seem to say people's names or everyday objects the right way. It's a part of her charm, I guess. Mika is more rebellious, but she's only six, so I haven't lost faith just yet. Her mother's leaving, abruptly in the middle of the night, affected her the most." A cloud passed through Madison's gaze. I paused, wondering if what I said triggered it. She blinked, and it dissolved, so I continued. "Mika thinks she's a grown-up and wants to be treated like an adult. I know she's struggling, and I get her all the help I can. Anyway, she's doing amazingly at school. Her bad attitude is mostly directed at me. She's a great kid with a huge heart. Justine and she are inseparable. Even when they fight for the most trivial reasons."

"If it's okay with you, I'd like to meet them. But only if you think your family and I could be a great fit. I don't want to impose, but I always like to make some sort of test run. Spend time with you guys and see if there's chemistry. The last thing you need is a nanny your children are hostile to. Nobody yearns to be unhappy."

Those words resonated with me. Yeah, I was done being unhappy too.

"I agree," Janice said when I didn't speak up, lost in my thoughts.

Who was this Madison Prescott, and where did she come from? One more point in favor of Riley being right all this time.

I scratched the side of my head.

Everything Madison said sounded smart—and logical. Could she be wiser than her young age? For everyone's sake, I hoped so.

The entire time I told her about Justine and Mikaella, she stared at me. As if she could swallow my words. As if I spoke some wisdom she craved the secret to.

Riley nudged me in the ribs.

"What?"

"Are you okay, Stevens? Janice has been talking to you, but you totally blacked out."

My face heated up. "Sorry. What were you saying?"

Janice offered me a warm smile. "No problem. I was saying that if you agree, Maddie could come to your house next weekend, and she could spend some time together with the girls and see if you all get along. And then we could meet up next week and discuss the details if you decide to go forward and hire her. How does that sound?"

I coughed to clear my throat, too many words trying to come out at the same time. "Sounds good to me."

"Me too," Madison echoed, her hands linked together in her lap, her general demeanor less strained than before.

Janice rose to her feet. "Great. I'll send both of your contact info in a joint email, so you'll be able to set up a date to get together." She held out a hand and I shook it. "It was great meeting you, Mr. Stevens, and I hope to see more of you soon." She circled her desk and kissed Riley on the cheek. "See you, cousin. Don't be a stranger."

"Take care, Janice. We'll keep in touch. Madison, I'm sure we'll see each other again soon. Thanks for giving this grumpy fellow another chance. I knew you two would hit it off, even if it got off to a bit of a bumpy start."

Madison offered him a lopsided smile before turning toward me. She fidgeted with the ring around her middle finger before her eyes caught mine and halted there for long seconds. She opened her mouth to say something but seemed to refrain. My gaze followed every movement of her lips when they bent at the corner as she said, "Thank you for giving me a chance."

"Sure. Let me know when you're available, and we'll set it up."

She returned my hesitant smile as we exited the office, and I made eye contact with her one last time over my shoulder.

Once out on the other side of the door, I exhaled and rotated my shoulders. The tension in my upper back dissolved bit by bit, and air didn't struggle to oxygenate my brain anymore.

I did it. I took the first step toward reviving my dying dreams. I was doing it—the gears finally in motion. I didn't know whether to feel excited or cautious. It all felt so surreal.

"Drink and dinner?" Riley asked as we walked to his car.

I fished my phone out of my back pocket to look at the time.

"Stop worrying. The girls are fine." My friend flipped his phone so I could see the screen. Devon had sent a picture of the three of them with rainbow pedicures, and another one of them baking cookies. By the giant grins on their faces, my daughters looked more than fine. "See? I told you. Carter is waiting for us at Wild and Country."

"Oh, how's the partnership with that Tucker guy going?"

"Great. It's a passive investment on my part. I only jump in when he has technical questions about music or is looking for the next best opening numbers for special nights. For a bar, the food he serves is freaking delicious. I'm telling you, it's the most popular new spot in town. The guy knows his shit."

"Any big names playing there these days?"

"Yeah, a guy I met a few times. Sam Stevens. You should hear him when he's onstage. People call him *The Legend*. You should come to see him play when you have some free time. He's worth the buzz. And soon he'll rock that stage. Give him a few weeks. Three months at the most."

"Tell me again why you never were my manager before?"

"Because you were too stubborn to see a great opportunity—aka me—when we met. You went with the big sharks, and they tossed you like an old pair of shoes the moment you didn't play by their rules anymore. It's never too late to recognize I'm the best in the business. Don't tell me now. Wait until you're at the top again, then I'll be all ears when you chant my praises and tell me how fabulous I am." Riley winked at me as he unlocked his car.

"Yeah, yeah. Keep dreaming, man." I shook my head, unable to hide my grin this time. Deep down, I'd always known my friend was the best in the business. I was just too stupid back then to recognize it.

———

We entered the bar. My eyes fought to adjust to the semi-darkness. This place had become an institution in Nashville since its opening. Back in the day, this used to be a pub where I met my friends regularly. When life was simpler and we still had dreams of making it big one day. A guy name Tucker Philips had bought the building, renovated it, and turned it into a hit venture in a short amount of time. When he asked for Riley's professional opinion about sound systems and acoustics, my friend offered to invest, swearing he could already see the potential of the place.

Tucker and Riley had friends in common, including Dahlia Ellis—Carter Hills's ex-bandmate—and her husband Nick. They became fast friends, bonding over investments, stocks, real estate, and good whiskey, as he'd once told me.

Riley Burns would do just about anything for his country family as he called them. Carter, Dahlia, Stud Burgess—the third ex-bandmate of the Carter Hills Band —Aisha Jones, his newest artist, and all their partners and children.

A family I wasn't a legitimate part of yet but aspired to be. Rightfully.

Carter waved from a booth at the back when he spotted us. Riley's phone went off, and he gestured for me to continue as he moved toward a room on our right, the device still glued to his ear.

My fellow country music star rose to his feet to pull me into a hug. "It's been a while, Stevens. I'm glad Ry convinced you to join us."

Rubbing my jaw, I sank into the black leather seat. "He has made it his mission to get me out of the house lately. He's adamant I should go back on tour, but I'm sure he's already told you all about his new plan. Anyway, why are you in town? You're barely ever here, now that you're living full-time in Green Mountain."

The first time I met the members of Carter Hills Band was when I'd just turned twenty-three and we both played at Green Mountain Fest. We all landed record deals and kept running into each other at every award show and music event after that. Carter, Dahlia, Stud, and I got along easily from the moment we first met, and a friendship quickly followed. Even if we didn't see each other as often these days, we were still close.

Carter brought the glass of water to his lips and took a sip before answering. "Had to go over some concert dates with Ry. And I wanted to see June. I missed her. We talk on the phone all the time, but it's not the same. April is with her right now. They planned a shopping date or something."

June was Riley's assistant and Carter's go-to person in his professional life. She worked almost exclusively for him.

"Where are the kids?"

"With their grandparents."

"April's parents?"

"No, her in-laws."

My eyebrow twitched. "April's in-laws? Which I'm pretty sure should be your parents... What am I missing here?"

"Remember the Bensons?"

"Yeah, the ones organizing that charity event every year in New York. What about them?"

"They're April's in-laws," he said.

"Let me recap. Mr. And Mrs. Benson are babysitting your children? How did you make that happen? Sure, you are a country superstar, but this is big. Even for you."

Carter snickered. "It's a bit complicated... April and they go way back. The time you canceled your appearance at the fundraiser because of Lisa's miscarriage, well... I replaced you, and they bumped into each other that night and rebuilt their relationship. It has progressed from there."

The mention of my ex-wife didn't hurt anymore. A sense of serenity spread through me at the realization I was done with that chapter of my life. She didn't own my heart anymore. Or my sorrow.

"Anyway, they are her family. So, by association, they're mine too. Where were you when it all went to shit? It was all over the news for weeks. When the media chased April away. Anyway, the Bensons gave that interview. They protected her...vouched for her... It was something else."

"Geez, I missed a whole chapter of your life. I've been living in some sort of cave for the last few years, and clearly I'd forgotten how entertaining your existence could be."

Carter Hills had been nicknamed the bad boy of country music. He had an attitude, could serve a mean left hook, and had had his face plastered on gossip magazines too many times due to a previous relationship. He was nothing like the media made him out to be. You had to be part of his inner circle to see the real version of him. The one he kept hidden from strangers.

A server approached us. "Can I get you anything?"

I ordered a beer, and then he turned to face Carter. "Another Smoky Stream, sir?"

My friend nodded. "Yes, please."

"Smoky Stream? Even water sounds fancy with you, man."

He shook his head and smiled. "The guy keeps calling it that, and I love it. Sounds almost like a high-end cocktail. Have you met Tucker yet?"

"No. Heard great things about him, though."

"Yep. Nick and he go way back. The three of us have become quite a trio over the last couple of years. Who would have thought? Let's say Nick sweeping Dah off her feet at first didn't sit well with me. But, in the end, I'm grateful, because I wouldn't have met April if I hadn't survived all the pain of unrequited love and the betrayal of the evil witch who made my life a living hell… Whoa, I haven't thought about her in a long time. All along, April was the one I was destined to be with. Anyway, I'll introduce you to Tuck later. He must be around here somewhere. You two will get along." His gaze fused to mine. "Now tell me you're really thinking of going back on tour. Country music misses some new Sam Stevens material. It's been too long. You're *The Legend,* and I can't hold the fort all by myself."

"Look who's talking, Mr. *Every One of My Songs Is Still a Hit.*"

Carter shrugged, not an ounce of smugness shadowing his face. "It's not about me. I'm happy for you, and I hope it all works out. You deserve it. I walked away by choice. You didn't. That's a big difference."

The server brought us our drinks, and Carter swirled

the water in his glass, the ice cubes clinking. "I don't have any real competition when you're taking time off, Stevens. I used to love competing with you for the top spots on the charts. I haven't retired, just doing smaller crowds instead of stadiums now… It suits me better. So…your return…is this serious or not?"

I inhaled, trying to put some order into my jumbling thoughts. "Yes. No. I don't know. Now that the possibility is real, I guess I'd like to give it a try. There's so much to think about, though… So much at stake. The girls… I gotta make sure they won't suffer because of it."

"What about that girl Ry set you up with? The nanny?"

"Yeah, what about the nanny, Stevens?" Riley asked as he took the seat next to Carter after they hugged, a tumbler of whiskey in his hand.

I dragged my hands over my face. "I'll give her a chance. I'm not agreeing to anything yet. We'll see how it goes."

A voice in my head told me there was no going back, whether I was ready or not.

"Yeah, we'll see how it goes," Riley echoed, his tone teasing, and a grin stretching across his face, practically begging to be punched.

Chapter 5
Madison

Emily, my older sister, was waiting for me when I returned from my meeting with Sam Stevens at the nanny agency. We had both moved to Nashville to attend college and never went back home to Kentucky. Emily was studying to become a surgeon. We shared the townhouse she was renting in East Nashville with two other doctors. Since I was always in and out, due to my work, she offered me one of the guest rooms to stay in every time I was in town or between jobs. It suited my hectic lifestyle since I wasn't ready to commit to a nine-to-five career just yet.

"How was it? Did you get the job?" she asked after I dropped my purse on the table, kicked off my shoes, and slumped onto the couch beside her, resting my head on her shoulder.

"No clue. That was the weirdest interview ever."

I straightened and rubbed my throbbing temples with my fingers as I felt a paralyzing headache coming my way.

"I thought you said it was a done deal after you met with his manager and his wife." I could hear all the questions in her voice and imagined the wrinkles around her eyes without even looking at her.

"I did, but the guy shook my hand, studied me for a few seconds, and announced it was a mistake, then bolted out of the room as if it were on fire." I sighed and risked a glance at her.

Emily coughed, her eyes widening. "He left? You're kidding, right?"

"He stormed off. I swear, it felt like I'd injected poison into his bloodstream with a handshake… He couldn't get away from me fast enough." She gasped her surprise as I continued, "But then he came back a few minutes later, said he panicked and was sorry, and now we agreed to meet again next weekend so I can spend time with his daughters."

"And you're okay with that?"

I blew out a long and loud breath. "The truth is, I really want the job. Riley made it sound so much fun. So different from what I've done in the past. Deep down, I feel for the kids. Their mom left without saying goodbye…or something like that. It's heartbreaking. With what you and I went through when we were their age, it's like I'm even more qualified for the job." To understand what they were dealing with.

My sister nodded her agreement. Nowadays, we were both at peace with our childhood trauma. Over the years, we had become more than just sisters. Best friends who always had each other's backs.

I let out a long sigh, and Emily watched me with a

puzzled expression. "High tension swirled between us, but I think I can handle it. I won't be there to care for him, but for the girls. His manager said he has trust issues. So, it might explain his cold reaction toward me at first. I checked him up online. Most articles are from before he stepped down. In the past two years, he hasn't given a single interview—at least, none that I could find. It's like he vanished from the limelight entirely, shutting out the rest of the world. The man I saw in the old pictures had an edge that the one I met today lacked…eyes that seemed to burn into the soul. It's hard to explain, but I have a good feeling about this. Imagine, going on tour with someone who once topped all the music charts around the world. This feels too good to be true. And yet, they picked me. I'm trying not to look too much into his past and just skim the surface so it doesn't influence how I act around him. The last thing I want is for him to think I'm some sort of groupie. Anyway, I'd love to live on a tour bus. See what the fuss is all about. Most kids my age are still in college or have just graduated. I'm not ready for a steady teacher's position just yet. I love my lifestyle."

"You've never loved things most kids your age enjoyed anyway. You're weird, but a good kind of weird. You're way too intelligent and mature for your own good. You know that, right? I could tell when you were like nine that you'd do great in life. That fire in your eyes, that will, it was already shining bright." Emily nudged me with her shoulder. "Let's be serious for a minute, though. What if the guy turns out to be a dickhead and you're in the middle of New Mexico with no cell phone reception for me to come to your rescue?"

"Like I said, I'll be there for his daughters. As long as I get along with them, the rest will be just fine. Remember

Mr. Cruz at first when I lived on the yacht with his family last year? He warmed up to my presence after three months. It can't be worse. I don't scare easily."

My sister rested her palm on my thigh. "You're right. I just don't want you to end up hating the guy if he messes with your opportunity to live a great experience, that's all. We should go out tonight. To celebrate your potential new job. It's still early, and I have the day off tomorrow. Please say yes. I'm putting in an official request to have some fun with my little sister before you're too busy to hang out with me. And since you're still unemployed as of right now, drinking on a Wednesday night is no big deal. Plus, it's ladies' night, so we'll drink for cheap. Are you in?" My sister's eyes clouded for a moment, and she sighed before looking away.

"Ems, what's going on? Talk to me."

She shook her head. "Nothing. I just need a change of air. Long shifts at the hospital are weighing heavy on me. My entire existence is dedicated to my job right now. Some days, I find it dreadful. Don't worry. Plus, I think Becks is playing somewhere on Broadway. Could be fun. To be young and carefree for a night."

She tugged at my dress sleeve giving me puppy dog eyes.

"Why not? We haven't gone out together in a long while. Let me change, though. This dress isn't suited for a night out," I said with a huff, recalling the earlier interview that had left me with a sour taste.

Two hours later, I was leaning against the counter in an overcrowded downtown bar with a glass of sangria in my hand when a guy about my age neared me.

"Hey," he said, aligning his body with mine, making me the center of all his unwelcome attention. His red T-shirt, a size too small, clung to his broad shoulders, biceps, and defined chest. And he smelled like he'd bathed in after-shave and hair gel.

I scrunched up my nose and stepped aside to avoid the overwhelming fragrance.

"Hey," I replied, giving him my most fake smile that screamed *stay away*.

He clearly couldn't read between the lines—or my facial expressions—because he moved closer. I leaned back. I hated this. I wasn't the type of person who made small talk with strangers in a bar.

"You wanna go somewhere?" Biceps Guy asked.

I winced. "Sorry, not interested." I sipped my drink and pivoted to my right, putting an end to our conversation.

"C'mon, let me at least buy you another drink."

Chills ran down my spine while he edged closer.

I took another step to my left, escaping his suffocating presence. My eyes scanned the crowd for my sister and her friends. They were supposed to head to the ladies' room and come back, but it had been a while, and there was still no sign of them. Maybe they'd gone upstairs. The bar had three stories, including a rooftop terrace on the third floor.

Biceps Guy clutched my elbow as I moved further away from him. "Let's have some fun, baby."

I cringed and wrenched myself free from his grip. He'd just called me *baby* and fucking touched me.

I discarded my cocktail on a nearby table, the taste making my stomach churn. Amazing. He was ruining my night.

Fishing my phone out of my pocket, I called my sister. *Please pick up. Please pick up. Please, please, please… Where are you?* It rang five times before going to voicemail.

Fantastic, I had no money and no way to get home since my wallet and keys were in Emily's purse.

Biceps Guy leaned even closer, his breath brushing the shell of my ear. Too much. Too close. He was too…everything. Icky. My pulse raced and I breathed fast. My insides coiled. I retreated until my back touched the wall. "Don't be afraid, baby. I won't bite you. Not yet at least."

Everything in me screamed to run away.

He trapped me between his arms. At least a foot taller than me and twice my width, I felt tiny in comparison.

To appear taller and stronger than I really was, I straightened my back and lifted my chin. I wouldn't let this guy intimidate me. "Move," I said, my tone leaving no room for argument, my voice firm.

"Don't be afraid, baby. I'll take care of you."

I raised my hands, ready to push him back when a voice behind me stopped me mid-action.

"Here you are. I've been looking everywhere for you. Don't get out of my sight again, honey." A guy in black jeans, a white T-shirt, and motorcycle boots, with an eyebrow piercing and brown hair, closed in on us. He arched one dark brow, smiled at me, and moved closer to take my hand. I wanted to be looked at like that for the rest of my life. As if I were the sun, the moon, and the entire universe.

What was going on? Who was this guy?

"Honey, is this man giving you trouble?" the mysterious stranger asked. High cheekbones, angular jaw, turquoise eyes, and thin lips. He looked like a fashion model. The ones you gotta to look at twice to get the complexity of their beauty.

Biceps Guy raised his hands in surrender. "Sorry, man. I had no idea she was yours. I'll go now."

"Yeah. Do that. And don't creep out the ladies. It's sick, man."

Biceps Guy muttered something and slinked away, leaving me with the fake boyfriend who had saved me. I tried to avoid his eyes, but they were like two abysses swallowing me whole. And I loved that. A little too much. We studied each other, neither of us able to look away.

"I'm Jacob. You are?" he asked, his fingers still laced through mine, his warmth spreading through me.

"Maddie."

His grin widened. "Well, it's nice to meet you, Maddie."

"Thanks…huh…for that. That guy, he—" Why was I unable to form a complete sentence?

"I know. I've been watching him from the other side of the bar. He's a douchebag. I'm glad I was there this time around."

"Me too. You come here often? Is saving ladies hit on by jerks your night job?"

Jacob smiled, and I got hypnotized.

"My first time. I wish I could be that kind of hero."

"You should consider it as a side hustle. So far, your track record is impressive."

We shared a chuckle. Somehow, Jacob and I clicked, and we spent the next twenty minutes talking about everything and anything.

"Hungry?" he asked after a while.

"Famished." After my interview with Sam Stevens, I'd barely eaten dinner, my stomach too tied in knots.

"There's a food truck outside, and they served the best Southern chicken fries in Nashville. My treat. You in?"

I bobbed my head, a stupid grin spreading across my lips, completely entranced by everything Jacob was. He took my hand in his. We were about to leave the bar when I remembered Emily. Where was she? I'd been so caught up with him that I'd completely forgotten my sister had gone MIA a long time ago.

Digging my heels into the wooden-planked floor, I spun in his direction. "Wait. We can't go just yet. I gotta find my sister. She's here. There…huh…somewhere." I gestured around the crowded bar with my hand.

"Let's find her then."

Hand in hand, we squeezed through the patrons, dancing and mingling, though I wasn't tall enough to spot my sister.

"What does she look like?" Jacob asked, speaking close to my ear so I could hear him over the music.

My body vibrated at the sound of his deep voice.

"About my size, wavy brown hair reaching past her shoulders, yellow tank top, and a mole on her right cheek. Oh, and she has my eyes. Other than that, you wouldn't guess we're related."

"Copy that," he said with an irresistible grin. One I wished could stay anchored to his face all night.

We searched the third and second floors. No trace of her anywhere. I was about to tell Jacob we had to come up with another plan as we returned to the first floor when I bumped into her.

"Hey, Ems. Been looking everywhere for you. Even tried to call you. Are you okay?"

She squeezed my upper arms. "Oh, Maddie. I thought I'd lost you. I'm so sorry. Cecilia drank too much tequila, and I had to hold her hair while she was puking her guts out. She's fine now, but we have to go. We'll drop her at her place on the way home." She moved closer and spoke into my ear while pulling me into a hug. "Who's that?" she asked, pointing to Jacob, who was busy watching the live band, with her chin.

"Someone I just met. We were going to grab a bite. Go with Cecilia. I'll stay here."

"You sure? You don't even know this guy."

"His name's Jacob. And I have a good feeling. Don't worry about me. I'll be fine."

Her gaze traveled between Jacob and me for a moment. She offered me her big sister's *be careful* look and smiled. "Maddie, you gotta have some fun. Doctor's orders. Enjoy yourself for once. Don't be too serious for a night, okay?"

"I'll try."

Growing up, Emily and I had been homeschooled by our mother until she got too sick after I turned fifteen. For as long as I could remember, my sister and I had always fended for ourselves and been more mature than most kids our age. It all explained why we'd both graduated early from high school and college. Our father had taught us to save our money, to be responsible. And self-sufficient. Sometimes, I felt more like a *thirty going on forty* girl than a *just-turned twenty-one-year-old*. People my age bored me. I'd never really connected with them the way I should have. No wonder I had such a hard time making friends.

In the short time we'd known each other, I realized Jacob got me. I could tell he was similar to me in that way.

Emily dropped a kiss on my cheek and pushed two twenty-dollar bills and my credit card and keys into my hand, then spun around to face my new friend. "Take care of my sister. Don't make me chase you down 'cause I will. Now gimme your phone."

His eyes flared, but he said nothing and handed her his device.

She typed fast and gave it back. She grabbed her own

phone and nodded. Seconds later, a deep frown appeared across her forehead, and she brought her fists to her hips. "Be warned. I have your phone number, so don't try anything, or I'll hunt you down."

"No worry, ma'am. I'll take good care of Maddie."

Emily sighed. "Fine. And don't *ma'am* me ever again. Second warning."

Jacob winked and interlocked his fingers with mine, leading me away. "Is your sister a psycho, or does she take great pleasure in intimidating men?" he asked, amusement clear in his voice.

"Believe me, you don't want to find out." I plastered my most devilish grin on, and he pretended to be spooked.

In a half-empty parking lot, we sat on the pavement against a red-bricked wall, drinking soda and sharing a plate of the best Southern chicken fries I'd ever had.

"Gotta say, you were right. I can't believe I've never tried these before," I said, licking my fingers.

Jacob smiled. I could watch his expression all night. It fascinated me. He looked like a boy with the dimple on his chin and glints in his eyes. A great contrast to his dark biker appearance.

"You know you're beautiful, right? I can't keep my eyes off you."

Was my face fire-engine red right now?

I wasn't used to getting compliments. And I wasn't used to flirting with strangers either.

"Don't be shy, Maddie. Your energy is contagious. It drew me in the moment I laid my eyes on you in the bar."

My heartbeat picked up. I didn't know how to react. Should I run for my life or savor his words?

Jacob cast a glance down and brought another piece of fries to his mouth. I zoomed in on his lips. They looked soft and were the perfect shade of pink.

Nothing about him screamed "serial killer." I just hoped my instincts were sharp and not off.

"Sorry. Didn't mean to freak you out. I just had to tell you." He shrugged, and I relaxed.

"It's okay. I'm not used to this," I said, motioning the space between us and around with my hand. "I don't go out a lot, and I'm dedicated to my work, so meeting new people and getting compliments isn't something that happens often to me."

"It should be." He sipped his drink, looking in the distance. When he turned his head and his irises met mine, nothing existed but us. "You said you're dedicated to your work, so what do you do when you're not eating with a stranger in a deserted parking lot at night?"

"I'm a teacher…sort of. And a nanny. I enjoy going on adventures with families and teach their kids while they're away from home. I spent a year on a yacht across the Atlantic last year. In a couple of months, I'll be on a tour bus for six months…if it all works out."

"Wow, I'm impressed. I wouldn't have pictured you as the adventure-seeking type. I like that. A lot."

I shut my eyes, trying to calm the flutters inside me and keep my expression blank—and breathed out.

"Tell me something not a lot of people know about you," he probed.

"Let's see." I hesitated for half a second. "I often feel like I can't find my place in this world. That's why I love to try new experiences. I rarely connect with people my age. I guess I'm trying to find out my true purpose… See where life takes me… It's a confusing process sometimes."

"Aren't you too young to think about all this?"

"My parents have always said I have an old soul. My friends have always been older than me. Instead of running around and pinning donkey tails at birthday parties, I was the kid chatting with the parents. Sorry, it's weird."

"Nah, I like that you can be vulnerable with me and able to speak about things honestly, as they really are."

"Trying to get the most from this life, I guess. And be authentic," I said.

"No one wants to live a life built on lies. I can relate to this. Honesty is something I value a lot."

"What about you? What do you do for a living?"

"I'm a biologist. I work at the university lab. We're testing ways to decontaminate soil using bacteria. It's quite captivating, and so far, our research is promising."

"You're a scientist? I had pegged you as an artist." I let out a weird giggle.

"Yeah. Most people do. I don't exactly have the geek vibe going on for me. I just love sciences. Always have." He raked a hand through his mass of brown hair, messing it up, and for a second, images of Sam Stevens doing the same gesture earlier flashed through my mind. I pushed them away and brought my attention back to the man beside me, losing myself in his gaze once again.

"Ready to go?" he asked, jumping to his feet and holding out his hand for me to grab.

"Where?"

"Wherever you want. I'm not ready to let go of you, Maddie." I could've freaked out, but the manner he said it sent a wave of calm through me. Jacob had a way of making me feel comfortable around him. There was something peaceful about him. Something that put all my demons to rest. Like I didn't have to pretend or be anyone else around him.

Without a word, I slid my palm into his, and we strolled through Nashville. We stopped midway across the pedestrian bridge, pausing to admire the city's night skyline from a distance.

Leaning on the banister, we listened to a country music concert in the open-air amphitheater below. Jacob circled one arm around my waist from behind, and I tilted my head back until it rested on his shoulder as we let the music soothe our souls.

"I don't want this night to end," I whispered, not sure if I wanted him to hear my confession but hoping he would at the same time. I loved the freedom our time together had given me so far. Closing my eyes, I etched it into my memory.

"Me neither," he said, his cheek pressing against my temple.

"Can we stay like this forever?"

"Yeah," he said, pulling me closer to him, curling a hand around my hipbone.

"We should do this again. Spend time together. You and I," he said.

I whirled around to face him. "I'd love to."

The chime of my phone broke the moment. I grabbed my device and smiled at the screen.

EMILY

Hope you're having fun. Don't be an idiot. But enjoy every second. I love you xx

ME

I am. Love you too xx

"Everything's okay?" Jacob asked.

"Yes. Everything's perfect. I have a serious question to ask. Hope you're up for the challenge. What's your opinion about ice cream?"

"Swirled. With a waffled cone."

I grinned. "You passed the test. Let's get some."

Two hours later, I hauled my tired self into a cab as Jacob kissed my cheek.

"Good night, Maddie. Are you free this weekend?"

"I have a job meeting, but I don't know the specifics yet. We could meet again Friday night, though."

"Have dinner with me," he proposed.

I nodded, smiling like a fool.

"It's a date then." He closed the door after me and hit the cab roof twice to signal it could pull away.

Jacob watched me go, his eyes following me until the vehicle turned at the next intersection, and our gazes lost their connection.

Lying on my bed a bit later, I replayed the entire night in my head. My awkward meeting with Sam Stevens earlier. The heaviness of his stare as he had studied me. Almost powerful enough to rip my dress to shreds. For a moment, I had believed he liked what he saw until he ran away as if I suffered from a contagious disease. The guy was both fit and hot, but he clearly lived behind a thick fortress, keeping people at a distance. I could tell from the moment our eyes met together for the first time. No matter how aloof he became, I felt an instant pull toward him. With his square jaw, short stubble, and straight nose, he was the living picture of my definition of a perfect man. Even the conflicting energy radiating from him appealed to my senses. On top of that, he still projected confidence in his nervous state. Yes, I could read the anticipation in his body language. The warring thoughts as he battled with himself about the meeting.

And then my brain traveled to Jacob. In a way, he resembled a younger and more grunge version of Sam Stevens. Dark hair, similar poise, manly energy, self-assurance. Easy-going, just a tad mysterious, and way less broody than his counterpart. I felt attracted to him the instant I laid eyes on him.

My mind zigzagged between the two men, so similar and yet so different all at once. How could I be attracted to both? I was way over my head and being ridiculous, so I shoved my silly thoughts away. Soon, sleep claimed me, and I forgot all about the encounters of the day.

On Friday, I woke up early to indulge in some yoga before starting my day. I was still unemployed, but Sam Stevens had reached out last night, and we'd agreed to meet on Saturday at his house so I could meet his daughters. I fixed my hair in a knot at the top of my head, rolled out my mat, and positioned myself, ready to start my practice, but my mind kept drifting back to the possibility of this new job. I had a hunch about this position, and the idea of living on a tour bus for months got me excited. It was unlike any job I'd had before. Cramped living quarters, random sched-ules, and a different city every night. How could I not be curious about experiencing life on the road for a while? Usually, yoga helped quiet my overactive mind, but this time, it barely did anything.

Draped in a towel thirty minutes later, I exited the shower, and a notification flashing on my phone screen caught my eye.

Jacob.

Since we spent the evening together strolling around Nashville two days ago, we'd been messaging each other nonstop. At twenty-five, he had a sense of humor matching mine, and my instincts were right the night we met. We got along, and I enjoyed our blossoming friendship. I wasn't the kind of girl with a huge circle of girlfriends…or even many friends at all. I usually hung out more with Emily's friends than with people I went to college with. Being away for work most of the time made meeting new people even more challenging. But I was fine with it. I was good at being on my own. Still, something about Jacob made me yearn to see what we could become.

JACOB

> Good morning. About to leave for work. Just wanted to know if tonight still works for you. We talked about lots of things yesterday but never actually made plans.

> My apartment is a ten-minute walk from downtown. We can meet there or someplace else. Let me know if it's still good for you.

> Have a great day. Can't wait to see you again.

I cracked the widest smile, unable to tune out the flutters in my stomach at the idea of spending time with him again.

I typed a fast reply, already thinking about later.

ME

> Yes, works for me. Your place is fine. Send me your address.

> How about Billy's? We can eat out on their covered deck. Nobody serves better pulled chicken in this town. We can walk there. Together.

> Or there's the Music City Market. Always wanted to try their renowned turkey legs. Never visited since they opened last fall.

My chest swelled at the sight of the three little dots bouncing at the bottom of my screen.

JACOB

Billy's. I'll make a reservation. Seven?

ME

Perfect. I'll meet you at six.

JACOB

It's a date.

Have a beautiful day, Maddie.

The day passed in a blur. Emily and I shared the house with two other med students working with her. They were barely ever here due to their hectic schedules. I spent my day running errands and tidying up the place so my sister and her roommates could relax once they got home.

At six, I rang Jacob's apartment buzzer from the side-walk. Before I could even announce myself, he appeared in front of me. The warm late-spring breeze tousled his hair. Dressed in black jeans and a Henley shirt with the sleeves pushed up to his elbows, a leather band around his wrist, and boots, he looked even more handsome than I remembered. Especially in the daylight.

The dimple in his chin gave him a boyish charm.

He scanned me from head to toe, and when he stepped closer to press a kiss to my cheek, I caught a whiff of his mountain-fresh cologne. "Maddie, you're beautiful."

"Thanks," I murmured, warmth rising to my cheeks. His compliment had me giddy all over again. "You're pretty nice-looking yourself."

"Shall we?" he offered. "Our reservation is in fifty minutes. Let's go for a walk first." Grabbing my hand in his, he led the way.

Jacob was everything I loved in a guy, and I enjoyed the

easy comfort we'd been sharing since the moment he saved me in that bar the other night.

Strolling by the river, we eased into more conversation after we finished dinner.

"When will you know if you got the job?" he asked, smiling at me, never releasing my hand. The kind of smile that heated my core.

I shrugged. "Hopefully tomorrow. I'm meeting with his daughters. We'll see how it goes. I really hope it works out. I'm not sure this kind of opportunity will present itself more than once."

"I think it's admirable what you're doing. Those kids will be lucky to have you in their lives."

We exchanged timid smiles. All night, we had grown closer, our chemistry impossible to ignore. We paused to watch the opposite shore when he traced the side of my face with his knuckles, sending addictive shivers through me. I felt his gaze burning into my skin.

The flutters I had felt before mushroomed in my stomach.

"Can I kiss you?" Jacob asked after what felt like forever.

I turned, rested one hand against his chest, and nodded. "I'd be really unhappy if you didn't."

Tilting my head back, I met his lips. Careful and warm.

My head spun.

My heart cavorted in my chest.

With my hands locked around his neck, I drew him closer and deepened the kiss. Jacob entangled his fingers in my hair while his other hand wound around my waist.

Neither of us required fresh air anymore.

Someone wolf-whistled behind us, and we pulled apart.

Jacob skimmed my lips with his thumb, then traced his own, as if to make sure it had really happened.

A satisfied smile brightened his features, and I was sure I wore one just like it.

We resumed our walk, our fingers now intertwined, and no gap between our bodies. Whenever we paused at a street corner, he pressed his mouth to mine in a slow, intoxicating kiss that made my toes curl.

The breeze picked up, sending a chill through me. Jacob held me closer, casually tracing the skin beneath the strap of my summer dress with one finger.

"Thank you for tonight," I whispered, rising to my tiptoes to kiss his lips once we reached his building.

"Wanna come upstairs?" he asked. Before I could reply, he pulled me to him, and I buried my face in his chest. "I'm not ready for the night to end."

"What's on your mind?" I tilted my head back to meet his gaze and blinked.

"We don't have to do anything other than cuddle. I kinda want to hold on to you for a bit longer."

"I'm not ready to go either," I admitted.

As soon as we stepped inside his apartment, Jacob gripped my hips and lowered his mouth to mine, claiming it in a kiss that weakened my knees.

We kissed for what seemed like hours. Until my lips felt too sensitive to continue.

"Make yourself at home," he said once we broke apart. "Snack? We could watch a movie."

"Movie sounds awesome. Want any help?"

"Nah, I'll be right back. Beer?"

I shook my head. "Can't. I'm a lightweight, and I'm driving. Better not."

While he busied himself in the kitchen, the scent of freshly popped kernels tickled my nostrils. I perused his living room. Jacob lived in a one-bedroom apartment in a five-story brownstone. It was small but cozy. The walls were painted white, and most furniture was black. The place looked a lot like its tenant. Classic and mysterious. Science books occupied most of the bookshelf along the wall opposite the TV. A couple of thriller and fantasy fiction titles I hadn't read yet were in the top section. "You're an Avery Davis and Tessa Salinger fan?" I asked from where I stood, my back turned to him.

"Yes. I love the worlds Avery Davis creates. Salinger, I've been a fan since I got a copy of *Spite* on my sixteenth birthday. Are you?"

"Kinda. I've only read two of Salinger's books so far. I'm more of a Brandon Clifford type of girl. Avery Davis, I've heard of her but never read anything she's written. I think her husband, Carter Hills, is a friend of Sam Stevens, my *fingers-crossed* future boss. Who knows, maybe I'll meet her someday if I get that job."

Jacob didn't reply, and seconds later, his warmth coiled around me and so did his arms while his lips grazed my nape. "You and I, we're already a great match." His smile caressed my skin, and I swiveled between his arms to press a quick peck to his lips.

It wasn't even midnight, and I struggled to keep my eyes open as the credits rolled across the screen.

"Spend the night," Jacob offered.

I straightened, and the gears of my brain engaged. I enjoyed the comfort he brought me. I felt safe in his arms and relished the connection we shared. But would I hate myself for spending the night with him?

"Sorry, I didn't mean to scare you. I just spoke my mind. I should have added that we can just sleep. Nothing more."

The frantic beating of my heart calmed down.

I inhaled and relaxed, folding my legs beneath me. A yawn passed my lips. *Be a grown-up, Maddie. You can go back to being a mature twenty-one-year-old in the morning.* I splayed my hand across his chest, feeling every thump of his heart under my palm. "I'd like to stay."

His brows shot up. "You would?"

I nodded and moved to my knees to kiss him. His scent enveloped me, and I felt good about my choice.

"No pressure, okay?" Jacob tipped my chin up with a finger, as if to make sure I knew he was speaking the truth.

"I wanna stay. I'm not used to having sleepovers, though."

He grimaced. "Me neither."

I let out a nervous smile. "Cool. Because it's a first."

"Are you—? Have…huh…have you ever been with anyone?"

"I had one boyfriend. We dated for a couple of months. It wasn't meant to last… I think we were too different… We expected opposite things from life."

Jacob cradled my face with one hand and searched my gaze. "For the record, I don't either. Invite women over, I mean. I'm not a people person, so I usually prefer being on my own. I had one serious relationship. And one… well…less serious. With you, it already feels different. Not only new, but like it could be the beginning of something."

We exchanged knowing glances that carried a lot of weight. We were both trusting someone we barely knew and getting out of our comfort zones. Together.

Jacob and I were much more alike than I had ever thought.

Knitting his fingers through mine, he led me to the bedroom. "I was serious before. I only want to sleep. And to cuddle. Nothing more. There's something special about you, Maddie. I have no intention of spoiling it. Everything about you is beautiful."

"Can I kiss you?" I asked, repeating his own words, feeling bold for once in my life.

His eyes darkened. "Yeah. Then we'll stop, because if we don't, I might have a hard time resisting you."

I nodded, not wanting to risk the moment by saying something stupid.

With my eyes shut, I quieted my breathing and my thundering heart when his lips molded to mine, deciding not to miss a second of how amazing he made me feel.

Breathless, we both pushed apart at the same time.

"Okay, bedtime," Jacob announced, his voice husky.

We grinned at each other, our foreheads pressed together, oxygen flooding our mushy brains.

Feeling the flush on my cheeks, I followed him to the small bathroom. Black tiled floors and ceiling, white walls, and a touch of orange in the towels and square rug. It was all masculine, jut like him.

"There are toothbrushes in the first drawer, and I'll bring you a shirt to sleep in." He watched me, waiting for an answer.

"Sure. Sounds good." Was I really having a sleepover at a guy's place? Remembering my sister's warning from the other night, I sent her a text. Including the address we were at. It would prevent her from going ballistic. Yes, Emily had a tendency to be a bit overprotective of me.

EMILY

Enjoy your night *smiley face*

A stupid smile peeked out as I slid my phone back into my pocket after setting the alarm.

Jacob knocked on the door at the same exact moment. "Can I come in?"

"Yes."

"Here, I brought you two. Pick one."

Once he left, I undressed and slipped on the white T-shirt. It fell to mid-thigh. His perfume lingered on the fabric, and I found myself hooked on the masculine scent, feeling at ease as it wrapped around me.

With soap and water, I removed most of my makeup and joined him in his bedroom. I gasped at the sight of him—shirtless, wearing only his unbuttoned pants.

He twirled on his feet, catching me ogling him.

"Sorry," I said with a lopsided smile.

Jacob inched closer, kissed my forehead, and disappeared into the bathroom.

Not sure what to do, I slipped under the covers, wondering whether he slept on the left or right side. I felt inexperienced in that moment. This was all new territory to me.

The bathroom door opened, and our eyes locked onto each other like magnets, unable to resist. "I love the image of you in my bed," he said, with mischief lighting up his features, only wearing pajama pants that hung low on his hips. He turned off the lights and slid under the covers, pressing his body against mine from behind, his face nuzzled into the crook of my neck.

He wrapped one arm around my waist, his hand resting on my stomach at the junction of my T-shirt and the waistband of my panties. He traced circles on my bare skin with his thumb, sending shivers of pleasure through me.

With a sway of my hips, I scooted closer, his hard-on now nesting between my ass cheeks.

"Good night, Maddie."

I swallowed. "Good night."

Unable to fall asleep, I listened to his steady breathing and stared into the darkness. I'd missed this.

Affection.

It'd been too long since someone held me like that.

As if I was his.

As if I was precious.

I felt every thump of Jacob's heart between my shoulder blades.

His hand ventured to rest on my hip. I wriggled on the bed as one of his arms held me tighter against his chest.

My eyelids fluttered close.

His breathing steadied.

And I dozed off in no time.

Chapter 6

Sam

Why was I nervous like going on a first date? Madison wasn't here to interview me, for Christ's sake. She was here to meet the girls.

When we had talked yesterday, we decided to spend an hour or two at the house, then go to the park at the end of the street to have a picnic and talk about logistics and expectations while my daughters played around.

Dressed in faded jeans and a black T-shirt, freshly shaved, I joined my kids downstairs as they watched cartoons.

"Oh, you smell good," Justine said as I squeezed myself between them on the couch.

Mikaella leaned in and sniffed my shirt. "Yes, you smell *gooood.*"

Busted. I might have used cologne. Did I overdo it? Would I scare Madison away? Why did I put it on in the first place? What was I thinking? I just wanted to look presentable. Nice. Was that a crime? Okay, I was being ridiculous. My rustiness with people—and women in particular—ran deeper than I'd realized.

"Maybe I should change."

Justine climbed onto my lap and hooked her arms around my neck. "No, Daddy. I love when you smell good." The smile she offered me melted all my fears, and I chased away my apprehension with a deep inhale.

"Okay, fine. You win." I tickled her belly, and the sound of her giggles filled the room.

"Is *Mallison* here?" she asked once I stopped the torture.

"Not yet. Her name is Madison, with a *D*, like *dinosaur*, and she should be here in about ten minutes. What are we watching?"

"Something stupid Justine chose. I don't like it. It's for babies," Mikaella whined, her arms crossed over her chest, giving me a pointed look. Yep, her teenage years would be so much fun.

"I'm not a baby, Mika. You are the baby," Justine replied.

I placed a hand on both their thighs. "Stop. No one is a baby. Justine is allowed to enjoy this…this… What is it anyway? Are those pink kangaroos even talking, or are they only making those weird sounds?" I asked, my eyes now glued to the TV screen. "Don't tell me. It doesn't matter." I shook my head. Mikaella was right. This looked awful. The sight of the kangaroos alone gave me a headache. "Madison will be here shortly. I'd like you girls to be nice, okay? Can you do that for me?"

Justine nodded.

Mikaella shrugged.

I cursed in silence.

"What's wrong, sweet pea? We've already talked about this. You promised you'd give Madison a chance, remember?"

"I changed my mind. I don't want another mama. I already have one. And one day, she'll come back to get me."

The already fractured pieces of my heart turned to dust.

I wrapped an arm around the shoulders of my eldest daughter until she rested her head against my chest. "Mika, you're not getting another mama. No one is. Madison will only help us so Daddy can go back to the work he loves to do. If you want to live on the big camping bus like we've talked about and travel the country, then we need Madison to come with us. Either that or we're not going. I need some help. I'm sure you'll like her. She's nice and—"

The doorbell rang, and Justine rushed to the door before I could tell her to wait.

"*Mallison*," she said as she yanked the door open, jumping around. "Daddy, *Mallison* is here. *Mallison* is here. *Mallison* is here. Daddy. Daddy, come."

"Hey, you must be Justine, right? You can call me Maddie," Madison said as she kneeled to level her face with my little girl's. "I've heard so much about you. And if I remember correctly, you're a princess. Am I right?"

I watched the exchange from a safe distance.

Justine's face brightened up. "You can tell I'm a princess? For real?"

Madison smiled, and a chunk of my heart that was dead came back to life. "Oh yes. Look at your purple dress. It's really princess-y. Later, I'll want you to show me around your kingdom if that's okay with you?"

Justine bobbed her head, her smile widening, happiness radiating from her.

My heart melted a little more, filled with an exciting buzz.

She slid her little hand into Madison's and pulled her forward. "Come. Mika is not a princess. She thinks pink is only for babies. She only wants to wear black clothes, and the other day she put marker in her eyes. She looked scary."

"Marker in her eyes? Are you sure? It sounds painful."

Justine snickered and closed her eyes, sliding a finger across her eyelids. "Not in her eyes, silly. Black lines here and here."

"Oh, I see. Your daddy must have had a great time removing it." Madison's eyes met mine for the first time, and I shrugged, offering her a slight smile that she mirrored.

My heart flipped a little. Just a tiny bit. Maybe this could work after all.

"Come on. Mika is in there," Justine told our guest, pulling her toward the den.

I followed close behind, letting Madison introduce herself to my six-turning-sixteen-year-old daughter.

"Hi, Mikaella. I'm Maddie. It's nice to meet you. I've heard great things about you. What are you watching?" She took a seat on the opposite side of the couch where Mikaella sat.

My daughter said nothing, ignoring the woman conversing with her.

"It's fine. You don't have to talk to me. We can just watch this show together if it's okay with you. Do you mind?"

Mikaella shrugged.

Justine neared Madison and climbed onto her lap, twirling the loose strands of her dark hair around her fingers. "You look like a princess too. Your hair is pretty. I love pretty hair. Princesses love pretty hair too. You're missing a crown. Wait for me." My daughter jumped to her feet and disappeared, only to come back a minute later with two sparkling plastic crowns. "Here," she said as she fixed one on Madison's head. "Now we are both princesses."

From her end of the couch, Mikaella studied them. I could tell she wanted to join in but refused to break her walls. Nowadays, I wasn't the most trusting guy myself, so I couldn't blame her for having trust issues too. My heart bled some more for the pain Lisa had inflicted.

"Now that you're a real princess too, want to visit our castle?" Justine asked. "It's back there," she said, pointing to the back door.

"Sure," Madison said, rising to her feet, and holding out her hand to take Justine's. "Do you want to come with us, Mikaella?"

"It's Mika."

"Oh, sorry. Are you coming with us, Mika?"

My daughter shrugged but finally nodded. Her curiosity would get the best of her. No way would she ever be able to resist Madison for too long.

"Great. Show me the way then."

Madison and I exchanged another hint of a smile as she walked past me. This was awkward. Having another woman in this house. No, a college-aged girl. Anyway, I wasn't sure how I felt about a stranger spending a lot of time in our day-to-day lives yet. All of us would have to get used to this new dynamic.

Leaning against the living room archway, I watched the

three of them as they exited through the back door and emptied my lungs, the knots around my stomach tightening, instead of loosening, once space separated us.

My brain started making up scenarios.

Could this really work out? Going back on tour? Madison taking care of the girls? Our being a happy family once again?

Or was all this just a mirage? A fake sense of possibilities I had no right to expect anything from.

The three of them laughed, already at ease with one another. Even Mikaella couldn't refrain from joining in. The sight and realization that my little girls had missed so much in the last two years while I was busy mending my own heart hurt as much as they fixed a broken string inside me. For the longest time, I didn't infuse laughter into our household, and it pained me to come to the same conclusion as Riley did. That all three of us needed this new experience. Together. A new opportunity to connect and move on with our lives. For good.

I shut my eyes, exhaled, and busied myself in the kitchen, watching Madison interact with my eldest daughter and giving Justine a piggyback ride, through the bay window. She said something, and the girls laughed their hearts out. Madison grabbed her phone, and the girls started dancing. Did she put music on? From where I stood, I couldn't tell for sure.

At some point, I couldn't contain the smile that broke free on my face. Madison looked like she belonged here. With them.

Tension rolled off me in waves.

For a moment, I could see the clouds over our heads parting and the sun shining brighter upon us. Yes, perhaps Riley's crazy idea could work out after all.

Peace tinted the air and calmed my worries.

"Okay, girls. You'll spend the day with Madison. Daddy has a meeting with Uncle Riley, and I'll be gone until the evening. Promise me you'll be nice."

"Yes, Daddy," Justine said as I lowered her to her feet.

"Here," I said to Mikaella after I finished braiding her hair. "What about you, sweet pea? Will you be a good girl with Madison?"

She glanced away. "It depends."

I sat on the edge of the mattress and pulled her closer. "Give her a chance. A real one. Do it for me. Madison really likes you, and she's been nothing but great with you guys so far. You always have fun when she comes over. I know two weeks is not a long time to get to know someone, but I'm positive you'll enjoy your time together. She has a whole day of activities planned for you two. We already talked about it. School is over, and it's time to enjoy your summer."

"Fine," she said, forcing a smile.

In the past two weeks, since Madison came over the first time, we'd spent six full days with her, and she had dinner with us twice. So far, the girls got along with her just fine. Even though Mikaella acted as if spending time with her annoyed her, she always let her guard down within five minutes of being around her. Madison had a way of reaching my daughter through the glass cage she had built around herself. My six-going-onto-sixteen sported happy grins these days. And that was worth more than any performances I'd give in my life. Worth more than any amount of money I could ever earn.

In the end, I had warmed up to Madison looking after my daughters in my home faster than I thought I would.

Springing to my feet, I scooped Mikaella over my

shoulder, tickling her at the same time. "Come on, sweet pea, stop brooding. Put on your cheerful face now. Do it for me."

We rolled onto the bed, laughing. My little girl cupped my cheeks. "I will. I love when you put your cheerful face on too, Daddy. *Grinchy* isn't a good look on you."

Fog clouded my vision, and I blinked my emotions away. I swallowed the boulder in my throat as her words wound their way into my heart. Yes, joy and giggles were more frequent these days in the Stevenses' household. And lightness had invaded our home too.

Justine joined us, sitting on my stomach.

"Girls, listen." I caught a wheezing breath in. "I'm sorry for everything. The last two years have been hard on me too. I'm ready to change things up around here. For us to have a fresh start. To be cheerful and smile more, so much that our lips are stretched forever and our happiness can't be erased."

Justine leaned forward and pulled my cheeks out, creating a huge, ridiculous exaggeration of a smile. "Like this?"

I had to laugh at that. "Yes, baby girl."

Mikaella shook her head. "No, please, you look scary. Don't grin too much. It's freaky."

"I'll stop smiling if you stop with the moody attitude. *Grinchy* isn't a good look on you either," I said, repeating her own words. "Do we have a deal?" I sat and held out my hand.

Her eyes darted from my palm to my eyes for a long beat. An I-mean-business frown appeared across her forehead. My daughter already possessed way too much backbone for her young age. She'd be a tough opponent growing up.

She groaned, putting her best game face on. "Deal."

We shook on it, and Justine climbed onto my back. "Let's get ready then because Madison will be here in fifteen minutes."

With Justine still clinging to me and Mikaella in my arms, we made it downstairs, the three of us laughing.

We were done with breakfast when the doorbell rang.

"*Mallison* is here, Daddy," Justine screamed as she ran toward the front door, her sister in tow.

I put the dishes away and wiped the kitchen island as they sauntered back in my direction.

"Good morning, Mr. Stevens," the nanny said. Coming from her mouth, Mr. Stevens made me feel like my old man. Damn it. I was older than her, sure. But I wasn't *that* old.

"We've already talked about this. Sam is fine. Don't Mr. Stevens me. Please."

"Then it's Maddie. No more Madison."

I ran a hand through my hair, taking in the woman before me. Dressed in black shorts and a cream tank top, she looked even younger than I remembered. Dewy complexion and rounded eyes. With hardly any make-up on, only her lips painted in a soft shade of pink. A few strands of her hair had drawn loose around her face from the low ponytail she was sporting.

She bent over to pick up Justine, and I got a peek at the swell of her breasts.

A fuzzy feeling worked through me.

I hadn't been close to any woman, except for my friends' wives or the girls' teachers, in two years. Having one in my kitchen, nonetheless, had a weird way of making my testosterone spike.

I cleared my throat before my mind wandered to uncharted territories. "I should be back after dinner. There's chicken in the fridge I made last night. And snacks in the pantry. My phone number is by the sink in case you erased it by mistake from your phone, and I made a set of house keys for you. Also, all the emergency numbers are on there," I pointed to a paper on the countertop, "and—"

Madison inched closer and put her hand on my forearm. She barely brushed my skin, and I almost shot my load in my pants. I really was a sick motherfucker.

"Mr. Stev…Sam. Stop. We'll be fine. I've been here almost every day in the last week. You don't need to worry. We've been over this more than once. And no, I haven't erased your contact from my phone, and I can dial 9-1-1 from memory."

She offered me a sweet smile, and I stepped back, desperate to move out of her magnetic field. All my poles were off. I had to get them back in check.

"Yeah, you're right." Warmth swirled inside me. I must have looked like a complete lunatic, not a father of two who had all his shit together and who was about to leave on tour for months.

Mikaella walked into the kitchen and broke the sort of daze I'd fallen into.

Thank you, sweet pea.

"Can we bake a cake? You said last time you'd show me how to ice one."

Madison's grin widened. "Sure. I even brought little sugar flowers I made to decorate it."

"You did? Can I see them?"

Justine came running. "Cake," she cheered with her adorable, overflowing enthusiasm, a trademark of hers.

Madison fished a small container out of her bag and showed the girls. They both screamed with excitement. They'd be fine.

From my office slash music studio, which I had

reclaimed as mine, I grabbed my guitar case, ready to get out of here.

When I walked back into the kitchen, the girls were already deep in baking mode.

Justine sat on the counter, cracking eggs, a white—did Madison bring it?—paper chef hat on, and Mikaella was propped on a stool, wearing a banana yellow apron, busy pouring flour into a measuring cup, white powder sprinkled all over her. Madison stood between them, a priceless, pride-filled grin stretching her face, her eyes sparkling, giving them instructions.

They'd be more than fine.

Why was I so worried about leaving them for a few hours? Standing in the kitchen doorway, I felt silly.

For a long minute, I watched them. The three of them looked at ease working together. The kitchen consisted of an island with an oversized butcher block countertop, stainless steel appliances, and a large window overlooking the backyard. The room had been neglected over the years. When the girls were little, Lisa and I used to bake pies on Thanksgiving together and cookies on Christmas day. On Sunday mornings, she made hot chocolate while I flipped pancakes, to my daughters' greatest enjoyment. Our own family traditions that had gotten lost after her departure. A fleck of nostalgia hit me, followed by a draft of happiness that took root in my chest. I relished the sight of this room, that contained so many good memories, being animated once again.

"What are you baking?" I asked as I landed a kiss on Justine's head.

"*Crotchcolate* cake, Daddy. Your favorite." Joy radiated from her.

"You mean chocolate," Madison said before I could correct her.

"Yes. *Crotchcolate*."

I sighed, and Madison snickered behind her hand.

"We'll practice it, sweetie," she told my oblivious baby girl.

I leaned forward, careful not to get flour all over me as I kissed Mikaella's cheek. "Mika, you're doing good. I can't wait to taste that cake tonight."

"Can we stay up until you come home to eat it together?"

"Absolutely. I wouldn't have it any other way."

"Justine, we'll make Daddy the most beautiful cake he's ever seen. Careful. Don't drop the eggshells into the batter."

I spun around to leave but bumped into Madison, squeezed between Mikaella's stool and the refrigerator behind us. My eyes darted to her chest, rising and falling, for a quick second before I brought my gaze back to hers.

"Here," I said, wiping the flour from her cheek with the pad of my thumb unable to help myself.

Her breathing picked up. So did mine.

High-voltage electricity gushed through me, and I yanked my hand back. I scowled to avoid sending her the wrong signals about a nonexistent attraction between us. Our relationship wasn't about this. I'd hired her to care for my daughters. Nothing more.

"Thanks," she whispered, eyeing me as if she were trying to understand the switch in my demeanor.

"I-I gotta go. You call me if you need anything, okay?"

She nodded. "I will. And we'll wait for you to eat that *crotchcolate* cake." A flush appeared on her face as she used my baby's word.

"I'm counting on it."

Before I could say something stupid and my brain started making double-meaning jokes, I walked away.

Outside, with my back resting against the shut door, I breathed in and out, trying to find a reasonable explanation for my sudden lack of boundaries.

Coming short, I shook my head, pushed the thought away, and climbed behind the wheel of my SUV, ready to get far away from here.

Chapter 7
Madison

W hy was Sam looking at me with a frown? As if I'd done something wrong. Nothing had happened. The girls and I were baking a cake when he walked in. At first, he had looked relaxed and happy. What had changed? His eyes had darkened when he'd glanced at me from up close, his pupils stealing the color of his eyes.

I had tried to swallow but failed when his heated gaze landed on me.

No matter how I flipped around our last encounter in my head, I couldn't come up with a reason why Sam Stevens would have been suddenly annoyed with me.

Justine spilled milk on the countertop as she lifted the measuring cup.

"Justine, you're making a mess," Mikaella complained.

The little girl's bottom lip quivered, and tears pooled in her eyes.

"It's all fine. Don't worry, okay? You're doing a great job, sweetie," I said, patting her head once she poured the remaining white liquid into the bowl.

"Like that?"

I nodded, and her cheerfulness returned. The girl's delight was contagious, and a wide grin split my face.

"Can I add the *crotchcolate* now?"

"Chocolate, dummy," her sister said.

"No, Mika. Enough. Don't use this word around your sister. Be nice and help her out instead." I crossed my arms over my chest, and Mikaella studied me for a moment, probably wondering if I was being serious. "What do you have to say to Justine?"

She muttered something under her breath.

"What did you say?"

"Sorry." She spoke so low that I wasn't even sure I heard it right.

"Come on, Mika, you can do better than that."

"Sorry, Justine. I am sorry I called you dummy. You're not. Happy now?" she asked, angling her body until we faced each other.

I clasped my hands together. "Better. Now let's finish this cake because we're going to the park before lunch. I brought a swimsuit, and we can play in the fountains."

"The fountains? I love the fountains," Justine singsonged, her happiness fully restored now.

"You're coming in with us?" her sister asked, stopping midway as she poured the batter into a mold.

"Sure. Why not? I like to have fun too."

"Daddy never comes in. He always watches from the side. Says he's too old."

"I'm not your daddy, girls. Age is just a number. Anyway, I wanna play in the fountains with you two. It's hot outside, and no way am I staying on the sidelines. What about a picnic? We could eat there."

"Yes," they both screamed at the same time.

————

When Sam came back, looking his usual mix of handsome, serious, and sexy but more tired than usual, the girls and I were in the backyard, tossing water balloons around.

Even though he wasn't always the most pleasant man —someone who ought to smile more often—he had everything women swooned over. Tall, a couple of inches over six feet, I bet he hid delicious chest muscles underneath his clothes. The ridges of his body, visible through his T-shirt, had me hot and bothered. His broody attitude made him mysterious and inaccessible, and his voice, rough and low with a Southern drawl, added to his magnetism, husky enough to melt panties.

No doubt he was a country music superstar. Just his presence could steal the breathable air from a room.

Did women throw their bras at him when he gave concerts in the past? Did they follow him to his hotel room and try to seduce him? Did they tattoo his face on their backs or ask him to autograph their breasts?

A twinge started in my toes and reached my skull.

I shouldn't think about my boss this way. I was the hired help. Nothing more. Nothing less. My job was to take care of his two adorable daughters, and I'd never do anything to jeopardize that. Ever.

My mind wandered to Jacob. His hooded eyes and sexy bed hair in the morning, the intensity of his gaze each time it roamed over me, the softness of his kisses, and the strength of his arms that one time he held me at night.

Our friendship was blossoming, and neither of us was in a hurry to take it to the next level. We enjoyed each other's company, and for now, it was more than I could ask for. We hadn't discussed it, but since I was leaving in the fall, we were both aware that a relationship would only complicate things between us.

Our easy friendship, common interests in literature and music, and our introverted lifestyle, added to our burgeoning attraction and made us a perfect match.

It also prevented me from entertaining a forbidden crush on the man who had hired me, one that had the potential to hurt me and screw with my job.

The other night, curious about him, I'd watched a video from three years ago of Sam rocking a stage. His hair had been longer back then, and his eyes glinted with joy—something missing nowadays. The present version of Sam Stevens always sported dark circles under his worry-filled eyes, and a permanent sadness lingered in his gaze. No matter what he did, it was always there, tinting his irises.

"Oh, you're home already?" I asked him, pushing the wet hair glued to my forehead back to clear my vision. "What time is it? We haven't had dinner yet."

Sam stepped closer, his hands floating between us. "It's only four. My meeting ended early, and I didn't feel like eating out, so I just came home instead. I prefer a night in to fancy restaurants or clubs anytime." He shrugged. "It was a no-brainer."

His eyes lowered to my red bikini top and snapped back to my face quickly.

"Sorry. I-I usually don't parade half-naked around you…people. I usually…you know…wear clothes. I had them, huh, I had them on earlier, then I got hot and undressed when I decided to get wet." *Uh-oh, that's coming out all-wrong.* I sounded like a lunatic. And a sex-crazed exhibitionist. Dear God. I paused, trying to regroup my thoughts and stop my rambling.

Sam watched me, his lips pinched together, barely containing the smile that threatened to burst out—*jerk*. It was clear from the crooked smile uplifting the corners of his mouth, he wouldn't help me out of this one. I was on my own.

I gave a loud, theatrical sigh as if he was forcing me to give an explanation and wasting my time. "I should use a towel now. I'm still dripping all over your deck. One slip and you might end up sliding right into my puddle… and me."

Sam cocked an eyebrow.

Gosh. Why were all my words sounding like innuendos while talking to my boss, half-undressed? My brain was either on strike or defective. These words didn't even sound like mine. *Geez…someone please kill me right now.* "I'm soaked, and being drenched isn't comfortable. Sorry, I'll get changed. And…huh…shut up." Oh, for crying out loud. Every time I opened my mouth, it got worse. "I'll go now." *Smooth, Maddie, real smooth.* I felt my face heating up.

He studied me a little longer, pleasure written all over his face.

"Daddy, watch out," Mikaella warned as she and Justine ran toward us and shot water balloons at Sam, dousing him in no time.

I pinched my lips together to fight the fit of giggles stirring deep inside me.

Sam stood there in his damp jeans and shirt, an unreadable expression overtaking his face and chasing his amusement away.

The girls froze, water balloons still in their hands.

I stopped breathing.

Would he get mad? I wrinkled my nose, waiting for his reaction. Instead, he grabbed a handful of ammunition from the bucket beside me and tossed them at his daughters. They both started running around, laughing and screaming for more.

His eyes twinkled and I exhaled, relishing this playful side of him.

From the lounger, I picked up a towel and wrapped it around myself, ready to leave.

My job here was done.

Just when I was about to open the back door, Mikaella caught up with me. Her eyes rounded as she stared at me. "Are you leaving?"

I kneeled before her. "Yes, I am. Your daddy is back. I'll let you spend time with him. I'm sure he missed you today."

She tugged at my hand. "But I like it better when you're here. You could have dinner with us. You can't leave without tasting the cake. We worked hard to make it pretty for Daddy."

My heart expanded in my chest. These little girls already owned my heart. "Maybe you could save me a slice, and I'll taste it tomorrow."

She shook her head. "No. I wanna taste it with you tonight like we were supposed to. I'll tell Daddy to come back later." She twirled on her feet, but I grabbed her wrist before she could rush to him.

My eyes followed Sam, now completely soaked, being chased by Justine, both of them zigzagging across the backyard and giggling. The sight of them brought a curve to my lips. "Mika, it's better if I go now. We'll have many more occasions to eat together. Go play with your daddy."

She shook her head. "I don't wanna play anymore if you leave."

Pieces of my heart cracked, and I pulled her into my arms. "Mika, listen to me, I—"

"What's wrong, sweet pea?" Sam asked, closing in on us, his hair falling over his eyes, giving him a rakish look.

My entire being pulsed at the sight of him, free of all the icy control he usually kept close around him.

"Why don't you play with us?"

Mikaella pushed away from me and firmed her shoulders, her attitude back. "Maddie is leaving. I'm not playing anymore if she goes. We were supposed to eat our cake together. She was supposed to have dinner with us. You were supposed to be at your music work. It's not fair. I want Maddie to stay."

"You leaving?" Justine asked as she moved between all of us, her eyes big and full of question marks. "Why? You don't wanna play with us anymore?" Her lips shuddered, and another fragment of my heart cracked.

"I love spending time with you two, but your daddy is back home, so it means I must go. I'll see you both tomorrow, okay? Don't be sad. We'll have a great time, I promise."

Justine circled my neck with her arms. "Can we go to the fountains again?"

"Sure, I'd love to."

"Can Maddie stay, Daddy?" Mikaella asked, her eyes bright with hope.

Sam cleared his throat and took a step in my direction. He locked his dark gaze on mine, swallowing me in. "Why do you have to go? The girls are right. Why don't you stay? You guys were having fun. I intruded on your game."

A shiver ran through me. "I shouldn't. It's your time with the girls."

"I brought everything for a barbecue on my way home. We can eat outside and—" He shrugged. "We can taste that chocolate cake you promised this morning. I've been looking forward to it all day. What do you say?"

"I..." Why wasn't I able to come up with a good enough reason to walk away?

Sam's heavy stare pinned me on the spot, and my brain lost the ability to think clearly.

"Say yes," Justine pleaded.

"Please," Mikaella added, giving me puppy dog eyes.

Sam took one step closer, and before I could add something, he popped two water balloons over my head. "Oops. You're soaked again. I guess you can't leave just now and must stay a little longer so that you don't ruin the floors when you go in, dripping wet. You know because if you're drenched, I could slide into you...or your puddle."

"Ohmygod. No, you can't do this. It's unfair. Using my previous humiliation against me in a battle of words is a cheap shot."

He winked, and I nearly melted into a puddle right there on his deck. How bad was the flush on my face right about now? That word again. I should never, ever think or say 'puddle' again. From now on, it would always be tinged with memories of this moment—with him—and my utter humiliation.

"Your words, not mine," he said, lifting his arms in surrender.

A fit of laughter escaped both our lips. I supposed the ice was broken between us. Maybe it would help melt the tension that always swirled between us whenever we stood close—the same tension that had been there since the day we met—for good.

"I can't believe I said that." I shook my head, trying to get rid of the moment.

Oblivious to the exchange, the girls laughed at my dripping face. Sam looked like he'd already forgotten my little embarrassing moment because he tossed missiles at his daughters before running after them.

With a sigh, I discarded my towel. "Girls, I think we should come up with a revenge plan." They both bobbed their heads, still laughing their hearts out as we devised a scheme to get back at their father.

For the next twenty minutes, we threw all the remaining balloons we had at Sam, now rolling around on the lawn, grass stains on his jeans, his arms folded over his head like a shield, begging us to stop our attack.

The girls helped him to get to his feet when we were short of projectiles before disappearing into their castle in the woods.

"You're sure it's okay for me to crash your family dinner?" I asked, still unsure if it was a good idea.

Sam busied himself removing the bits of grass stuck to his wet shirt. "I'm sure. I'm the one who disrupted your plans."

I nodded, avoiding his eyes.

"And Madison—"

"Maddie," I replied, savoring the sound of my name rolling off his lips. *Focus, girl. Enough with the misplaced crush. Grow a spine and get over it. Not happening.*

"Yes, *Maddie.* Thanks for bringing joy to my little girls' lives. Thanks for putting smiles on their faces. They haven't had as much fun as they should have had in the last two years. It-it's all my fault… For over a year, I was in a very dark place. I'm grateful you're here to show me what I've been missing. And how I can get better."

"Stop it. You're a great father."

"Yeah. Well, I try to be. But I screwed up. A lot. My life was a mess, and it impacted my children's happiness.

Without you around, I'm not sure I would've realized it soon enough. So, thank you. For everything you are doing for our family. I don't say it often enough."

I bowed my head, at a loss for words. Vulnerability looked good on him. Almost dangerous.

The air between us heated up.

When I tilted my head back, I met his eyes, dark and cryptic. He watched me for a beat as if deciding whether to tell me something or not, before breaking eye contact.

"I should get changed."

"Me too," I said, following him close behind toward the house but making sure to keep enough space between us. "Careful. Don't get the floors wet," I teased.

He watched me over his shoulder, choking on a laugh. The air charged around us. Sam blinked, cracked a tiny smile, but said nothing as he stared ahead and retreated inside.

———

"They're both fast asleep. I don't know what you did today, but I'll buy your recipe. Neither one complained when I told them it was bedtime. Mika, who usually always has something to argue about, stayed quiet."

"I can't tell you my secrets, or they won't be secrets anymore. All I can say is that we ran around all day. And can you believe Justine napped for an hour and a half this afternoon? Mika didn't, but we rested anyway."

He nodded and motioned to stand. "Drink?"

"No, thanks. I'll stick to lemonade. I'm a lightweight. I don't drink and drive. One is enough to get me dizzy."

Sam fetched a can of beer and resumed his seat across from me on the back deck.

The terrace ran almost the entire length of the back of

the house. Accessible from the kitchen door, the outdoor cooking space—featuring a grill, a sink, and an under-counter refrigerator set into a stacked stone structure—was to the left of the dining area. Matching loungers and a set of dark couches were two steps up on our right, positioned by the door leading to the den and dining room.

Both side neighbors were far enough, and the thick line of mature trees bordering their land created natural fences, allowing enough intimacy.

The girls' castle was nestled in the woods that outlined the far end of the backyard, surrounded by an expanse of manicured green lawn. A wooden swing set with a corkscrew slide and a guitar-shaped covered sandbox were on our right, where the back deck ended.

"Listen," Sam said. "I was thinking… Before the big tour, I'd like to throw a party for the girls. With their friends. Something special. I might ask for your help. You're amazing with kids, so your intake would be useful. I know it's months away from now, but I'm putting it out there…so I don't forget."

"Let me know what you have in mind, and I'll be happy to brainstorm ideas with you and help out."

"Are they giving you trouble?"

"The girls?" I asked.

"Yeah. Mika can be stubborn sometimes."

"Nah. They're good kids. And let me tell you they love baking. It doesn't seem like it, but cooking is a mix of literacy, math, and sciences. It's a great way to teach kids without them feeling like you're trying to force knowledge into their brains."

"Whoa. I'd never seen it like that before, but it makes sense."

"Plus, it's fun since we can eat our creations afterward.

It's great for their self-esteem. Has Mikaella told you about Stella's birthday party on Friday? They stopped by earlier to drop off the invitation. It's from late afternoon till the evening at the park. Justine is invited too, but you gotta be present."

"Mika said nothing. We're auditioning musicians to form the band on Friday. It's usually a long and exhausting process. I'm not sure I'll make it on time."

"I can go if you want," I offered. "The girls are really looking forward to it. Stella's mom said there would be a magician and a petting zoo."

"You don't have to. I can talk to Stella's mom. She'll understand."

"I insist. Since Mika will be away for six months, she should enjoy time with her best friend while she's still in town, don't you think?"

Sam sipped his beer, drumming his fingers on the table, appearing to debate the idea in his head. "I'm still not comfortable asking you to put in more hours."

"When we first met, you and Riley told me there would be evening and night shifts. I'm prepared for all eventualities. I'm telling you that I'm happy to go if you agree."

Sam huffed. "I won't fight with you over this. Just make sure you still get some free time too before we leave. Because once we're on the road, it will be intense. Fun, but tiring sometimes."

I flipped my phone over on the table to check the time. "It's late. I should leave. Thanks for dinner. You didn't lie. I gotta say, those ribs were spectacular."

We both rose, and Sam shoved his hands into his pockets, looking a lot younger and vulnerable in the sunset. In the last few hours, some of the creases around his eyes had receded. "We'll see you tomorrow?"

"Sure. I'll be here at nine." I waved at him as I walked to my car, a vehicle I'd bought with the money I'd piled up, working two jobs at eighteen.

In the safety of my car, I blew out a long breath.

Why was the air tense every time Sam and I were alone in the same room?

My imagination was playing tricks on me. That had to be it.

I pulled away from the driveway and parked on the side of the road to text Jacob.

ME

I'm done with work. Want to hang out tonight?

His answer came within a minute.

JACOB

Wanna come over?

ME

I'll be there ASAP.

After Jacob buzzed me in, I climbed the stairs to his apartment, two at a time.

"Do you wanna go out or stay in?" he asked me, locking a hand around my waist and tugging me closer.

I leaned back and studied his face. "Night in would be awesome, but I kinda have somewhere to be later tonight. I was hoping you'd join me."

"Do we have time before leaving? There's something I'd like to try with you first."

I raised an eyebrow. "What is it?" I asked, the air molecules around us charging with possibilities.

"Do you trust me?"

"I do."

"Close your eyes then."

I heard a door being opened—or closed. Something that sounded like a zipper. And plastic on plastic rubbing together. The suspense was killing me.

Jacob fixed something on my head. Was it a helmet? Or a hat? My pulse kicked up a notch. Should I be worried?

"Okay, look now." He spoke in that pleased tone he only ever used around me, mostly shy with everyone else.

My lids fluttered open, and my hands flew to cover my overexcited heart. I mirrored his gorgeous smile. "Ohmygod, you got these for us?"

"Nah, I borrowed them from a girl at work. She actually gave me a lesson during lunchtime so I wouldn't break my bones and would be able to stand for more than thirty seconds straight."

"You roller-skated in the lab during your lunch hour?"

"Kinda. I have to be able to care for you if you have a hard time staying upright. These are way tougher to manage than inline skates."

I took in the retro white roller skates. The ones people wore in eighties movies.

Without a word, I jumped into his inviting arms. "This is the best idea ever. I love it. I would break my neck with you any time, Jacob Williams. Only with you, though."

He fixed the helmet properly over my head. "Promise me you won't put them on without this."

I nodded, and he kissed my forehead.

"I promise. When can we go? Tonight? I always wanted to try roller skating. I used to watch old music videos when I was a kid and pictured myself skating around a rink, wearing them."

"I remember your eyes lighting up when you saw those

girls skating around in that clothes ad the other night. Thought you might be onboard."

Jacob was always noticing the small details about me. Things I didn't say out loud, from my expressions alone. It amazed me how well he could read me.

"Thursday. There's a vintage-themed night at the rink. Black lights. Laser beams. Disco music."

I fastened my grip around him. "I'm so ready to fall on my ass and be the worst skater on the face of this Earth if I'm doing it with you."

"I was hoping you'd say that. If we like it enough, maybe it could become our thing. Rocking the skating rink to old pop songs in mismatched, vibrant clothes once a week."

I bobbed my head. "Yes. I'm glad we're doing this together. Speaking of tonight, Becks—one of Emily's friend—is playing at a bar downtown. His set ends at eleven thirty. It's almost ten, but would you join me? It's a big deal for him, and I'd promised a while back I'd make an appearance."

"Let's go then. I'm always more at ease around people when you're beside me."

"I know. I am too. Before we leave, can I try those skates for just a minute?" I asked, batting my eyelashes, my hands linked together in a prayer—or a plea.

"I was wondering why you hadn't begged until now. Come on, let me give you a quick lesson. I'll move the couch and table while you get set. And don't be scared. I won't let go of your hand."

His contagious smile turned my chest into a firework show.

Our friendship was the highlight of my days. With Jacob, I could just be myself. No pretense. No complication. We connected on so many levels. I had never experienced a relationship like this with anyone else before. Except for my sister, but that didn't really count. I never had a best friend before him.

I put the skates on, unable to hide my happiness overload.

"Need help to tie those?" he asked.

"Nah. I think I'm good." I winced. "Oh, maybe you could tighten the left one. It feels a bit loose."

Jacob kneeled before me and got to work. "Earlier I was thinking… When you get back from tour, I'd love for us to go somewhere."

"What do you mean?"

"I've never traveled the world. If I go on a plane and visit another country for the first time, I want it to be with you. It would be out of my comfort zone, but backpacking in the jungle or climbing a mountain sound like things you would enjoy. If we do this together, I bet I'd love it too." He shrugged. "I don't know. I always feel braver when I'm with you."

I rested my hands on his shoulders, and his gaze found mine. "You do?"

The tilt of his lips got my heart racing. "Yeah."

"Jake, I'd love to go on an adventure with you. And for what it's worth, I feel more courageous around you too. I never told anyone about my childhood. You're the first person I ever confided in. I don't know… It seems right. Thanks for saving me in that bar. I can't imagine a life where we never met."

His lips brushed mine. "Then let's do this. Get up and show me your skills." He extended his arms, helping me to my feet.

When I rolled backward, his hands secured my waist, preventing me from falling.

"Ready?" Jacob asked.

I exhaled and firmed my back. "Yes."

For the next ten minutes, like a baby giraffe learning to take her first steps, I roller-skated around Jacob's living room, laughing so hard my abdominal muscles hurt and my eyes leaked happy tears.

For the first time in years, I felt content. And light-hearted.

Chapter 8
Sam

I came home in the middle of the afternoon, exhausted. Rehearsal had lasted forever, and the band and I had made so many adjustments to three of the songs, I could no longer decide which version I loved best. All I craved was some quiet time and a cold beer. Something I started buying again, now that I'd decided to reclaim my *Sam Stevens, the man* title and not just be defined as *Sam Stevens, the single father of two.*

The last month had come and gone in the blink of an eye. It felt like it was just yesterday when I had walked in on Madison and the kids running around and throwing water balloons in the backyard.

Madison's presence in our lives had turned out to be a blessing after all. Every day, Mikaella laughed a little more —and smiled a whole lot more. I had no idea if it was due to the fact there was a woman in our house most days of the week or if Madison just possessed some magical power that appealed to my daughter, but I noticed the subtle changes every time we were together. Even her psychotherapist asked me what I did differently that brought her out of her shell. A few weeks with her nanny had achieved what almost two years of therapy couldn't.

Like a magnet, my eyes found Madison the moment I stepped into the kitchen. Dressed in denim cut-offs and a loose white T-shirt, her back made an enticing picture. Her hair was tied in a knot at the top of her head, and colorful bracelets dangled around her wrist. She looked like a vision I could easily fall for.

A *too-young-for-you vision*, I chastised myself.

On her tiptoes, she tried to grab a pan from the cupboard. Cursing under her breath, she stretched to her full length, still unable to reach the upper shelf.

Feeling like it was my duty to help her, I neared her from behind and placed my hands over hers. "Here," I said. "Let me get that for you."

She gulped a sharp intake of air, nodded, and stepped back.

My body powered up at the proximity, her citrusy fragrance whirling around me, but I ordered it to shut down.

"Thanks," she said in a soft voice I had a hard time resisting. "I didn't hear you come in."

"Where are the girls?"

"Napping. I put them to bed for a nap a bit later than usual. I'll wake them up in about thirty minutes. We had an active morning."

I grabbed a can of beer from the fridge and took a seat on a stool, facing her across the island.

She studied me. "You're home early."

Something was different between us. Madison was different. Distant. Something had changed in the last couple of weeks, and I couldn't pinpoint what it was exactly. Gone were the sideways stolen glances and the easy connection we'd once shared.

"Everything fine?" she asked

I shook off my questioning thoughts. "Yeah. All good. Just tired." I chugged half the beer in one gulp, relishing the coldness down my throat, and watched her pour a mixture of something chocolaty into the pan. "What are you baking?"

"Brownies. You guys always devour them within the hour every time I make them. I thought you'd like to have some for dessert tonight. I also told the girls they could have a piece after their nap."

"Are you staying for dinner? I'm sure the girls would love you to," I said, trying to sound casual. Since the day we had a water-balloon fight and I'd barbecued, Madison had refused all our requests to stay for dinner on the days I was home early. In all honesty, I missed the company. Her company. She possessed some special power—not only with my kids, but with me too—able to put my mind at rest. To keep my annoyance simmering low instead of overpowering.

She shook her head. "Sorry. I already made plans for tonight."

"How are you going to make it home? I noticed your car isn't in the driveway. Need a ride?"

Was I being too inquisitive? Was I overlapping boundaries? No. I was just caring for her safety. Nothing more.

"Nah, thanks. I have someone picking me up later."

A light pink flush crept up her neck and cheeks. She looked like a little girl caught doing something naughty.

"Wanna hear something funny?" she asked, leaning forward and resting her forearms on the countertop to stare at me.

"Always."

"The girls and I talked about New York, and I showed them pictures of the Statue of Liberty. Justine decided she looked pretty and spent almost twenty minutes with a blanket tied around her shoulders and one arm over her head, holding the TV remote, pretending to be her."

"She did?"

Madison nodded. She showed me a picture of my baby girl on her phone. "She lowered her arm when I served lunch and couldn't resist my mama's mushroom chicken recipe."

"Rewind a sec. Mushrooms?" She bobbed her head as I scratched my forehead in awe. "Once again, you gotta tell me your secret. How did you get her to eat those? She's a picky eater. She never even takes a bite when I serve them."

"We pretend they are fairy's houses, and they sprinkle magic dust in her stomach. I'm telling you, she can't resist then."

She returned to her pan and placed it in the oven. After using a dishcloth to wipe her hands clean, she twirled on herself, ready to exit the kitchen. "Be right back. I'll go check on the girls."

Why did I have the feeling she was avoiding me? Did something happen? Did I do or say something that had bothered her? I raked my mind. No, I couldn't think of anything.

Before she could get too far away, I grabbed her arm. Why was I always drifting toward her…always fighting not to touch her? What was wrong with me?

She's your children's nanny. My conscience jumped in, trying to berate my kindled, traitorous body once and for all. Easier said than done. Something about Madison was waking up the primitive side of me. *Me. You. Cave. Babies.*

With a deep breath, I shook my head, trying to erase the intimate images of us forming in my mind.

I'd been alone for so long. It was the fact she was a gorgeous woman, and I was a man, single and lonely, that was messing with my hormones. Nothing more. I was only receptive to her feminine charms. It had nothing to do with her, per se. After all, she was the only woman I saw almost daily. We were always around each other. Breathing the same oxygen.

Madison halted and stared at me.

Why did she have to look at me with those sea-green eyes of hers? Like she could swallow any word I'd throw at her.

Trying to ease the air surrounding us, I broke the charged silence. "Mika and Justine are fine. If they wake up, they'll come downstairs."

She nodded, looking away, her teeth imprinting on her lower lip as she chewed on it.

I took a deep breath. "I'm gonna ask you a question." Her eyes darted back to mine as I stared at her face. "Did I do something that…huh…hurt or annoyed you?"

She glanced down to where my hand still clutched her arm, and I released her.

My heart went off-beat the moment we broke apart. Why was my body so responsive to hers?

"Every time I'm home, you-you can't leave quickly enough. We'll be living together on a bus for months. If you've changed your mind or if something is bothering you, you have to tell me. We must be honest with each other. That's the only way we'll get through this without harboring murderous thoughts about each other. Tour life isn't always easy. People cramped together for long periods of time with no room to catch a break more often than not. It can get ugly fast. I'm speaking from experience."

Before she could answer, Justine came barreling down the stairs, wearing a glittery pink princess dress, and rushed toward me. My heart burst from too much happiness at the sight of her happy demeanor. I pulled my baby girl into my arms, spun her around, and nuzzled her hair.

"Daddy. Daddy."

"Baby, oh, I've missed you so much. Where's your sister?"

She cupped my cheeks with her small hands. "Sleeping. She sounds like a monster. Why is she making weird noises?"

I fought a smile. "She must be snoring. That means she's really tired. Aren't you tired too?"

"No. I want to eat *browkinies*. And play in the castle. And draw."

"First, it's brownies, and they're not ready yet. Second, why don't you draw something I can hang in my studio? Third, when Mika is up, you two can play outside. Sounds good?"

"Yes, Daddy." Those two words. They could melt my heart and heal every broken piece. Justine jumped from my grip and hurried into the den where her pencils and coloring books were stacked.

As soon as she scurried away, I brought my attention back to Madison to continue our conversation, but she was nowhere to be seen. Well, we'd have to do this some other time.

I emptied my beer and went to find my daughter. Sitting in the chair by the fireplace, I fished my guitar out of its case. "Wanna sing with me?" I asked her.

"Yes." She abandoned her coloring books to sit at my feet. "Doo-doo-la-la," she said, referring to a part of the chorus of "I Belong," the first song I'd written this summer.

…You and me (Doo-doo-la-la)
Are meant to be (Doo-doo-la-
la)
This is where you'll find me
Because this is where I belong,
baby

While I sang the last verse, I watched Justine, grinning, and said, "Solo, baby."

Goose bumps bloomed on my arms at the sound of her small voice. She took her time to articulate every word the best she could while following the melody.

…You and me (Doo-doo-la-la)
Are meant to be (Doo-doo-la-
la)
This is where you'll find me
Because this is where I belong,
baby

My eyes caught Madison listening to us from the archway. Her eyes weren't on my daughter, but on me, cold and unreadable. Not a single hint of a smile touched her face. She watched me with an intensity that sent a surge of heat to my core. My throat worked as the song ended.

She neared us, clapping. "Wow, you guys. You two were great."

"You heard my song?" Justine asked as Madison sat beside her and pulled her into her lap.

"Yes. And you were the best." Her voice turned to a whisper. "Don't tell your daddy, but I think you're even better than him. You are the star, sweetie."

My baby girl sprang to her feet, running away, "Mika,

Mika. Maddie said I'm a star and I sing better than—"
The distance drowned her words.

"Ever played music?" I asked.

"No. It's not something I've ever been inclined to learn. My mom and sister play the piano. Growing up, I preferred to sit and listen to them than to give it a try."

She moistened her lips with a quick swipe of her tongue, and my attention drifted there for a brief second.

I cleared my throat. "Wanna try?"

She hesitated for a second. "Not sure I'm talented."

I shrugged. "You won't know unless you give it a shot."

"Yeah… Makes sense."

On my knees, I settled next to Madison and handed her my instrument.

"What do I do now?"

"Place your hand here," I arranged her digits, "and your fingers here and there. Yeah, like this. Now your other hand should be positioned like this," I said, shifting it into place. "Let's try it."

In a hesitant motion, she strummed the cords. "Oh, I did it. It almost sounded like I know what I'm doing."

"You did. You played your first chord," I said, smiling at the contagious grin stretching her face. "If you'd like, I could give you lessons now and then."

"That would—"

The sound of stomping little feet interrupted us. A barely awake Mikaella neared us, a bouncing Justine in tow.

"I wanna sing too," my eldest daughter said.

Madison handed me the guitar back.

"Pick a song, sweet pea."

For the next half-hour, we all sang any song the girls came up with. Laughter filled the room. Madison turned out to be quite a singer. If she weren't so shy, she'd be really talented.

"This is fun," she said as I put my guitar away. "I understand now why the girls can't stop raving about it. Thanks, Sam, for giving me a peek into your life."

"Anytime. You can bake one hell of a cake and sing in tune. I'm impressed."

"Don't worry, I won't go after your job. I would be petrified to stand on a stage in front of so many people. I'll stick to teaching and baking instead."

"I won't object to any of those," I said.

Justine linked her hand with mine and grabbed Madison's with the other as we made it to the kitchen.

———

The four of us were eating brownies, positioned around the kitchen island, when the doorbell rang. Who could it be? I wasn't expecting anyone. Mikaella and Justine raced toward the front door, debating who would open it first. This was such a bad habit. One I should forbid. Running after them, I caught up just in time when they yanked the door open.

A man, about twenty-five, with messy dark hair, dressed in black clothes, stood there, his hands stuffed into his pockets. Didn't he get the message that it was summertime and it wasn't some goth party? Without a word, we eyed each other. A hunch in me told me I should give him all my attention.

"Who are you?" Mikaella asked. "Are you a friend of Daddy?"

"*Yesss*. Who are you?" Justine echoed, pressing her tiny fists to her hips.

"I'm... My name is Jac—" His eyes landed on something, or rather someone, behind me and lit up. I could see the whole galaxy shining in them. What the hell did that mean?

"Hey, you're here," Madison exclaimed from behind me. "I thought you were supposed to call when you arrived."

The guy, whose name I still ignored, frowned. "I was, and I called you, but you never picked up."

I turned as slowly as possible to study Madison's reaction, her face now bright red as all eyes were on her. She patted the back pockets of her cut-offs. "Shoot, I must have forgotten my phone in the castle in the backyard. Wait for me. I'll go get it." She left us all in the entryway as we studied one another some more.

"Castle?" the guy asked, looking confused as he scratched his temple.

"It's a treehouse Daddy built for us," Mikaella chimed in.

Justine tugged at his hand. "Are you Maddie's special friend?" The guy, who still didn't have a name, smiled. Even I had to agree he looked kinda mysterious and handsome as his face brightened up. "If you are her friend, I want to be your friend too. I'm a princess. And Maddie is a princess too. What's your name? Do you want to play with me?"

I pressed a hand on her shoulder. "Easy with the questions, baby," I said, when all I wanted to do was beg her to get every truth out of this guy using her four-year-old irresistible, charming power nobody could resist.

The guy raised his hands. "It's okay. My name is Jacob. And yes, we can be friends. I think princesses are awesome. And I'd like to play with you and visit your castle one day."

"Do you love pink?" Justine asked next. "It's my *favoritite* color. Do you wear princess crowns too?"

Rocking on his heels, Jacob focused his attention on her. "Pink is nice….huh…I guess. I've never worn a crown before. Think it would look good on me?"

Justine bobbed her head fast. "Mika doesn't like—"

Before she could continue, the door opened, and Madison joined the party, a lightness in her steps I had never noticed before. I let out a relieved breath—and so did Jacob. A huge grin parted her lips, her eyes shooting sparkles all around her, dissipating the suffocating tension that had permeated the air.

She positioned herself between all of us and kneeled to pull the girls into her arms for a hug. "I'll see you two tomorrow, okay? Be nice to your daddy." She touched Justine's nose, grazed Mikaella's cheek, and stood. "Bye, Sam. Thank you for the music lesson. I'll be here at nine."

I unfroze. "Sure. See you then."

Her gaze met Jacob's, and they exchanged a smile.

She returned the girls' waves as she traipsed away.

I rubbed the back of my neck, watching them pull away. A foreign emotion swirled inside me. The skin there felt raw and sensitive, and only then did I remove my hand.

The girls' chatting reached my ears. They both tugged at my hands.

"Daddy, are you okay?" Mikaella asked.

"You look like a statue," Justine added. "The *Libersilly* Statue."

I shook my head, still hanging low. "All fine, ladies. Let's prep dinner. And it's Statue of Liberty, Justine."

Armed with glue sticks, a bucket of glitter, and paper, I set my daughters and the arts and crafts supplies on one side of the kitchen island while I chopped vegetables to make chili on the other side. Glitter required constant supervision because it often ended up in places even the vacuum couldn't reach. Complete chaos.

Lost in my mind, my thoughts wandered to uncharted territories. I attributed my angst to the upcoming tour and my growing loneliness. Since Madison had started to care for my daughters, I had more time on my hands, and more time to think about the next chapter of my life. Lately, the idea of meeting a woman took more space inside my head each day. Madison's appearance in my life had triggered my ache for company. Love and sex. With the new album consuming my time and the rehearsals and tour fast approaching, a steady relationship was out of the question for now. Maybe a consensual, part-time friends-with-benefits agreement could be an option…or not. There were so many changes happening in my life right now, and I had to focus on what mattered the most. My children and the tour. There was too much at stake here, starting with my daughters who shouldn't get mixed in the clusterfuck of my non-existing love life.

———

"Daddy, you have your angry face on. Why are you mad?" Mikaella asked as I placed the pizza I had ordered in the middle of the table. In the last couple of hours, my mood had downgraded from great to awful. I sighed and pushed some of my anger down. My daughter was right. I'd been a grump since Madison had left two hours ago. I was furious with myself, the circumstances, and the whole fucking world for things I had no control over—and the glitter bomb that had exploded all over my kitchen.

"Daddy is no fun," Justine added. "Daddy is mad, mad, mad."

"I'm not mad," I said, trying to defend myself when I knew deep down, they were both right.

Every time I tried to chase away the memory, my anger returned with a vengeance.

I'd burned dinner. Then I'd dropped a pitcher of lemonade that had mixed with the *glitterification* of my floor. It was impossible to clean up, so it would be sticky and shiny forever. Justine had dumped my phone in the toilet—luckily for me, she had flushed seconds before—so it had been sitting on the kitchen counter, covered in rice, for over an hour. Perfect. Amazing. Incredible night so far.

"*Mushy-brooms* are yucky," Justine said, pushing her slice away. "I like just cheese on my pizza."

Mikaella, the teenager in the making, rolled her eyes. "Don't be stupid. You gotta have sauce too."

"Mika, don't call your sister stupid. Say sorry."

"Sorry," she said with her mouth full, giving me a *that's the best I can do* look. Little devil.

"Justine, they are fairy's houses. They sprinkle magic dust in your belly."

"No, they're yucky. Yuck, yuck, yuck."

"You sure? They look delicious."

"No, they don't. I want just cheese. *I wantjustcheese. Justcheese.*"

I pinched my lips together to avoid getting angrier than I already was. "Fine. Gimme your plate. I'll fix it. See? I removed all the yummy things you don't like. All gone. Don't be mad if *I* turn into a fairy."

She offered me a grin big enough to split her face in two. "Love you, Fairy-Daddy. I hope your wings are pink."

Some of my annoyance vanished. How could children heal your heart with just three words?

I sat opposite them, and my shoulders slouched forward as I exhaled. "Girls, I'm sorry for being grumpy. It has nothing to do with you." I forced a curl to my lips and relaxed as I took a bite.

"Daddy, can we invite Jacob over?" my eldest daughter asked.

"Who's Jacob? A friend of yours? Was he in your class?"

Mikaella rolled her eyes again, and Justine snickered, cupping her mouth with both hands, her shoulders and the set of purple butterfly wings strapped to her back bouncing.

"Daddy is funny," she said. "Do you think Daddy is funny, Mika? I love Jacob."

"You know Jacob too?" I traced the length of one eyebrow with my thumb. They had never spoken about that kid before today. "Does Jacob live down the street? Did you meet him at the park?"

Both my girls shook their heads, looking annoyed.

"What?" What did I miss?

"Daddy, Jacob is Maddie's special friend," Mikaella whispered as if I were in on the confidence. Oh, *that* guy. "I think he's pretty. Can he be my special friend too?"

"You're silly, Daddy. Mika, is Jacob Maddie's *bote-friend*?" Justine asked with a snicker.

And now even my kids were smitten with him. Perfect.

Craving some alone time in my home studio, I put the girls to bed early. Me. My guitar. My music. It always transported me into a new universe far away from the rest of humanity.

Feeling inspired, I penned, in less than an hour, the lyrics to a melody I'd been working on.

The more I played it, the more the storm inside me lessened. Confident about how it sounded, I adjusted it until I was fully satisfied.

Unable to come up with a title, I put my guitar on its stand and lay back on the cream couch, one arm folded under my head and the other resting on my stomach, staring at the high wooden ceiling. It usually helped me clear my overactive mind and see the situation from a different perspective. As predicted, my thoughts traveled far from here. They went back to the last time I gave a show, to the night Lisa quit on us, to my first encounter with Madison at the nanny agency, to tonight, when I came back from work and she looked at home in my kitchen, baking. It traveled from the four of us singing in the den to the girls and me sharing a pizza and practicing my newest song at bedtime.

Images of Madison were conjured in my head. For a reason I failed to explain, I had a hard time not thinking about her whenever she wasn't around.

I'd never survive six months on a tour bus around her if my fascination with her didn't die. This would just complicate my life. All our lives. How did my existence go from boring to messy in just a matter of weeks?

Resigning from the tour now made no sense. Even less for a forbidden crush I had no intention of pursuing. This opportunity was my chance to get my life back on track, to prove to myself I could do this. And decide if the two sides of me, the father *and* the artist, could co-exist together.

The other option would be to find a replacement for Madison. A dude or a lady old enough to be my parents.

Nah, Madison fitted in our lives, and the girls loved her. I'd never be able to extract her from their existence. If I chased her away, I feared they'd never trust another grown-up woman ever again.

Now that she had infiltrated our lives and made a huge impact on us, I believed no one else would ever be good enough for them, except for her.

Why did everything have to be so complicated?

Without Madison around, I couldn't embark on this six-month adventure.

With a loud sigh, I shut my eyes, my mind drifting to my resurrected career and the new song I'd just written.

"Sam?" A pause. "Sorry to bother you."

Was I dreaming? I struggled to open my heavy eyelids.

"Sam?" The voice, filled with softness, spoke my name. The voice that had been haunting my dreams lately.

Was I dreaming? A hand landed on my forearm, and I jumped awake. My pulse quickened. It wasn't a dream after all. God, I really had fallen asleep.

The guitar. The song. My messy thoughts. Yeah, I must have dozed off in the middle of this.

Oh, right. The title. The last thing I remembered was trying to come up with a title for the song I'd just written.

My lids fluttered open.

There she was, crouched beside the sofa, watching me. A twinkle shone on her face, and her hair fell loosely over her shoulder in waves, the copper highlights from days spent under the sun adding a glow to her aura. Madison looked ever more angelic in the low light than I had pictured her in my head. Her lips parted, and she smiled. At me.

How much would I give to be kissed by an angel?

The title. It fit. I loved it.

"Hey," she said in a gentle tone. "I'm so sorry to wake you up."

I propped myself up on my elbows, scanning the room, urging my brain to return to the present. "What time is it?"

Her smile widened. "Ten. I forgot my purse here earlier, and my sister is working a night shift, so I couldn't get home. I didn't want you to think there was a thief or whatever, and that's why I decided to let you know I was here. Again, sorry I disturbed your sleep."

"How did you get in?" I remembered locking the front door earlier.

"The back door. I hauled myself over the fence." She grimaced. "Sorry. I texted you and knocked, but you didn't hear it and never replied. I didn't want to ring the doorbell in case it woke the girls up. I-I'm rambling. I have my stuff now, so I'll get going."

Madison motioned to stand, but I circled her wrist, the pad of my thumb resting over her frantic pulse point. What was I doing? Why was I touching her—again? We held each other's gaze, neither of us looking away.

As they did so many times before, her sea-green irises sucked me in.

Her bottom lip trembled.

I breathed in, fighting the urge to trace its length with my finger. My attention darted back to her eyes, and I coughed to clear my airways, breaking the moment that had settled between us. "Stop saying you're sorry. You did nothing wrong."

A strand of her hair fell over her eyes when she tilted her head, and my fingers itched to tuck it away.

"I should go."

"Do you need a ride home?" Could I slap myself? If she said yes, I'd have to call her a cab. Waking up the girls wasn't a viable option.

A flush spread across Madison's cheeks, and she avoided looking at me. "No, my…huh…Jacob is waiting in the car."

I nodded.

Her scent, that citrus blend, tipped all my senses. Could I bask in it for just a little longer? Her heart rate synced with mine. I felt every beat under my touch. In a jerky movement, I let go of her wrist and jumped to my feet. With the heels of my hands, I erased the remnants of sleep from my eyes. "I'll walk you out then."

She bowed her head and followed me.

The air in the house warmed up and became a heavy blanket enveloping us.

Oxygen barely reached my brain, and I got dizzy.

"My phone… Justine…huh…she dropped it in the toilet earlier. I'm trying to save it. I didn't *not* reply to your message on purpose." For a reason I couldn't justify, I wanted to explain myself. To let her know I'd never ignore her by choice.

"Oh no."

I offered her a noncommittal shrug. "It goes hand in hand with the night I had."

"That bad?" she asked.

I exhaled. "Yep. It was awful."

"Sorry to hear that. Tomorrow will be another day."

"I suppose."

We stopped by the front door.

"I should go," she said, pointing to the idling car.

Neither of us spoke for a whole minute.

"Yes," I finally said.

"Night." She traipsed away and approached the car where her friend was waiting. "See you tomorrow," Madison said, her voice strained.

My gaze followed her movements. Before she got too far, her head twisted in my direction, and I captured her gaze for a couple of endless seconds.

"Good night," I repeated, mostly to myself.

Jacob waved at me, and I returned the gesture.

His lips connected with hers before they drove away.

Standing in the dark for a little longer, I wondered what the nagging feeling that crawled over my vertebrae meant. "Probably nothing," I muttered before retreating inside.

Chapter 9
Madison

Wearing a silver cocktail dress I'd borrowed from my sister, I kept my gaze trained on the entrance. Beside me, a man in his sixties was going on and on about the Neoclassism influence of artists from the eighteenth century, something I really had no interest in.

I sipped my champagne, trying to forget how much the strapped heels on my feet hurt. Why did I agree to wear those? Oh yes, because I wanted to look pretty for my date. The same date who was almost half an hour late.

I closed my eyes for an instant, the alcohol already bubbling through my brain and making me unsteady on my feet, to block out the voices around me.

I hated large crowds. For no reason other than I disliked feeling like I lived in a cage. Being surrounded by too many people just didn't sit well with me. Another thing Jacob and I had in common. Living on a yacht for months had been the perfect setup last year. I was aware going on tour would probably force me to deal with a lot of people at times, but I'd decided I was ready to tackle my aversion and face it once and for all. With the girls or Sam around, I believed it'd be easier. For some reason, I felt at ease around them. And it calmed my nerves.

I inhaled through my mouth and reopened my eyes.

"Miss, are you even listening to what I'm saying?" the man asked.

"Sure." I faked a smile and brought my focus to the rim of my glass where my lipstick had left an imprint. I wasn't that girl. Pretending to be interested wasn't who I was. "You know what," I said. "I'll be right back. I need some fresh air and to call someone."

"Oh, okay," he replied, looking dejected.

"I'm sure a lot of people will be interested in your theory about *The Enlightenment*. If you'll excuse me." I discarded my half-empty glass onto a tray as a server passed by.

Threading through the patrons, I finally made it onto the sidewalk.

The thick summer air did nothing to ease the pressure in my lungs, but at least I could breathe on my own here. To my left, a group of people was having an agitated conversation. In front of me, two parking attendants dressed in black were joking around. The wide poster announcing the museum's newest exhibit glowed in white light on the building's facade.

"Jacob, where are you?" I asked no one, checking my phone screen for the umpteenth time.

Just when I was about to put it back into the fancy purse Emily swore I had to carry around tonight, his face flashed on the screen.

"Maddie. Ohmygod… Sorry… Supposed to meet like

thirty minutes ago… Car broke down on the highway… Waiting… Towing…Presentation in Memphis… Be back… Afternoon… Middle of nowhere and… Reception is bad." His voice sounded distant, and I could catch only about half of what he said.

"Oh no. I was getting worried. You're always so on time, and running late is so unlike you. Can I do something? I can't drive because I had champagne, but I can call a cab to come get you."

"Nah… State patrol with me. I'll call you later… Better reception. Again, I'm—" The line cut before he could finish his sentence.

"Great. All this," I said, looking at my outfit, "for nothing."

I opened the app on my phone to call a cab when a silhouette I recognized strolled in front of me and stopped mere feet away.

"Maddie?"

"Sam?"

"Wow, you look stunning," he exclaimed, before rolling his lips over his teeth and glancing down as if he'd said something wrong. His eyes returned to mine. "What I meant is…huh…what are you doing here? Not that you don't look great…but… Okay, let's start over. Hi, it's nice to bump into you. Are you here for the—?" His eyes traveled behind me. "Are you here for the inauguration of the new exhibit?" He frowned. "Sorry, I know nothing about museums."

I let out a snicker. "Me neither. I guess you can call it that. Jacob got invited by one of his peers at the university, and I was supposed to be his plus-one, but his car broke down, and I'm here, figuring out how to get away from this place as quickly as possible." I lowered my voice. "I really don't feel like I am in my element in this cesspool of art intellectuals."

"Yeah, I understand the feeling. A few years ago, I gave a performance at a museum in Texas, and I felt out of my element too. I can tolerate the children's museums and the natural history ones because they're fun, but this"—he pointed to the building behind me—"I cannot. Where are you going now? Anything I can do to help?"

I sighed. "Home. I got all dressed up for nothing." My shoulders dropped forward. "One thing I'm excited about, though, is removing these blistering pumps. They are killing my feet. I'm not drunk enough to forget they are skinning my feet alive every time I take a step."

"I'd give you mine, but not sure they'll fit you." He gazed down. "And those will definitely not fit me."

He laughed, and I relished the deep baritone of his voice. Sam Stevens looked handsome when he let his guard down and laughed without restraint. Tonight, he appeared younger than usual. He had a calm about him, hard to ignore, and it drew me in like never before.

"I have a question," I said. "Where are the girls? How can you be out on your own tonight? A night off is unusual for you from what you've told me in the past."

"My parents are in town for the weekend. They arrived last night. Surprise visit. They insisted I go out and enjoy some me-time. That's what I'm trying to do. It's all new to me, and I'm not sure I'm doing it right. Was on my way to a small hotel bar to watch the game. I know it sounds pathetic. I'm just a little rusty when it comes to social inter-actions. It's been so long that I'm not sure how to proceed. How do we meet people these days, other than through an app? How does anyone?"

I shook my head. "You're not asking the right person.

I'm such an introvert. Somehow, I think it's just a question of timing."

A chime on my phone announced the cab was a minute away. When it pulled along the sidewalk, Sam scratched the side of his neck and averted his gaze before speaking again.

"I know it's spur of the moment and all, but do you… do you want to maybe grab a bite or something? The night is still young, and I could use the company. You won't have wasted your night and dressed up for nothing." He stuffed his hands into his pockets. "What do you say?"

The idea of sitting alone in front of the TV at home didn't appeal to me. And I'd never hear the end of it if my sister found out I came home at seven on a Saturday night.

"Why not? Could be fun," I said.

Sam opened the passenger door and said something to the cab driver who drove away.

He winced. "I shouldn't have sent him away," he said. "Your feet. Can you walk the three blocks from here?"

I bent down, and soon my heels dangled from my fingers. "Problem solved. For three blocks at least."

We exchanged small talk for the first few minutes. It was different. Being here with him on our night off. It didn't feel like I was with my boss, but just a guy friend.

"I'm not gonna spend the night going on and on about the girls, but I did try feeding Justine mushrooms, and it backfired. Big time."

"For real?" I asked, giving him a sideways glance, a grin threatening to form on my lips. "How so?"

Dressed in a casual button-up deep frost-blue shirt and a pair of dark jeans, Sam looked both relaxed and sophisticated tonight. He wore brown cowboy boots and a matching belt. Beside him, minus the heels, I didn't feel *that* overdressed. Just a tad.

"They were on her pizza. She complained she hated them. I told her, like you said, that they were fairy's homes, and they would spread magic dust in her belly. It didn't do the trick. She started screaming and pushed her food away."

I couldn't help but burst into a fit of laughter. "She did not?"

"Yep. And when I told her I would be the one turning into a fairy, she said she wished my wings were pink."

I used my fingertips to wipe the tears building in the corners of my eyes. "Oh no. She's the best. Your children are so adorable."

He shrugged. "Guess so. At least, when they put their minds to it."

We kept talking, not giving the world around us any attention.

"Oops, we passed it," Sam said after a moment. He spun around. "I think it was like five minutes that way." He pointed to where we just came from. "Well, this is embarrassing. We can either go back or we——"

I surveyed the city around me. "There's a country bar two minutes from here. I used to go there when I was in college and pretended to have fun getting wasted for the three months it lasted. Wanna go? Unless you think people will come to you and ask for pictures and stuff."

"Nah, it's fine. People here are laid-back and rarely care."

At the entrance, I slipped my heels back on and winced as I stepped forward.

"That bad?" Sam asked.

"Yep. Heels should be illegal. I never found a pair I could wear without wanting to rip them apart." I took another cautious step, feeling—and probably looking—as if I were walking on a bed of nails.

Sam offered his bent elbow. "Hold on to me. It might take some pressure off your poor feet."

"Thanks."

We exchanged a soft smile and entered the establishment. Country music blared from the red jukebox on our left. A few pool tables were set in the far back. In front of us, a wide bar dominated the space, shelves of alcohol bottles lining the wall behind the bartender—an old man with thick glasses. A makeshift dance floor, surrounded by high tables and stools, took up most of the room to our right, with a small stage holding a single microphone and two chairs in one corner. The rest of the bar was filled with wooden tables and chairs for those coming here to enjoy a meal.

It was everything I remembered, just older than the version in my memory.

The host led us to a table and set down the menu after listing the night's specials.

Sam and I sat across from each other. The table was so small our knees brushed underneath the surface. With the dim-lit chandeliers casting a soft glow, the setup almost looked romantic.

Tilting sideways, I slipped off my heels, sighing in relief.

"Better?" Sam asked.

"Yeah. My feet are relishing their freedom."

"I'm lucky I'll never have to endure such torture," he said with a wink that got me smiling way too big. "Hungry?" he asked as he perused the laminated two-sided piece of paper.

"*Yesss.*" I said it with too much enthusiasm before I could rein in some of my excitement. "Sorry. I haven't had dinner, and the champagne went straight to my head."

The server came to take our orders, and we both asked

for a beer. "Do you want a bit of everything?" Sam asked me.

"Sure. Why not?"

"You okay to share?"

I nodded and mirrored the faint curl of his lips. Gone was the pain masking his face most of the time. Tonight, Sam Stevens appeared relaxed. And happy.

"We'll have the large nachos, extra guacamole, a plate of chicken wings, potato skins, the mozzarella sticks, a side of raw veggies, a plate of mini-burgers, shrimp tacos, and the fries with gravy and brisket."

"Anything else?" the server asked.

"Ohmygod, no," I let out. "I think we're good."

We handed our menus back and settled in as we waited for our drinks.

"Can I ask you a question?" I asked Sam.

He nodded.

"How do you deal with fame? How weird is it to have strangers call your name or tell you they love your stuff?"

"Truth?"

I nodded.

"I don't think I'll ever get used to it. Those two sides of me live in the same body, but it's like they're different identities. In my everyday life, I'm a private person. I love the anonymity. When I'm onstage, this other side of me lights up. Takes over. I crave the music. The energy only an amphitheater full of people can provide. It's hard to explain. I have a friend who can't tolerate the limelight that comes with the job. It gives him anxiety. I guess we all deal with it differently. For me, it's really about separating those two versions of me. The regular guy, single dad, and the musician slash celebrity or whatever name you wanna call it."

"I could never do what you do. Having all those

people, obsessed with me, scrutinizing my life as if I was a social experiment, voicing any opinion they deem fit about me and my character."

"It took me a while to develop a thick skin. When I was younger, other people's opinions of me mattered…a lot. Well, I thought they did. Until I realized looking up my name online and reading those heinous reviews was only hurting me and my self-confidence. Now I don't care anymore. I do my own thing. People like my sound, fantastic. They hate it, I won't miss sleep over it. They're entitled to their own opinion. There are people out there who seem to be born to always find negativity in everything other people do. Not sure they're happy, though. If they were, they wouldn't feed on the high they got from bad-mouthing others."

"Wow, that's impressive."

"What?"

"Your vision of things. I like that. And you're so right. So many people nowadays feel free to say anything they want about anyone, without giving it a second thought. It can be hurtful. They forget they are addressing their heinous comments to human beings…people with feelings. Criticizing their lives, their choices, their careers. But those same people would never accept themselves being ripped apart for the sake of entertainment. It's sad. It's frustrating how some people choose to be mean just because they think their voice gives them the right to project their insecurities onto anyone trying to do what they love. It's nobody else's business if they're unhappy in their own lives." I paused. "Sorry about my ranting. Human beings are a weird species. They should lift other people up instead of finding ways to belittle their work or character. Encourage them. Cheer them on. Help them get better. We should all have each other's backs. Spread happiness instead of hate. I love that you can block the negative out and feed on the positive." I shrugged. "It's inspiring."

Sam sipped his beer. "It's much more empowering to tell someone *keep going, you're doing a good job* or *I love your stuff, you inspire me* than to break their spirits and call their stuff mediocre or any other detrimental adjective. I'm trying to teach my kids to be empathetic, to think with their hearts. We all have it in us…you know…what it takes to be mean. It's a choice we make to opt to be better than the greater majority."

"And it's rewarding," I agreed.

"Yep." He pushed his drink toward me. "Let's drink to that."

We clinked our glasses just as the server brought our food.

"Whoa, that's a lot. Do you think we can eat it all?"

Sam stared at me, amusement dancing in his irises. "Guess we'll find out. I have all night. I'm free tonight. For once, I don't have to be anywhere."

I clinked his glass again. "Let's drink to that. A free night."

"Cheers," he said.

We talked about our families as we indulged in our food. I hadn't had a proper junk meal in a long time. After licking my fingers, I wiped my hands on a napkin.

"How was it?" he asked next. "Teaching kids in Africa."

I clasped my hands together. "One of the most rewarding experiences of my life, without a doubt. Children in developed countries take school, and learning in general, for granted. Those kids… Their eyes lit up every time I walked into the classroom. They were thankful. I had an all-girls class. They have so much to learn from us, but we have just as much to learn from them—their strength, their resilience. It's hard to believe we live on the same planet, yet our lives are so different. I was only eighteen back then but could sense how what we were doing was important to them. These little girls were thriving. I would love to go back one day and try to see where they're now."

"It's amazing what you do. I'm here, being paid big money and being adulated because I can play the guitar and sing songs. What you do means so much more for our world. Our children are the future. There shouldn't be distinctions between them, no matter their background or where they are born."

"Thanks. For recognizing the value of my work. It means a lot."

"Maddie, I've witnessed the changes in my own daughters. It's amazing what you've succeeded in accomplishing with them in such a short amount of time. Mika is back to being a kid. She laughs, smiles, and is happy again. This is priceless. I don't know how you do this, but your talents are underrated."

I could feel a blush taking over my face. I returned Sam's smile. "Thank you."

"No," he said, shaking his head, his eyes glued to mine. "Thank *you*."

Hours later, we enjoyed more beer as people started line dancing on the makeshift dance floor.

Barefoot, I tapped along to the intoxicating rhythm. Despite my efforts, I couldn't conceal my love for the group dance.

"You love that song?" Sam asked.

I leaned back, angling myself toward him. "I love *the* dance. Do you know the steps?"

He massaged his temples. "I used to. A long time ago. Do you?"

"Yep. It was part of my three-month *let-loose* challenge in college, to tour bars and play drinking games. All in the name of experience. To understand why people love it so much." I blamed the booze for the next few words escaping my mouth. "Wanna give it a try?"

He pointed at his chest with his thumb. "Me?" I nodded. "Nah, I think I'll pass."

"Come on, you're called *The Legend* of country music and you're afraid of some line dance?" I waggled my eyebrows as if to prove my point.

Sam exhaled sharply. "Don't you dare me. I'm super bad at resisting those. I used to always get in trouble as a teen because I was the dare king."

"Dare King, show me what you're made of." I poked my tongue out playfully.

Sam frowned. "Maddie, are you being serious?"

"I got dressed up. Better enjoy the night, no?"

On wobbly feet, thanks to the champagne and beer I'd drunk tonight, I kicked the heels I had removed when we got seated further under the table and reached for his hand.

"I'm too old for this," he teased.

"Age is just a number. You're twenty-nine, not seventy-five. Come on."

We reached the dance floor and stood side by side. After a few seconds, the steps came back to me, and soon I was dancing in perfect sync with everyone, laughing my heart out. Sam tried to follow me, off-tempo and mixing the steps. Concentration etched across his features as he kept trying until he got it right. When the song ended, I lost my footing, and strong arms coiled around my waist to steady me.

"Thanks." I swiveled to face him, his arms still

wrapped around me. A soft ballad began to play, and couples paired up all around us.

Sam shifted me so we faced each other. We locked eyes for a long beat. His Adam's apple worked, and I followed the movement with my gaze, entranced.

"Wanna go back to the table?" I asked, feeling like he was still standing here because of me.

"Not really. I'm having fun. Are you?"

A wide grin broke free on my face. "I am."

Without overthinking everything, I splayed my palms across his hard chest and closed my eyes, letting the slow tempo of the music control my feet.

Sam's scent—musky, woodsy, and entirely him—clung to all my senses.

When I opened my eyes, he was staring at me with an unreadable expression.

The song eased into another, and before we knew it, we spent over an hour on the dance floor, breaking apart just long enough to take sips of our beers.

"Where does *The Legend* moniker come from?" I asked.

"When I released my second album, I sold a million copies within forty-eight hours. Back then, it was a big deal. Not many artists had done that before me. The nickname passed the test of time. I don't really like being called that. It just puts unwelcome pressure on me." He shrugged. "Why would I enjoy being put on a pedestal? I'm just a regular guy who enjoys a low-key life. There's nothing legendary about me."

"Don't be so hard on yourself. You're allowed to be the best at something. Nothing to be ashamed of. For what it's worth, I like it. It's flattering. Don't put too much thought into it, but I think it's fitting."

"Maybe. Still, I don't consider myself special in any way."

"Be proud of what you have achieved. Sometimes, it's okay not to be humble and to acknowledge what we've accomplished. This is the perfect example. Everyone is special in their own way. You are too."

"How can you be so smart at your age? You see the good in people—and in life. It's a great quality. Never lose it. It's precious."

"Born this way." I shrugged. "Are you excited to go on tour? It must be an adrenaline rush to come back into the spotlight after two years."

"I am. But parts of me fear I'll be rusty. Or that I'll forget how it's done. It sounds silly."

"It's not silly. It's normal to have doubts. But you're *The Legend* after all, so I'm confident you'll be fine." An idea hit me. "Do you still consider yourself the dare king?" I asked.

"Not sure. I haven't thought about it in years. Why?"

"Because I dare you to ask the barman for a guitar—I saw one behind the bar when we walked in—and to play a song. Here and now. On that small stage. I'll be the judge of whether or not you've lost your title."

"You're kidding, right?"

"Try me," I said. Yep, the beer should be blamed for my newfound confidence tonight.

Sam's voice was a soft murmur against my skin when he said, "Maddie—"

I stepped back. "Sam, time to prove yourself you still got it. You said earlier you can't walk away from a dare. This, right here, is me challenging you."

"Maddie—" he repeated.

I pushed him back with both hands. "Impress me."

Our eyes were transfixed on each other, a conversation of unspoken words that I couldn't vocalize but understood. It awakened something deep in my heart. Sam's irises went from shiny to dark, a hidden emotion simmering in them. One that lured me in. And stole my breath away.

He twirled me one last time on the dance floor before letting go of my hand and sauntering away, shaking his head.

With his back straight, chin tipped up, and a newfound determination pouring out of him, he neared the bar.

When he stared at me over his shoulder, I saw a glint in his eye I'd never witnessed before.

"Show time," I murmured.

Chapter 10

Sam

With steady steps, I reached the bar. I still had a hard time comprehending how Madison had ended up challenging me. Tonight, I had discovered a new side of her, and for the first time in years, I felt free. Like I could do anything or be anyone and nobody expected anything from me. With Lisa, I used to always walk on eggshells. She had expensive tastes, demanded and expected a level of commitment from me that always seemed exaggerated.

Other than Riley's trick to send me back on the road and with my own children, I hadn't been challenged by another person in a long time. Deep down, I relished the feeling and the adrenaline rush that came with it. I didn't lie earlier when I'd told Madison I was the dare king as a teenager. Running down the street bare-assed, climbing the tallest trees, going to school dressed like a cheerleader, I had done it all.

Right now, I missed the version of myself I once was—the carefree guy. Responsibilities, a quickly ascending career, and heartbreak had buried that Sam. Madison had just dug him out earlier when she had convinced me to line-dance with her.

If I were being honest with myself, I hadn't laughed this much in years.

It felt good to feel alive. To just be. And have an honest conversation with someone. In the past two years, I had closed myself off a lot, not letting people in. Talking with Madison felt different. As if she could understand me. Without judgment. As if she got the whole fame thing without making too much out of it. Tonight, I was presented with the side of her I'd only ever witnessed around my daughters. Her caring side that she had never extended to me until now. The woman in her. The funny, beautiful, and easygoing person she was inside and out. I already knew her heart was made of gold, but I had the certitude tonight she was genuinely a wonderful human being.

One thing was certain: she cared. And she was a lot more perceptive than most people I knew.

As I walked away, I caught her gaze over my shoulder. She watched me traipse away, her hands clasped in front of her and her chin jutting forward as if she believed I needed encouragement to go through with the dare.

For the first time since we'd met, I could see she had taken off her responsible-adult suit too, enjoying the night, without questioning anything.

"Hey, man. Listen, I was wondering… Is there a possibility I could borrow that guitar for a song or two?" I asked the bartender, pointing to the instrument resting against the wall.

"What for?"

"See, I'm going back on tour in a couple of months and my friend back there," I gestured behind me with my thumb, "the one in the pretty dress, thinks I should prove to myself I still have it in me."

"Have what?" he asked.

Okay, he's not going to make it easy for me, is he? The last thing I wished for was to use my name to convince people to give me a chance.

"The stage presence. The jitters. The excitement."

"What are you? Another guy trying to make it big? Over the years, I've seen enough young men your age arrogant about their talent when they couldn't sing for shit. If you're booed, please walk down that stage, even if you're not done. I'm telling you, this industry is overcrowded. Don't expect too much from it."

"Thanks for the advice. I'll remember it when I am on tour. So, can I?"

"Sure." He grabbed the guitar and handed it to me. "Be careful. And good luck."

"Thanks." I saluted him with one hand as I adjusted the keys with the other.

I climbed the four steps up and sat on a chair in the middle of the stage. I waited until the song from the jukebox ended and reached for the microphone after I turned it on.

"Hi, folks. I was challenged by the brunette down there," I gestured to Madison, who was standing so close that, even in the low light, I could see the pink hue coloring her cheeks as people turned to look at her, "to sing a song tonight."

I heard people whispering my name, but I chose to ignore them, continuing to pretend I was that eighteen-year-old Sam Stevens, praying that one day he'd be able to play his music for a larger audience and make a living writing love songs.

Someone wolf-whistled as I strummed the first chords of "When You're Far Away."

More people cheered and clapped. Standing in front of me, never blinking, stood Madison. Her contagious smile rubbed off on me, and I started grinning like a fool while I played.

"Again," a group of women hollered once I was done and about to climb down the stage.

"Okay. If I do this, though, I'll need some help." Many patrons lifted their hands. "Sorry, guys, only one person knows this song. Maddie, come on up here."

She shook her head, her cheeks now bright red.

"She might require a little encouragement from you guys. Everyone, please welcome Maddie to the stage."

Sam, she mouthed. *Why?*

I offered her a one-shoulder shrug. "You know the lyrics," I said, my hand covering the microphone, as I bent forward. "Plus, you're all dressed up. You made me dance earlier. It's the pendulum swinging back. Pretend it's just me and the girls like we rehearsed the other day. I'm the king of dares, remember? And I'm daring you to do this with me. You'll see, it's not as intimidating as it seems. You'll be able to decide for yourself if it's as scary as you believe up here." I held out my hand in invitation.

Muttering something under her breath, Madison exhaled in a dramatic fashion and squeezed my offered palm as she stepped up the stairs and settled next to me.

After I adjusted the microphone between us, I added, "Forget about them. No one is listening. You have a beautiful voice. Sing with me, okay?" I squeezed her hand for an infinitesimal instant, and a shiver passed through her before she nodded her agreement. I let go of her and strummed the first few notes.

We sang "I Belong," the song I had played with Justine the other day. Madison joined me on the chorus. Her voice quivered as the words initially escaped her lips. We locked eyes, neither of us breaking the contact, and soon enough, confidence coursed through her, and she looked more at ease. We exchanged smiles, and I relished watching her come alive beside me. No doubt, people were falling under her charm too. How could they not? Madison had a magnetic aura. One that made it painful to leave once she cast her attention on you.

When we finished the song, I jumped down the stage and helped her back to the floor.

"See? It wasn't that bad," I teased, bumping her shoulder with mine.

She blinked. "You're joking, right? I did it. I faced a fear of mine." She spun on the balls of her feet and looped her arms around my neck. Heat crawled where our skin connected. "Thank you, Sam." She detached from me and averted her eyes for a split second, as if she feared she'd crossed some lines.

Trying to push away the sensations rising from deep within, I handed the guitar back to the bartender.

"You should have told me, son, you were *The Legend*. Sorry I didn't recognize you. My sight is not so great these days. Cataracts are a shame."

"I loved being anonymous for the time it lasted. It reminded me of my younger days."

He offered me two beers. "For you and the lady. Thank you for singing at my bar. It means a lot to an old fellow like me who's been following your career since the beginning. I'm excited you're getting a new album out. It was about damn time."

I thanked him with a nod.

Madison and I returned to our table. "I'm still floating in the air," she said. "Now I understand the adrenaline rush you get from being onstage. I still wouldn't do it, given a choice, but I loved it for the length of one song."

We cheered to that.

"Ready to go?" I asked later.

"What time is it?"

"Around two in the morning."

"Two?" Madison exclaimed with round eyes.

"Yep. We'll share a cab ride. I'll feel better knowing you get home safely."

"Sam, you don't have to."

"I insist." She fished her credit card out, but I stopped her with a hand. "Let me. You saved the night. Trust me, it's the least I can do."

She grabbed her heels and grimaced as she put them on.

"Still hurting?"

She shut her eyelids and tilted her head back. "It's awful. You have no idea."

"Sit," I ordered.

Confusion took over her gaze, but she did as I said.

I leaned down, removed both her shoes, and turned around. "Jump on."

"Sam, what are you doing?"

"Doing my part to heal your feet. Come on."

She shook her head. "I can't."

"Come on. It's already too late. Our picture is probably already plastered all over the internet as we speak. You're the one who challenged me earlier. Just don't read the news for the next week. The press will insinuate lots of things. Ignore it. Soon, they'll fabricate stories about other people. The gossip never lasts. There's always some more riveting news to cover in the entertainment industry."

"Huh…okay…all right."

Perhaps giving the nanny of my kids a piggyback ride wasn't super ethical since technically, she worked for me, but right now, I just didn't give a shit about it. Tonight, we were just two friends watching out for each other.

When the cab halted in front of Madison's townhouse that she shared with her sister, she turned toward me and hesitated. She held out a hand, then pulled it back. I leaned forward to kiss her cheek but decided it would be awkward. In the end, we waved at each other.

"Thanks for tonight," she said. "I had fun."

"Me too. See you on Monday."

"I'll be there."

For the next minute, my eyes stayed trained on her as she made her way inside and closed the door behind her.

Madison had opened a portal in me in the last few hours we'd spent together. I now felt energized and ready to conquer the world.

When we had danced tonight, her touch had woken up something in me. It made me want to be better. I did my best not to make a big deal of the electricity her hand in mine sparked through me. This couldn't mean anything. We already had a couple of drinks, so it was probably my imagination playing tricks on me. Yeah. I glanced down at my palm and massaged it with my thumb, stretching my digits to remove the memory of our connection.

"Sir, you can go now," I told the cab driver who pulled away from the driveway. Through the back window, I noticed the curtains moving on the second floor and wondered if, just like for me, the deception that the night was over filled her too. A tinge of nostalgia hit me. My stomach knotted at the thought of stepping back into our roles when we'd see each other again on Monday. I couldn't remember the last time I had felt completely like myself, or when the weight pressing on my shoulders had finally receded.

I wished it never came back because I loved the freedom my night with Madison had provided.

———

"What the hell, man," Riley said as I took his call the next morning. I cracked my eyelids open and decided it was too early to deal with him at eleven in the morning. I hadn't slept in…in, huh, forever. Nope, I couldn't remember the last time I had done so.

"Can we talk later?" I asked, burying my head under a pillow. "I'm tired."

"Nah. I need an explanation. Why are there pictures of Maddie and you looking cozy all over the web? Singing together. Dancing together. What did you do last night, Stevens?"

I scrunched up my face. Damn. I had forgotten all about it. "It's nothing. Just the press making up a story for the sake of it. Don't worry."

"*Who is Sam Stevens's new love interest? Is Sam Stevens in love again? Sam Stevens is coming out of his retirement and paraded his girlfriend all over town.*" He huffed so loud that I could hear his lungs deflating. "I'll ask the question again. What happened last night, Stevens? Because there are pictures of you two singing together, of you two looking intimate on the dance floor, of you giving her a piggyback ride. A piggyback ride, man. Are you serious? What is this all about?"

I sat on the bed and rubbed my eyes with a finger, trying to shake off the grogginess. "Ry, you should know that nothing in the press is ever what it seems. Why are you even grilling me about last night's whereabouts right now?"

"June is overwhelmed with calls and emails. I just wanna hear the truth from you. No doubt Janice will ask for an explanation too when I talk to her later."

For the next ten minutes, I described my night to my friend.

"Madison is not used to this kind of attention. What were you thinking? You should be aware ending up on a cover of a magazine can break someone. You're aware what happened to Carter and April. It almost destroyed them. She didn't want to be known as Carter's girl. The media painted her as a gold digger. They spread lies to sell copies of their trash. Be careful. Madison is inexperienced with fame. The last thing we need is for her to panic and back out of the tour. I'm not mad at you two... Just concerned."

I dragged a hand over my face. "I'll talk to her. I warned her last night. Kinda. Geez, I'll meet with her and explain. Make sure she stays away from any gossip rags."

After a hot shower, I made my way downstairs. My parents had taken the kids to spend the night at a hotel with a pool and a waterslide, so I had the entire house to myself.

Last night had long-lasting upsides. I felt refreshed. For once, I didn't feel ten years older than I really was.

The doorbell rang as I was pouring myself an oversized cup of coffee.

"Coming," I said, nearing the front door in nothing but a pair of lounge pants. I had ditched the shirt, thinking I'd be alone most of the day. "Maddie?"

She stood on the front porch, her hands linked before her, dark shadows under her eyes, wearing a look on her face I wished I could forget.

"Come on in. I was just about to call you," I said.

"Sam. We gotta talk."

Chapter 11
Madison

"Coffee?" Sam asked after he closed the door behind me and led me through the house as if I'd never been here before.

As I followed him, I did my best to avoid looking at his naked torso.

"Yes. Please." Caffeine would help settle my nerves.

After he put on a faded black T-shirt from a past world tour, Sam carried two mugs to the kitchen table as we took a seat next to each other.

My pulse hastened, and I wrapped my palms around the mug, entranced by the billowing steam instead of the man studying me from up close. I could feel the weight of his gaze on my skin, and I wondered if I'd dreamed of the connection we shared last night. Or if my boozy brain had conjured the ease and familiarity with which we challenged and confided in each other.

"So, I suppose you searched the internet?" he asked,

going straight to the topic that brought me here on a Sunday morning.

"About that... I...I know you said to ignore the rumor and to avoid it. But...huh...even though I've tried to, people I love and care about sent me links to multiple outlets that shared pictures of us and insinuated we're a couple. Even my mama called me first thing in the morning to ask questions."

Sam said nothing for a minute. I risked a glance at him. His face had lost his easy composure, a somber mask tightening his features.

"Listen, Maddie, I'm aware of how this looks. Trust me, I never meant for your face to get plastered all over gossip rags. It was never my intention to put you on the hot seat. For what it's worth, I'm sorry. If you want, I'll give an interview or ask June to write a press release. But in my years of experience, it's better to let the story die. It will... Eventually."

I drummed my fingers, and Sam reached for my hand, putting my fidgeting to rest.

"Stop. It will be all right, Maddie. I promise. You can trust me. I'll make sure of it."

I abandoned my hand to his comforting squeeze. After a moment, I realized something was off and scanned the room around me. "It's oddly silent in here. Where are the girls?"

"They spent the night at the hotel with their grand-parents."

"Wow, you're really going all in for your first me-time weekend."

"Trying to. Since I went to bed too late, I was glad to have the morning to myself."

Sam released my hand as if he'd just noticed he was still holding it in his.

"Huh…do you really think those pictures will go away?"

"Yep. They may resurface at some point, but we did nothing wrong. All they show is two people having a great time. They can come up with the narrative they want, but you and I both know the truth."

I finished my coffee and rinsed and placed my mug in the dishwasher. "I'll go. For what it's worth, I trust you. It was just weird to wake up to my face splashed all over the internet. Not sure I'd ever get used to it. Sometimes, it's hard to remember people actually know who you are. Strangers speaking about you like they're part of your everyday life." I sighed. "This is surreal. Anyway, thanks for reassuring me."

"Anytime."

I turned to leave when I spotted the half-built structure at the far end of the backyard, in the corner across from the girls' castle. "What is it?" I walked toward the window, which offered a view of the green lawn, to try to make out what it was.

"A greenhouse. To grow herbs and veggies. I thought you and the girls would love it. A project to tackle this summer. I'm supposed to finish setting it up today. My father and I did most of the work yesterday."

"For real?"

"Yeah. I thought it could be fun to teach the girls how nature works."

"Ohmygod, I love DIY projects. Can I give you a hand?"

Sam neared me, angling himself so we faced each other, a perplexed expression overtaking his face. "You sure? It's your day off."

"Unless you wanna do it on your own, I have nothing planned today, and I really like working with a hammer. I used to do all kinds of construction projects with my daddy when I was little."

"In that case, gimme a sec. I'll never refuse help. Let me gather the tools we need and I'll be right back."

For the next few hours, Sam and I finished assembling the greenhouse. While he painted the exterior walls in a sky-blue hue, I used the small paintbrushes to add embellishments of fake grass, butterflies, and flowers, sitting cross-legged on the lawn.

"Other than being the king of dares, were you more like Mika or Justine growing up?" I asked.

"Neither one. For the longest time, I was a shy kid. Then I started playing music, and I was good, like really, really good. It gave me confidence. I was thirteen when I wrote my first song and nineteen when I signed my first record deal. Since then, I've never stopped working."

"Do you feel like you missed out on things by working full time from an early age?"

"Whoa. I never actually asked myself that question. Would I do things differently? Hmm... Not sure. It brought me to who I am today. In the grand scheme of things, I consider myself lucky." He paused. "Do you feel like you're missing out on something?"

"Not really. I'm doing exactly what I've always dreamed of. If I didn't, I'd be scared to wake up one day and feel like I didn't follow the little voice in my head begging me to go for it. Even when it's out of my comfort zone."

"Like singing on a stage in a country bar?"

I burst out laughing, and Sam joined in. "Yeah. Well, I'm glad I did it. What are the top three craziest things that have ever happened to you in your career? Any women throwing their panties at you or asking you to marry them?"

"Let me see… I've seen a lot of crazy over the years." He paused. "Top incident for sure was this one. I was twenty and signing autographs at a VIP event. A woman I never saw before waited for over two hours in line, and when she walked up to me, she handed me a newborn. I thought it was for a picture, but it turned out he was supposed to be my son and I was to recognize and accept my paternity. The woman had a fair complexion and red hair. And the baby, let's just say his skin was so dark there was no way anyone would have assumed we were related. She started screaming I was an egotistical jerk and refused to feed my own child. Security had to escort her out. It was…surreal."

"I thought such stories were rumors. The ones we heard sometimes."

Sam shook his head. "Nope. I can assure you there are some weird people out there. Second was when a fan wrote lengthy posts online and wouldn't stop bashing my new album because he didn't like the title of a song. He said it reminded him of his cheating ex. He went on and on, writing on blogs, social media, and anywhere he could post his words, insulting me. It's insane how your work can trigger people, and instead of dealing with their own pain, they mirror it back to you, calling you out for things that have nothing to do with you. He even threatened to sue me for psychological distress."

"Geez. I'm not sure I'd be able to deal with haters. What's the third?"

"This one you'll like. A guy reached out to a friend of mine. He wanted to ask his girlfriend to marry him, and they had tickets for my show in Cleveland. I called him one night, and he explained his plan. We set everything up, and during the show, he came onstage, and in front of an entire stadium, he asked his high school sweetheart for her hand.

It was so emotional. Turns out the guy had been fighting cancer for years and had just learned he was in remission. I sang at their wedding a year later and offered them tickets to Fiji for their honeymoon. We're still in touch. They live in Spain now and have two kids. They named their son Samuel. Those are the stories that stick with you."

Moisture dampened my eyes. "Wow, this is beautiful. I'm…wow. Thanks for sharing with me."

"What's your best memory?" Sam asked.

"When I was around eight, we adopted a dog. A stray. I was having nightmares, and Cooper, that was his name, slept in my bed at night. We had so much in common. He became my confidant. Other than my sister, he was my best friend. We shared a deep connection, he and I. Did you ever have a pet?"

"When I was a kid. A cat named Peluche. One day, I'd like to get one for the girls. I'm just not convinced the timing is right. I may reevaluate the idea after the tour."

I finished the last touches to my design and studied the flower pattern I'd just painted. "I think we're done here." Back on my feet, I admired the work we just did.

"It looks great. It exceeds my expectations," Sam said, pride radiating from him. He smiled at me, and something swelled in my chest. I loved being on the receiving end of his happiness. "I've also bought everything we might need to build a garden in there."

"I can't wait."

Once we put all our tools aside, he stood next to me, and we high-fived. "It really does look sharp," I stated. My phone chimed in my pocket, and as I swiped the screen to unlock it, I realized it was almost four. "Oh shoot, I gotta go. I have dinner plans tonight."

"Go," Sam called after me. "Thanks for the help."

I waved at him over my shoulder, crossed the house,

and hurried down the three steps leading to the cobble-stone pathway. Once in my car, I slid my shades down over my eyes, ignited the engine, and pulled away. Sam Stevens's front yard was more like a big parking space, separated from the street through a curved driveway, making the house almost invisible from the main road. In the rearview mirror, I noticed him standing next to the alley leading to his backyard, watching me with a serious expression and his hands stuffed in his pockets. Had Sam and I become friends in the last twelve hours?

———

"Hey, how is it going?" I asked as Jacob let me in. His face didn't reveal the signs of the easy cheerfulness he usually carried around me. "What's going on?" I stepped closer to kiss him, but he yanked away from my touch. "Talk to me. What did I miss?"

His eyebrows bunched as he eyed me with an expression I'd never seen before.

"Jake…"

"Maddie, what's going on between Sam Stevens and you?"

I blinked. "What?"

"Don't play the innocent. I saw the pictures. The entire world saw the pictures. You both looked lovely together. Are you leading me on?"

"Me?" I said, gesturing to my chest. "Am I leading you on? Are you being serious?"

"I'm not blind, Maddie. The guy's a catch. And from what I've seen online, riding on your boss's back doesn't exactly scream a professional relationship."

"Wow, I can't believe you're accusing me of something that never occurred. Nothing went down. I was outside the museum, talking to you, worried because you never showed up, and the next thing I knew, I bumped into him. I was disappointed about going home after putting in the time and effort to look pretty for our date. He was alone and planning to watch a game at the bar, but we decided to grab a bite instead and ended up at that country joint. I dared him to play a song. People recognized him, and he played two. By then, my heels had wrecked my feet, so he offered to carry me until we caught a cab. End of the story. See? Nothing worthy of gossip websites or mass-media magazines."

"You'd tell me if it meant something more?"

"Yes. And by the way, I freaked out when Ems woke me up with the links to pictures of me online. They were taken and posted out of context."

"I sounded like a jealous asshole before. Sorry. I know we're not even officially dating and you don't owe me anything. For a moment, I felt played. It's silly." His lips claimed mine. Slowly. With care. "Just be honest with me. That's all I'm asking."

I nodded against his chest as he pulled me into his embrace.

"You have no idea how much I love this movie," I told Jacob a week later as we strolled toward the park where there was an outdoor presentation of the movie *Catching Up With You.* "I think I watched it a thousand times when I was a kid. That scene with the dog, it's the best."

Jacob reached for my hand as we neared the entrance. He did that every time we were surrounded by many people. As if I could ease something in him just by being by his side.

"I can't believe you've never seen it," I whispered in his ear as we followed the crowd, all of us on the lookout for the best spot.

"I was a book nerd as a kid." He pressed a kiss to the tip of my nose. "Come on, for once, I'll even sit in the middle of all these people so we're front and center." He handed me the rolled blanket tucked under his arm. "Go wild. I'll head over to the concession stand."

I scanned my surroundings. "See that free patch of grass over there?" I pointed through a sea of families and couples. "Meet me there."

"It's a date," he said, his smile lighting up his handsome face.

"Before I forget, don't make plans for Saturday night."

He cocked his pierced brow. "Why?"

"Remember when you said you missed the opportunity to see the monster truck show when you were sixteen because you got food poisoning?"

Jacob nodded.

"Well, they're in town for a night, and I got us tickets."

He blinked. "You did?"

I nodded and offered a half-shrug. "I thought you might like it."

He looped his arms around my waist in a tight embrace. "You thought right. This is very sweet of you." He stepped back. "Now go, or you'll miss that perfect spot."

"Oh yeah, sure." We broke apart, and I returned my focus to my mission. "Sorry," I said, weaving through the crowd and trying not to bump into anyone or step on their toes, heading for the green patch I had set my eyes on. Just as I was about to lay down the blanket, someone crashed into me from behind, and I fell to my knees.

When a hand reached down for me, my eyes lingered

on the long fingers, slowly tracing the corded forearm, muscular shoulder, and finally resting on the handsome eyes trained on me.

I blinked. "Sam?"

"Maddie?"

"Hi." I anchored my hand in his, rose to my feet, and brushed dust off my knees with my free hand.

He frowned. "Are you okay?"

"Yeah. All good. Okay, this is so weird. We gotta stop meeting like this."

"What are you doing here?" he asked.

"*Catching Up With You* is my all-time favorite movie. I wouldn't miss the screening for anything."

"It is? I watch it at least once a year. That dog scene gets me every time."

I blinked, speechless. Was he for real? "Wow, I didn't—"

"Girls, let's get ready to watch this movie," Riley announced, nearing us with Justine in his arms and Mikaella holding Devon's hand in tow, cutting our discussion short. He stopped when his eyes landed on me and gave Sam a puzzled look. "Hi, Maddie. I had no idea you were joining us tonight."

"Maddie," the girls hollered. Justine wiggled to get down, then both of them ran into my arms as I squatted, holding them to my heart.

"I'm so happy to see you." I glanced at the others from above their heads. "Actually, it wasn't planned," I told Riley. "Sam and I were battling for the same patch of grass to lay out a blanket."

"Now that you're here, you gotta watch the movie with us," Devon chimed in.

"Actually, I'm here with my friend."

"Jacob?" Mikaella asked.

I patted her head. "Yes. He went to get us popcorn. He should join me any minute."

"I wanna watch the movie with Jacob, Daddy." Justine bounced on her feet. "Please, please, please."

"You two are invited to join us if you'd like," Sam offered at the same time Jacob reached us.

"What's going on?" Jacob asked, his eyes darting across everyone, stopping on me.

"Huh, we happened to—" I began.

Justine jumped in. "Daddy and Maddie want to sit together, and Mika thinks you're pretty. Wanna watch the movie with me?"

Mikaella's cheeks reddened as her little sister bobbed her head, unapologetic about revealing her innocent crush.

I shrugged as Jacob asked me a silent question. Sam's daughters owned my heart. Even though I wanted to spend my night alone with Jacob—despite being surrounded by strangers—I could never refuse them time with me.

Justine curled her tiny body around his leg. "Please," she begged.

I cupped my mouth with one hand to stifle a laugh and noticed Devon doing the same.

Justine batted her eyelashes. How could anyone refuse her anything?

Jacob's arm slid across my waist, and he nodded. "Fine. The more the merrier, I guess." I could tell by his sudden rigid demeanor that the idea of spending our night with other people didn't please him. I leaned in so only he could hear me. "We can sit elsewhere if you prefer."

He breathed out. "No. It's okay. At some point, I gotta meet them. They are important to you, so they are important to me too."

I grinned way too big at the sound of his words. "Thanks. Girls, it's settled, we'll watch the movie together."

"Yay," they both cheered.

The moment we all sat down, Justine perched herself on Jacob's lap, her tiny arms circling his neck, and Mikaella curled herself under my arm while I brushed her hair back with my fingers. This, the concept I belonged somewhere, filled me with warmth.

Sam's gaze caught mine, and he shrugged, shaking his head.

They're perfect, I mouthed, at which he nodded his approval.

He offered me a lopsided smile, and I mirrored it. I loved this new friendship we had going on.

About forty minutes into the movie, Justine fell asleep. Sam set her beside him, using his hoodie as a blanket. Mikaella moved between Riley and Devon, snuggling with Hope, their dog. Jacob used his newfound freedom to scoot closer to me and wrapped an arm around my shoulders, and I sank into his embrace.

Minutes later, he nuzzled the side of my neck and kissed my temple. He was usually not a very PDA kind of guy, and this sudden urge to claim me in front of everyone else felt out of character for him.

"What are you doing?" I asked in a whisper.

"Enjoying the movie." He leaned in to silence me with a kiss, but I pulled away.

"What's going on?" I asked. We had agreed not to *date* date because I was leaving for six months soon, and if we got too invested in a relationship before my departure, leaving would break both our hearts. I didn't want to complicate or jeopardize the tour—and my heart—or feel homesick the whole time. So far, being just friends had worked well for us, even though I could tell Jacob yearned for more. But I wasn't ready to fall in love if it meant being heartbroken shortly after.

"Just enjoying the night," he said, tracing the contours of my face with his fingertips.

I pushed further away from his touch. "No. Stop. We're not making out here."

He toyed with the tendrils of my hair that fell down my back. "I'm tired of pretending we're not together when we both know we are. Why are you so scared?"

"Can we talk about it later? Now isn't the time or place."

Jacob slid to the left and folded his legs before him, a frown creasing his forehead. His eyes stayed glued to the giant inflatable screen positioned between mature trees in front of us. From the corner of my eye, I noticed the tick in his jaw and the hurt hardening his features. Tears prickled my eyes, but I blinked them away. I hated fights and the feeling I had deceived someone I cared about. Since the day Jacob had confronted me about the pictures of Sam and me in those tabloids, he'd been acting insecure. I was done reassuring him that they were just pictures meant to insinuate and provoke, and nothing more. I understood where he was coming from and why he was questioning me, but I was twenty-one, single, and free to hang out with whoever I wanted, without having to explain myself. We had agreed, Jacob and I, that we were friends. Who kissed sometimes. But friends, nonetheless. No label. No sex. Nothing to blur the line until I came back from the tour, and we decided if we wanted to give it a real shot.

I cocked my head to the side, and Sam's eyes reeled me in.

Are you all right? he mouthed.

I shrugged. Not really. But I wouldn't confide in him about my messy, nonexistent love life.

For the rest of the movie, I felt his heavy stare on me. I could tell he wasn't convinced by my act. More than once, I caught him watching Jacob intensely, a frown marring his forehead.

Since Jacob had shifted away from me, he'd kept his hands to himself and remained distant.

I placed a hand on his shoulder in a tentative attempt to bridge the gap. "Can we not fight here?"

He shook his head and sighed. "Sorry. It's stupid. It's weird for me to spend the night with your boss and his family and friends."

I leaned against him. "I know. It wasn't planned. Thank you for agreeing, though. It made the girls happy. I'll never hear the end of it. They'll chant your praises for weeks to come."

We exchanged tentative smiles.

"They love you," he said after a stretch of silence. "I'm glad they have you in their lives…because I'm glad I have you too."

The movie ended, and Sam lifted a near-comatose Justine in his arms. Riley picked up a tired Mikaella, who complained that her legs were asleep and she couldn't possibly walk back to the car on her own.

Devon grabbed my hand. "It was so good to see you again, Maddie. I hope we'll see more of each other soon." She waved me goodbye and followed her man, who had stopped to strike up a conversation with a couple he seemed to know.

Jacob left to look for the portable potty, and then it was just Sam and me—and a sleeping Justine. Like he did every time he was nervous, Sam stuffed his free hand into his pocket. "So, I was wondering if—"

No idea why, but I could finish his sentence. "I'm…

huh…okay… Jacob and I just had a disagreement." I decided to be honest. "He's not over the pictures…"

"I see." He sighed. "If I were in his shoes and saw my girl online with all those headlines, I'm sure I would've reacted too."

I lowered my shoulders. "We're not really…dating. We're just friends."

"Oh." He took a step forward, and skimmed my upper arm with his fingers.

The air around us charged. Time seemed to stop. All I could hear was the pounding of my own heart.

"I believed…" He never finished his sentence. Dropping his arm to his side, he backed away from me.

I swallowed, pretty sure I'd imagined something that never existed, and tried to return to my previous train of thought. "All I'm saying is—" I stopped. Why was I breathless?

Sam's throat worked, and he watched me, waiting for me to continue.

"I…huh…I understand his concern. I do. About the… about the pictures. It's legitimate. Why wouldn't it be?" And now I was rambling. "But…" I didn't remember where I was going with that. "Anyway, I'm free to do whatever I want. I'm aware those pictures weren't ideal, but we did nothing wrong. So why would I get carried away? We had a great time. I chose to do as you said and let them be. With the ugly, multi-million-dollar celebrity divorce going on in Hollywood right now, you and I are already old news. You were right. Those things get swiped away pretty quickly."

"See? I told you so." His amused expression made him look boyish, and I relished the sight of it.

"I should go," I said, pointing over my shoulder. "Jacob will be back. And you gotta put the girls to bed so…"

"You'd tell me if you weren't fine, right?" He raised one dark brow. "As your *friend*." Was it me, or had he put too much emphasis on the word *friend*?

"Yep. No worries."

Our eyes fixated on each other for a bit longer. Why was it so hard to move away from Sam's energetic field? Since the first time his eyes had roamed over me at the nanny agency, Sam Stevens's attention always sent flutters to my belly. It made me feel special—in a way I had never felt with anyone else. I had no explanation for it.

I pushed the thought away, knowing I was, once again, overthinking everything.

"I'll go now." Recalling the awkwardness in the cab the other night, I leaned forward, unsure if we should shake hands or kiss each other's cheeks. And, like that night, I decided against it and waved instead. Sam nodded his agreement but didn't budge, watching my retreat. I could tell because I felt his eyes on me. They burned my back.

Jacob joined me, and when I risked a look back, I noticed Sam hadn't left, a serious expression painting his face. A small knot twisted my stomach. Was he worried I had faked being all right seconds ago?

Whatever his expression meant, I preferred to be on the receiving end of his smiles. That I knew for sure.

Chapter 12
Madison

"Will Daddy be home before bedtime?" Mikaella asked, her hair still damp from her bath, dressed in a pastel-blue nightgown with a grinning, pink-glazed donut printed on the front. The one I'd gotten her the other day when we all went shopping together because she argued her father had no sense of girls' fashion. The memory of it sent a bolt of warmth through my heart.

Back then, we were fine—all of us. Or at least, I believed that was our reality.

In the last month, since that movie night, Sam had been colder around me. Even more than usual. His broody attitude had made a full comeback, reminding me of the man I'd first met at the nanny agency. His annoyance seemed solely directed at me, though. His patience ran thin these days. He argued with the girls more often too. Up until that night, we were getting along great, and our working relationship had even evolved into a friendship. Or I thought it did... Now, I didn't know what to think anymore. For a week, I'd blamed it on the anxiety of going back on tour, but now I wasn't so sure.

In the midst of everything, my relationship with Jacob had also gotten complicated.

He was asking for more. For commitment. A voice inside my head was telling me to be careful and to give it more time. To wait and see. And thus far, in my life, my intuition had been mostly right, so I usually chose to listen to it.

Many question kept me up at nights these days, and I often wondered if Sam was rethinking my presence on tour? That was the only logical explanation I could come up with for his iciness toward me.

When we were alone in a room, he always found a reason to leave. He never struck up a conversation with me anymore, just for the sake of it, nor did he ask random questions to get to know me or look me in the eye. My ego was hurt, and I feared what would happen with the girls if he decided my presence on tour wasn't necessary anymore. No way would I leave them of my own volition. Never.

I had been that kid—the one who felt like the adults in her life had turned their backs on her at some point. I would never subject Mikaella and Justine to the same treatment. They had already been deceived once. I wouldn't be the next adult in line to disregard them.

Needing more than a grown-up's bad temper to ruffle my feathers, I swallowed the whirlwind of emotions rising in me and kept giving my full attention to those two little girls, who had become my entire world over the past few months.

No matter how hard I tried to forget him, my troubled

mind always swirled back to their father whenever I was left alone with nothing to occupy my thoughts.

Sam and I had spent a great deal of time together before the movie night, and on each occasion, I'd felt we were getting closer…understanding each other on a deeper level.

The night I went back to his house after forgetting my purse, I was certain we shared a moment in his music studio. I'd bet my life we did. Supercharged electricity had infiltrated the room….and the intensity with which he'd stared at me… Whoa, I thought I would melt right there on the carpeted floor. I remembered I could barely breathe, my brain starved for oxygen.

Then we shared food in that bar, danced, and sang together. Though I'd tried to convince myself otherwise, I knew I hadn't imagined the powerful connection we'd shared. That night, I saw a new version of Sam Stevens—the man who enjoyed his freedom for a few hours, a man rather than just a single father. The one who thrived and shed all the walls around him.

He hadn't faked happiness that night. Sue me, but I could tell. I knew it deep in my bones.

At that point, my feelings for him had become conflicted. Once back home, I'd watched him leave through my bedroom window, my heart fracturing at the thought that it had been a one-night-only thing between us. Nothing more. Just a glimpse of a laid-back life—one where we could be ourselves, without anything or anyone standing between us. A man and a woman, simply enjoying each other's company for a few uninterrupted hours.

When I'd gone to bed afterward, I concluded it wasn't mere attraction we shared but undeniable chemistry. I had convinced myself that being friends with him was enough.

Things were simple between us. Nothing was forced. We got along great.

But now, over a month later, I'd realized I had completely misread the situation back then.

Gone was the easy familiarity between Sam and me. Every time we were around each other, he spoke as if I were just another employee, the warmth behind his words nonexistent. These days, he didn't grab my arm when I said something he disagreed with. We shared no eye contact. In fact, Sam had shut me out entirely. If the greenhouse hadn't stood as concrete proof that we once made a great team, I wouldn't have believed it myself.

I hurt as the rip separating us became a canyon. Wide and deep.

Mikaella tugged at my shirt. "Maddie, you're not listening. Will Daddy be home before bedtime?"

"Sorry, I got lost in my head for a minute." In one swift movement, I flipped my phone over on the countertop to look at the time. "He should be here within the hour." I cringed. "I…think. He didn't go over the day's plans with me this morning. I'm sure we can push bedtime a tiny bit to wait for him."

Justine met us, dressed in an almost-identical nightgown as her sister, but hers was pink with a toothy ice cream cone printed on the front. "I wanna dance. Can we do a *partly*? With music."

"A party, sweetie," I said with a smile. "You want to throw a party?"

The four-year-old nodded. "*Partly. Partly. Partly*," she repeated, jumping around the kitchen.

I wiped my hands on the dishcloth hanging over my shoulder. "Okay. Let's put some music on. Help me move some furniture around in the den, okay?"

Both girls bobbed their heads with unconcealed glee and infectious giggles.

We cranked up the volume of a pop song they adored, and Justine and Mikaella started dancing around. The room soon filled with laughter, and my heart brimmed with delight.

Lifting Justine in my arms, I spun her around only to grab Mikaella's hands next to twirl her too, swaying to the rhythm of the catchy melody.

"Again," Justine said once the song ended.

I put another song on, and this time, we held on to one another's hands in a circle and danced, laughing our hearts out.

This, right here, was why I would never be able to walk away from those girls unless I was forced to.

"I'm thirsty," Mikaella said, breathless, her cheeks crimson, after the third song.

"Keep dancing. I'll get you some water. Be right back." I put another song on, and the girls did all kinds of acrobatic moves, jumping, swaying their hips, spinning.

I watched them, unable to stop grinning as I walked away.

In the doorway, I bumped into a wall—a human wall —and lost my balance. Two strong hands clamped around my waist, and I nearly melted under the searing heat coursing through me.

I raised my head, meeting Sam's eyes. They fixed me in place, darkening more and more with every heartbeat. My throat felt dry and itchy, and I swallowed through a maze of sharp edges.

Trying to regain control over my senses, I blinked twice.

As if someone had nailed me to the floor, I couldn't move, his gaze pinning me in place.

My deafening pulse drowned out Mikaella's and Justine's laughter, its thudding all I could hear besides Sam's heavy, fast, shallow breathing.

Maddie, say something. Anything.

"I…huh… We-we've been… I mean, hi." *Real smooth, girl.*

Sam cleared his throat, and his voice sounded rougher than usual, pulsing through all my cells. "What are you doing?"

"Getting water."

His fingers dug into my skin, his grip tightening instead of loosening.

My head hovered just above his heart. Could I hear its drumming if I closed my eyes and listened closely? Would it beat in time with my own?

"I said, what are you doing?"

I leaned back, my brows bunched together, not sure I understood the meaning of his words.

"The girls should be in bed by now. It's almost eight thirty."

I met his gaze, my face probably betraying my bewilderment. Was he kidding right now? Since when did he become so stiff about bedtime hours?

It wasn't like I kept them up late often. It only happened once or twice in the past. And both times, he was glad they stayed up until he came home.

"They missed you. They wanted to wait for you. I'm sorry if I overstepped here. I thought you'd be glad to tuck them in yourself."

A storm rumbled in his irises. I parted my lips, but no words came out.

Would he lose his cool over this? What was going on with him? Where was the guy I got to know in that bar? The king of dares who enjoyed a good time.

His tone turned icy, sending chills through me. "You can't decide what's best for them, Madison. I'm their father. I call the shots." His words sounded lethal. What? We were back to Madison? What was happening? What did I do to deserve his unconcealed wrath?

I blinked again. Once, twice. A hundred times.

Fragments of fury formed inside me. How did I ever think Sam Stevens and I were on an equal level of friendship?

In the past, when I barely knew him, this grumpy side of him allured me. Not this time. The time, it affected me instead…a lot.

This version of the man I worked for didn't sit well with me.

I straightened my back and glared right back at him with the same fervor. He had no right to belittle my character or my judgment. No matter who he was or what he wanted, he had to trust me to know what was best for his kids when they were under my care. No, Sam Stevens couldn't stand there and intimidate me just because he was in a sour mood or had a bad day. Whatever was wrong with him had nothing to do with me and everything to do with him. It would be better if he kept his wrath for someone else—someone who had truly hurt him and deserved this angry side of him.

"I'm sorry if I kept the girls up fifteen minutes past their bedtime, Mr. Stevens. Won't happen again. You have my word."

His face flushed, and some of his anger evaporated as he studied me, blinking, as if taken by surprise, the storm in his eyes dissipating and switching to surprise. "Mr. Stevens? Are you being serious? What is this all about, *Madison*? Explain."

Why was it that every time my name fall from his lips,

it sent waves of heat through me? I felt like a popsicle in the sun whenever he called me by my full name. I sighed. Somehow, tonight, it even eased my irritation.

"You called me Madison so I'm calling you Mr. Stevens. Only fair."

Breathing the same air, neither of us looked away as we indulged in a staring contest. Tension ran high, swirling around us, taking us hostage in its claws.

We faced each other.

"It's a bit childish, don't you think? If I remember correctly, Madison is your name." He arched one dark brow in a sexy slash infuriating manner.

My ire clothed my heart, leaving knots crushing my stomach in its wake.

Using my most innocent tone, I mocked, "Mr. Stevens is *yours* too, no?"

If looks could kill, I'd be dead right now. Our gazes stayed locked, neither of us stepping down. Sam's nostrils flared. His eyes transformed into weapons, powerful enough to vaporize every inch of me. A new flame ignited in my lower belly. Great. Now desire and hate mixed together. Because, like some idiot, I relished the fervor of our exchange.

He watched me but said nothing, so I continued, "You told me once we needed to be honest with each other. Right now, I feel like you're upset with me for some unknown reason. You're the one acting like a petulant child." I clamped my mouth shut as soon as the retort escaped. Why was I engaging in a war of words with my boss? *No, no, no.* This was bad. I was crossing a line that couldn't be uncrossed. "Sorry. I...I...huh...didn't mean to be disrespectful. Won't happen again." In a twisted way, it felt good to get it out there and to express myself without restraints.

His somber expression morphed into amusement. A crooked smirk appeared on his face, and it disrupted my flimsy resistance. "I must say I'm impressed. I—"

"Daddy," Justine and Mikaella screamed as they ran in our direction. Sam released his grip on me, and my knees wobbled. I used the wall to hold myself upright as I regained my composure.

What had just gone down?

Once my legs steadied, I stepped back, creating space between us, determined to break free of Sam's gravity and reclaim my self-control.

I resumed my breathing, shaking away every lingering morsel of our heated encounter. Whatever I did, I didn't deserve his rant. But the way his stare had burned into me was hotter than any confrontation I'd ever experienced, making my confusion even more overwhelming.

"Daddy, we're having a dance *partly*. With music," Justine said as he lifted her in his arms and spun her around before she peppered his cheek with kisses.

"Maddie said we can go to bed later because we wanted to wait for you," Mikaella said, raising her arms to be picked up too. "We missed you."

"She did, didn't she?" he asked, his gaze slowly finding me. His Adam's apple bobbed, and I pushed down whatever heat his unyielding attention provoked inside me.

For a moment, I forgot how to breathe, intoxicated by the hostility raging in the room. My body overheated, and prickling sensations surged through me.

Gasping with each intake of air, I spun around and fled to the kitchen, desperate to create space between us.

I poured myself a tall glass of water, fighting my emotions down and cooling all my misplaced attraction. I was mad at Sam. And upset at how he'd addressed me. But

I also couldn't deny our altercation had woken up something in me that I had no words to define.

Tilting my head back, I tried to put a name to that rapture vibrating between us. The push and pull. That forbidden attraction we had felt in the past that had flared up again just seconds ago—more potent this time, more explosive.

The cold liquid eased some of the fire down my throat.

Not in the mood to have another face-off with my boss —since when did I start referencing him as my boss again and not Sam?—and fearing that for some reason I'd read the situation wrong and he wasn't rethinking my place in their lives, I gathered my stuff, ready to bolt before I combusted. My mind drifted to Jacob. I missed the comfort he provided me. His arms. His kisses. And the way he made me feel like I was the most important person on Earth. How he never took pleasure in submitting me to a battle of wills.

My heart changed its tempo as more thoughts of him filled my mind.

I wiped the tears pooling in the corners of my eyes with the hem of my shirt and sent him a text.

ME

Can I come over?

He replied within a second.

JACOB

Just got home. I was hoping I'd see you.

ME

I'll be there soon.

JACOB

Can't wait. Dessert?

ME

Yes.

I had dinner with the girls earlier, but dessert sounded great right now, as chocolate and ice cream always helped me sort out my troubled emotions.

I slid my phone back into my back pocket and poured two cups of water for the girls.

They were still in the den, telling their daddy all about their day. The twinkles in their eyes soothed some of my doubts. They healed the cracks Sam's earlier accusations had carved into my heart. Now that the heaviness suffocating us had lessened and my common sense had returned, I couldn't wait to flee the scene.

"Are you leaving?" Mikaella asked as I leaned closer to hug her goodbye.

"Yes. It's time for me to go." I coughed, my emotions lacing my voice, trying to erase all traces of my meltdown.

Still in her daddy's arms, Justine looped her small arms around my neck, pulling me forward. "Why are you sad, Maddie?" Why did she have to be so perceptive at such a young age? She was connected to people's emotions. All the time. She cupped my face and studied me for a moment, her eyes boring into mine as if she could read my soul.

I blinked, not ready to let her see through me. "I'm okay, sweetie. I just have to go. I'll be all right. You should go to bed now. It's late."

"I love you, Maddie," she said, burying her face in the crook of my neck. "Don't be sad."

Tears filled my eyes and rolled down my cheeks. Her compassion broke the dam I was trying so hard to contain.

I fastened my grip around her tiny body, my shoulders heaving. She moved from her father's arms to mine, and I squatted to level my face with a worried Mikaella.

"Did Daddy do that to you?" she asked.

I sniffled. Could I hold on to these girls forever? I wasn't ready to let their father see how badly our interaction had overwhelmed me.

"Girls, go brush your teeth. I'll be right up to tuck you in. Say goodnight to Madison."

His clipped tone propelled another wave of hot tears down my face. Great. Now I'd look like a mess. Just like a kid unable to face any criticism. Because when he confronted me tonight, Sam Stevens had treated me like a kid. He had talked to me like an entitled jerk. One I refused to acknowledge anymore for the time being.

I pulled away from the girls' embrace and wiped my tears with my fingertips. "I'm fine, sweethearts. Just a bit tired. I'll go to bed and be all good in the morning, okay? It's bedtime for you two."

They both nodded, hugged me one last time before walking away.

"Come on, Justine. They wanna have a grown-up conversation," Mikaella whispered to her sister. She huffed and stretched her arm to grab Justine's hand in hers and led her away.

I watched them go. They reminded me of how Emily had looked after me a long time ago, and it eased some of my emotional overload.

Sam held out his hand, helping me to stand up. He searched my eyes, shoving his hands into his pockets, looking less lethal than he did minutes ago. "What's wrong?" His tone softened. Kinda. "Was Mikaella right? Did I do that to you?"

I shrugged, avoiding his gaze.

"Fuck. I'm sorry. I overreacted earlier. You didn't deserve my anger." He hung his head low, chin nearly touching his chest, and burrowed his hands deeper into his pockets, an unmistakable sign he was uncomfortable. "I… I'm bad at this." He rubbed his scruffy jaw with a hand. "I'm trying hard to do the right thing here." I had no clue what his cryptic words meant. "Maddie, I-I didn't wanna make you cry. I swear. There's a lot going on in my head right now, and you paid the price. Again, I'm sorry for anything I might have said that hurt your feelings. It was never my intention. You do a fantastic job with the girls."

His words twined around my heart. They spread pride and warmth throughout my being.

When regretful, Sam looked vulnerable and charming all at the same time. A deadly combination. One that appealed to the caring side of me, and to some extent, to the woman in me too.

Again, it messed with my feelings. And my will to leave.

I was hurt—and sad—but I craved his devoted attention, nonetheless. How every time he smiled at me, it lit up my days and reminded me I was his equal. Not just the hired help or another employee. How when we'd had openhearted conversations in the past, I saw beyond his celebrity or daddy status and just witnessed the guy hiding behind those labels. They didn't define him. There was so much more to Sam Stevens than people could see. You had to work backstage and be in his inner circle to grasp a hint of it. Deep down, I was grateful I did. More than once. Yet there were times when he went back to being a jerk for reasons I still couldn't comprehend.

Without thinking it first, my hand moved to rest on his forearm, my fingers grazing the skin there. His annoyance dissolved. Sam blinked, avoiding my eyes for the longest time. I sucked in a shallow breath, trying to keep my composure.

His eyes darted back to mine. This time, gone was the aggravation. He looked at me with respect and reverence, and a new surge of never-experienced-before sensations bubbled up deep in me. Messy feelings I'd been trying for months to conceal returned and amplified. They went against all logical reasoning.

"Are we okay?" he asked.

I retracted my hand, praying it would kill the longing knotting my stomach.

This just didn't compute. Right now, I was attracted to Sam—more than ever before—but I was also attracted to Jacob. Intellectually, we were a perfect match. We enjoyed nights in and a laid-back way of living. Sam did too, but he was more complex. He and I connected on another level. Family, his children, music, and reaching for our deepest dreams in life while facing our fears. On the physical level, the resemblance between them was striking.

I was sick. How could someone sane be attracted to two completely different people?

This was bad. How would I ever be able to do my job if I had a crush on my boss? This situation had to go away. It needed to be resolved, and fast.

Sam's voice, like a drug I couldn't escape, brought me back to him. "…hear me out, okay?" Great, I'd missed most of what he was telling me. "I hate the tension between us. It's not good for the girls. They sense it. We should talk. Once they're in bed."

Still under the shock of my inner revelations, I folded my arms over my chest, trying to raise a barricade between us and hoping my heart would get the memo and leave it at that. "Another day. I'm not feeling well right now." My words sounded weak as they left my mouth. I had to retreat and assess my complicated feelings far away from here.

He shook his head. "No, I wanna clear the air tonight. It's the right thing to do. Let's not draw this out. There's a weird tension between us. It's unhealthy. Let's hash it out once and for all and move on." He touched my upper arm for a split second, his finger tracing the length of my triceps, leaving me spellbound.

I stood there, hair standing on end on my arms, a storm of inner chaos swirling in my stomach, and closed my eyes. What should I do?

Taking advantage of the time I had while Sam tucked the girls in bed, I hurried to the bathroom to splash cold water over my face and gave myself a pep talk.

"Go out there and face him. First, no getting all emotional when someone criticizes you. Second, he's your boss. Just. Your. Boss. Drill that piece of information into your head. Third, grow a spine and face the man, Maddie. He wasn't upset at you earlier. He overreacted and said he was sorry. You did nothing wrong. If he's had a bad day, it's not your job to fix it. Or to fix him. Nor to be on the receiving end of his annoyance."

I rolled my shoulders back and exited the room with a new resolve.

Sam Stevens wouldn't break me—or my spirit. I wouldn't let his vulnerable and handsome self get a grip over my heart.

After I poured two glasses of water, I took a seat on a stool at the kitchen island, waiting for him to join me.

Meanwhile, I sent Jacob a text.

ME

Will be running late. Have something to deal with here first.

JACOB

Noted. I went to get ice cream. Just in case that's the mood you're in right now. And a raspberry and cream cake in case I'm wrong.

Jacob's thoughtfulness made me smile, and it made my heart rate peak.

ME

Be there ASAP.

Sam joined me, and I flipped my phone over, hiding the screen, as if he'd just caught me doing something bad.

I relaxed my stance when his lips bent into a shadow of a smile.

He didn't sit down. Instead, he leaned against the opposite countertop facing the kitchen island.

"About earlier, again, I was wrong. And I'm sorry. I had no right to bark at you. Since you've come into our lives, the girls can't stop talking during bedtime, telling me all they did and all they learned during the day."

His shoulders relaxed, his stance softened, and I emptied the air stuck in my lungs. The one I kept in, in case I required a reserve if our conversation went south.

Repeating my pep talk over and over in my head, I lifted my chin and decided to get to the bottom of this. The source of this tautness between us that hadn't existed before. "Something's wrong. I feel it. It's been going on for weeks. I thought we were getting along just fine, the four of us."

Sam looked away, his upper back going rigid. He shut his eyes and breathed out, pinching the bridge of his nose. Gone was the easygoing posture.

I had no idea how to read the man. He was so closed

off most of the time that every once in a while when he got out of his shell and laughed or played with us, it felt like a small victory.

The girls and I didn't deserve his shitty attitude, though. I couldn't tell him that without overstepping, especially since I had reminded myself that Sam was my boss, not my friend.

"There's so much going on—"

"Stop. It's not that. I can tell. It's not about tonight. You're mad at me, and it's been going on for a while. Did I do something wrong? Did I say something that bothered you? Are you rethinking the tour? My position?"

My heart lurched into my throat, and my airways constricted as I spoke the words I feared the most out loud.

Chills moved along my spine.

An acidic taste filled my mouth.

Sam's gaze snapped back to mine. He moved toward me, as if an invisible string connected us, stopping just a foot away.

"No. Maddie, don't say that. We need you. The girls need you." The column of his throat rippled. "I...I need you." He glanced down, rocking on his heels. When his irises found mine again, they were darker than I'd ever seen them, and the sight had a powerful effect on me. His voice cracked as he spoke. "Are you...are you thinking about quitting?"

I parted my lips but couldn't speak.

"Are you second-guessing the tour, Maddie? Are you looking for an out?"

I shook my head, feeling myself softening like molten clay beneath his heavy stare.

"Y-you need me?" Why was my voice suddenly so raspy? Somehow, all I'd heard was his need for me. The rest of his words didn't even register in my conscious mind.

The room temperature shot up by a thousand degrees. Sweat lined my back.

My breath caught in my lungs.

Sam blinked and stepped back with a head shake, breaking the moment.

"We all do…" Not '*I* need you' this time… but '*We* need you.'"Your presence is essential for me to go on this tour. If you're not coming or are not fully committed to it, then I can't go. I won't let anyone else but you around my daughters. If you're having doubts, you must tell me now before it's too late and we can't fix things."

Back to business. The heart-to-heart had evaporated. Gone was the moment. The air cooled. He only needed the professional me to pursue his career, not the personal me to appease his heart or speak to his soul. I was wrong all this time when I believed we were friends.

How could he think that his newly raised barrier protected him from real talk? From opening up? From feeling anything?

Sam Stevens stood a couple of feet away from me but appeared much farther away.

My fingertips followed the condensation on the glass, caught by its quiet pattern. Would it be out of line to fight with him? To show him he could drop the false pretenses and speak his mind—be honest, like he had been in that bar? That being himself, not that robotic version, would benefit not only his daughters but himself too? I had seen that version of him, so I knew it existed somewhere inside him.

I weighed my words before speaking again. "No… I'm not quitting…or thinking about quitting. Unless that's what *you* wish. And even if it is, I'm ready to fight for my job. I don't back down from my responsibilities and engagements easily."

Something passed in Sam's eyes. A glimpse of his hurting soul. His lips twitched. Clouds shadowed his face. It had been a while since I'd seen that expression etching his features, and I had forgotten how it twisted my insides when it faded away.

"Good," was all he said, his voice lacking warmth. "In that case, it's settled. We go on tour as planned. End of discussion. Unless you have something else you wanna say. Now is the time."

I bit my tongue, choosing to avoid a battle I was certain I couldn't win—at least not tonight. I was drained and longed to be somewhere far from his orbit.

"Nope. All good." My words sounded insipid, not even convincing myself.

"And for the record, I'm not angry at you. If I made you believe I was, it's not the case. I'm mad at myself for different reasons." He turned around and busied himself with making coffee. "Want some?"

"No. I should go. I'm sure you have plenty to do. I'll get out of here. It's getting late."

"Yeah. Sure. Go. Do your thing." He did not even bother to turn around to look at me while I saw myself out. "Good night."

The more space I put between us, the cooler the air turned. As if an arctic breeze had replaced the chinook that had swept the room when we had our face-off earlier and minutes ago when he admitted to needing me.

With my hand around the knob and about to open the front door, I rethought my escape. Sam was hurting. I could tell. The friend in me should find the courage to go to him and offer him a way to vent it out. But again, I had decided earlier we weren't friends per se because it was safer for me to only see him as my boss. I hated the idea of leaving when things were still awkward between us. My heart hung by a flimsy thread in my chest. I debated my options in my head. Before I could come to a conclusion, his muscular hand pushed against the panel over my head, preventing me from leaving.

I jumped at the abrupt movement. My pulse spiked.

I swiveled around, trying to decipher Sam's mixed expression.

His irises, fixated on me, shone darker. Midnight abysses I couldn't flee from. They captured mine, and I swallowed to ease the tightness in my throat.

We stood too close for comfort. I could smell the hint of coffee on his breath and the lingering notes of his cologne.

My head spun. I backed against the door, my eyes still linked to his. His looming posture was anything but professional. It was dominating. I had become the prey he'd caged with his entire being.

He started talking, his voice rough, sending shivers through me. "Before you go, I just want to tell you I'm having some people I care about over for a barbecue on Saturday. Friends. For my birthday." His tone, still hardened, reverberated through me. "I'd like you to join us…if you're free. As a guest, not the nanny or anything else. There'll be plenty of food, good wine, beer, cocktails, music, and… Anyway, the girls made me promise to ask you to come."

My mouth went dry, and my heart thudded. A new wave of anger blossomed inside me.

"You're only inviting me because Mika and Justine asked you to. I'm no one's pity invite." No way would I be an imposter at this party and feel like a stranger amongst all his probably rich and famous country music friends.

Never. Anyway, why would he want me there in the first place?

Sam swallowed, taking his time to answer, his gaze fleeting away.

He cleared his throat, still not looking fully at me, but not moving back.

He spoke again, his tone gentler this time. "Maddie, is this what you believe? That I'd invite you out of pity?"

In the scant room between us, I folded my arms. "It sure sounded like it. Like it hurt you to invite me. Like you're only dealing with my presence because you don't have any other option and you'd rather stand anywhere else but here, in front of me."

He stepped closer. The slim gap separating us shrunk. "Maddie, I want you there. You and I... I-I consider you my friend. I wouldn't have asked if that wasn't the case. I'm sorry if it sounded rude. Believe me, it was never my intention. I swear. And I'm far from being annoyed by your presence. On the contrary... You call me out on my bullshit, and it's unsettling. *Petulant child. Pity invite.* I'm not used to people defying me when I go off track or when I'm wrong."

He finally met my eyes. I noticed the pleading in them. The apology. Fire ignited around us. What was this force messing with my whole self when we stood close? Was I the only one feeling the sparks?

Sam leaned in as if he couldn't evade the magnetism too.

"Saturday, I already——"

"If Jacob is around, he's invited too," he added before I could refuse. "Since that movie night, the girls have been talking about him nonstop. I'm sure all of us will get along just fine. When he visits you on tour, it's better if we're already acquainted."

"You'll let him come visit me?"

"Maddie, you're not going to jail, but to live a life not a lot of people are lucky to experience in their lifetime. Your friends and family are welcome anytime."

And now he was back to being the generous and caring man I had uncovered under his tough exterior. The one he was around his children—and around me when he wasn't pretending.

After the realization that had hit me earlier, mixing my personal and professional lives didn't appear to be a good idea. It screamed disaster in big bold letters. Jitters invaded me at the thought, and I could feel my will to stay away from him off the clock slipping away bit by bit. Would the nagging voices in my head just shut up for a minute so I could gather my thoughts?

I exhaled a shaky breath, racking my brain for a smart reply. "I, huh, gotta check with him because we had plans to go to this astronomy convention in Chattanooga. Can I give you an answer tomorrow?

Sam dropped his head, looking deflated, his confidence gone. "Sure." Why was he looking so defeated right now? "You're into galaxies and stars and planetary orbit things?"

I sighed. "Not really, but I said I'd accompany him. The road trip part will be fun. Perhaps we can go on Sunday… I'll have to ask him."

Sam backed from me and released the door. "Night, Maddie."

"See you in the morning," I blurted as I hurried outside, welcoming the summer breeze as it tickled the tip of my nose.

There, I could finally breathe.

With my back resting against the door, I tried to find an explanation for the complicated emotions that had invaded me tonight. Soon I'd be screwed if I didn't find a way to untangle the mess I was slowly creating inside me.

———

"Is everything all right?" Jacob asked after he greeted me.

I forced a smile, not wanting to worry him. "I'm fine. Just tired. Had a long day and it was kinda weird."

"Wanna talk about it?"

I shrugged. "Not really. Just my boss being his grumpy self for no reason."

We sat on opposite countertops in the kitchen, bowls of cookie dough ice cream in our hands.

"Maddie, I gotta tell you something, and it can't wait."

My spoon hung, suspended midair, just below my mouth as I waited for him to speak. From the looks of it, I feared the words that would leave his mouth. I could tell they would just add another layer to the entanglement I was already dealing with.

"You occupy every corner of my brain all the time. I want more with you." I parted my lips to protest, but he kept going. "I know what you're gonna say. That you're leaving and don't want ties here so you're not heartbroken because you'll want to be in two places at once and it will be difficult to enjoy the experience of the tour if your heart is here." He paused and sucked a long breath in. "We're already in a relationship....whether you like it or not. Knowing you'll come back to me after those six months are over is all I'm asking for. Please say yes. I want you in my life. I'm all in."

I stopped breathing. Ohmygod, I was pretty sure I stopped breathing. Yeah, I did.

I blinked, trying to jolt my lungs back to life.

My heart danced in my chest, its throb echoing through every fiber of me.

A fuzzy feeling filled my chest.

I blinked again.

Would I pass out or start breathing on my own soon?

Jacob jumped from the counter and inched closer. He studied me, waiting for me to say something.

All the words died on the tip of my tongue.

I blinked some more.

"What do you say? Maddie? Are you okay?"

I nodded. "I hear you, but…the thing is, it's not what we discussed. I know me," I said once I regained control of my speech. "If we do this, I'll never be able to walk away."

"Think about it. We're spending the weekend together. Let's give it a try. See what it would look like if we were together for real." He cradled my face with his palm. "I'm falling for you. Hard. There's nothing I can do to stop it. We're amazing together. Why wait? When you know, you know."

"You'd wait for me while I'm gone?"

"Yep. Because you make me happy, Madison Prescott. Now that I have you in my life, I don't want to let you go."

Jacob looked at me with reverence. Everything he said sounded good. Why was I so afraid to commit to a relationship?

"I'll be the lucky one you come back to when it ends. I'll hold the fort while you tour the country."

"O-kay. We'll give it a try." As I spoke the words, an uneasy feeling woke up inside me. Knots wrapped around my stomach. I wished to do this, but a part of me kept telling me I shouldn't agree so fast. For once, could I ignore that voice in my head?

Jacob's mouth claimed mine, and I lost myself in his

love. It silenced all those unwelcome voices in my head that knew nothing about what I desired.

Breathless, we broke apart.

"I can't wait for this weekend," he said, smiling like a fool.

"About that, can I meet you there on Sunday instead?"

His brows pinched together. "Why? We both have the weekend off. We planned this weeks ago. You know how hard it was to get tickets."

I pushed away to look at him. "I've been…well, we've been invited to a barbecue at Sam's place. All afternoon and probably all evening on Saturday."

A frown creased his forehead. "I don't understand. Are you working or not?"

I shook my head, chewing my bottom lip. "They're having friends over, and Sam invited me. As a guest. Well, he invited both of us, but I told him you already had plans. It's his birthday."

"*We* already have plans," he corrected with a sharp tone. I could read all the hurt painting his face. "Your country music superstar of a boss wants me at one of his infamous birthday parties with his friends?"

I nodded and remained silent.

"You sure? Our last encounter was a bit strained. Not sure he appreciates my company."

"I told you already. He's broody sometimes. Don't make too much of it. He's nice—well, most times—and has a huge heart once you get to know him. When he's in a good mood… Did you forget he walked out on me the day we met?"

Jacob tilted his head back and let out a warm chuckle. "God, you're too good. I can't believe you gave him a second chance after he stormed out without a valid reason. Only a dick could do that to you."

I shrugged. "Anyway, he probably had his reasons. Or maybe not… Remember, he said he was sorry because he panicked. It doesn't matter anymore. We get along fine now. Most of the time." I paused and stared at him. "The girls and I will be happy to have you over."

"You're really going?"

"You already met Riley and Devon. Since I'll be spending months with him on a tour bus, it's better if I get to know his friends beforehand, no? At least, I'll know what to expect. The underside of the country music industry is all new to me. I won't have this chance twice. I wanna immerse myself as much as possible in it. It's a huge opportunity for me." I studied his face. "If you don't wanna come, like I said, I can drive to Chattanooga early on Sunday morning and meet you there. Or take the bus if you want us to drive back together."

"Gimme the night to think about it."

I nodded.

Jacob's eyes drank me in as he gave me a slow once-over. "I was really looking forward to spending the entire weekend together."

"I'm sorry."

He huffed. "Don't be. We'll make it work. Somehow." He flashed me a pearly-white smile.

Jacob looked so sure of us. Why couldn't I share his optimism? I really wanted to. I was desperate to. The chatter in my mind wouldn't stop, no matter how much I tried to block its murmur.

"Are you staying over tonight?" he asked while he refilled our bowls.

After the night I'd spent here on our first date, I'd never stayed over again. Ever. Why was he asking me tonight of all nights?

I fixed a curl to my lips. "Nah. I should go, it's getting late."

Anyway, I still needed to sort out my feelings, and fast. I couldn't be attracted to two guys at once. With Jacob, I knew it would be safe and easy. On the other hand, Sam woke up something potent inside me. It was the worst-case scenario.

Once I showered and slid under my covers an hour later, I prayed the night would erase all my doubts and things would look so much clearer in the morning light.

Chapter 13
Sam

"When will Maddie be here, Daddy? She's better than you at braiding my hair."

"Sweet pea, I can do it." I emptied the grocery bags on the kitchen counter. "Gimme ten minutes."

Mikaella shook her head with enough velocity to detach it from her neck. She had a much better attitude when Madison was around. Her occasional bad moods were still mostly directed at me, but her therapist told me my little girl had made lots of progress in the past few months. I could only thank Madison for helping my girl through her struggles.

"Maddie's here?" Justine asked, bouncing our way. "I *loooove* Maddie. Maddie? Maddie? *Maaaaaddie?*"

I fought a smile while she looked around sporting a glittery emerald-green dress with lime-green satin ribbons and a yellow cape. A blinding combination of colors. For a second, I wondered who had gifted her that piece of ugliness. No matter how awful it looked, my youngest daughter glowed in it, and it was all that mattered.

"Maddie's not here, baby girl. She should arrive later this afternoon. At the same time as everyone else."

"But she gotta braid my hair," Mikaella argued.

"And I want Maddie to make pancakes," Justine said.

"Girls, I can do all this. If you'd give me ten minutes."

"NO," they both screamed at the same time.

"We want Maddie, Daddy," Mikaella said, not breaking her stance. "We need her. She's better at this than you are. She's a girl. She gets us. You're a boy, so you can't get our women complexities."

"Women complexi-*what*?"

She rolled her eyes. Great. "Women complexities, Daddy."

"Women complexities? Who taught you that?"

"Stella's mama told her daddy the other day after she got mad, and he said she was overreacting. See? Women complexities."

Oh wow. I hadn't seen that one coming. I huffed and tried a new approach. "Doing your hair and prepping lunch are two tasks I can manage on my own."

"Doesn't matter. We want Maddie to do it."

"Yes, Daddy, we want Maddie," Justine echoed. "She cooks special bunny pancakes. You don't."

"Girls, you want breakfast for lunch? I was thinking pasta."

"No. Bunny pancakes. It's *Saturnday*."

I kneeled in front of my little girl. "Saturday. And you'll have round and boring pancakes today. I'll ask Maddie to teach me how to make special bunny pancakes for next time. Deal?"

Justine frowned and stamped her feet on the floor. "No. No *dweal*. I only eat Maddie's pancakes."

"Since when?" I asked.

"And Maddie *has* to braid my hair. Not you," Mikaella chimed in.

When did my daughters team up against me? I usually had at least my youngest daughter on my side.

I should get a dog. Some old fellow—not a puppy who'd be all over the girls—too rusty to run around, who'd agree to be in my corner. Then it'd be two against two. Fair fight.

This house was lacking testosterone.

I'd be overrun by the time they were both old enough to go out and get into trouble.

Mikaella led her little sister away and whispered something to her. Justine bobbed her head, her smile reaching her ears.

They giggled some more before joining me.

"Fine, Daddy. We'll wait for Maddie," Mikaella said, her eyes bright with devilish sparks.

"Sweet pea, what did you tell your sister?"

"Nothing."

Justine snaked her arms around my legs, tugging at my shirt.

I squatted to level my eyes with hers. "What's up, baby girl?"

"I *loooove* you, Daddy," she said, mischief in her gaze.

"What are you girls up to?"

"Nothing, Daddy," Justine said, batting her eyelashes at me. "I love you *verrry* much."

I ran my fingers through my hair.

They both had me wrapped around their fingers. This was bad.

I shook my head and chuckled. My daughters would be

the end of me. One day. They would team up for real, and I'd be defeated.

"I love you too."

She ran after her sister, leaving me confused as I continued emptying the groceries.

The front door was yanked open less than twenty minutes later, and I jumped at the sound. I looked at the time. My friends should be here in three hours. Whoever arrived hadn't called beforehand.

"Ry?" Who else could it be?

A flustered Madison entered the kitchen instead, her hair in a messy knot at the top of her head, dressed in black shorts and a teal shirt, looking fabulous. Distressed. And in a hurry.

"What's the emergency?" she asked, panting.

I ditched the vegetables I was cutting and moved closer to her. "What emergency? I have no clue what you're talking about."

She sighed. "The girls. They called. They told me you were having an emergency and requested my help and to get here as soon as possible." She raised a brow, studying me.

"They what? I—"

"Maddie," they both exclaimed as they stormed into the kitchen, with matching, satisfied grins on their faces.

"You made it," Mikaella said with a crooked smile. "That was quick."

"Special bunny pancakes. Special bunny pancakes. Special bunny pancakes," Justine chanted, pulling her forward.

"There's no emergency?" Madison asked, a frown of confusion crossing her brow.

My daughters both shook their heads. At least they were honest.

"Not really. We just need you. A *lotttt*. Can you braid my hair?" Mikaella asked in a low voice, expectation dripping from each word.

"And cook pancakes," my baby girl added, looking at her with her big eyes and curled lips, still wearing that eye-bleeding dress.

Madison's expression softened. She sat on the floor, and both my daughters climbed onto her lap, caressing her face and her hair with their hands. The picture of the three of them cuddling on my kitchen floor offered me a glimpse of how different our lives would have been if their mother hadn't left. Would she have taken the time to just be with them? Comfort them? Throw water balloons on a weekday afternoon only because it was fun?

"Girls, listen. Emergencies are serious. You can't just call me behind your daddy's back to tell me something is wrong when it's not. I thought something bad had happened. That you guys were hurt. Do you understand what I'm saying?" They both nodded. "Next time, tell me you need my help, and I'll still come. I'll always be there for you two. You own my heart, and I love you. Just don't make me lose my mind, okay?"

They all hugged and kissed, everything forgotten.

Madison came back downstairs after tackling the girls' hair and helping them change into sleeveless summer dresses.

"I'm sorry. I had no idea they'd stolen my phone. I don't even know how they got hold of the password."

"I'm sure they have their ways. Ever heard of voice command? Anyway, they are kids, and technology has a sweet spot for them. Don't worry. It's fine. I just pictured the worst-case scenarios in my mind as I drove here. I'm glad everyone is safe and sound. Need a hand?"

"Sure."

"By the way, happy birthday."

We exchanged a smile. "Thanks."

"Oh, I almost forgot. Be right back." I heard the front door open and close, and seconds later, Madison set a square white pastry box on the counter.

"What is it?"

"It's for you."

I removed the tape securing the lid and opened the box. Inside lay two dozen chocolate-glazed cupcakes.

I blinked. It had been so long since someone had baked me a birthday cake that I couldn't even remember when. "You baked them?"

"This morning. Thought it would be weird for you to make a cake to yourself."

Emotions washed through me. "I'm touched. Thank you." I almost pulled her into a hug, because with anyone else that was what I would have done, but I refrained just in time. I didn't need to make whatever this was, awkward between us. Since our heated exchange a couple of days ago, things had been less tense, and I intended to keep it that way.

That night, after she'd left, I had stayed awake for hours, trying to figure out why I was so annoyed by her presence lately. I'd realized that over the last few months, Madison had taken over a huge part of my life. I enjoyed every moment we spent together. For reasons beyond my understanding, she appeared to get me better than anyone else. With her, I could let go of the control and social expectations and talk openly without fear of judgment. I could speak from my heart and be entirely myself. To be honest, this bond between us scared me. Fascination with a woman had become a rare occurrence for me these days. I met plenty of them in meetings, rehearsals, and at the recording studios, but at the end of the day, Madison was the one person I wished I could tell everything to. My fears. My dreams. And my hopes. A hunch told me she would understand them all and reassure me whenever I doubted myself. It freaked the hell out of me to be attracted to her this way—to feel like her presence in my life was essential and that she could calm the storm inside me. What would happen if I became dependent on our friendship? It was a scenario I preferred not to think about, because no matter what, it would lead nowhere. Madison and I, we didn't have that kind of relationship. She was my kids' nanny, not someone I could be attracted to. Yet somehow, the thought that we were destined to keep our distance saddened me more than it should have.

Next to me, she made a joke about me teaching her to play the birthday song on the guitar, and it brought me back to the present.

Just like that, we worked side by side, calmness settling between us, as if we'd done this thousands of times before and that it was the most natural occurrence in the world. Every time Madison smiled at me or we locked gazes, my heart did a somersault in my chest.

Beyond all expectations, I was falling for her—hard and fast—and had no idea how to stop the emotional disaster that was about to unfold. I'd never planned for this to happen, and I had no idea when it actually did. Last night, I looked at the pictures of us that the press had published, which I'd saved on my phone. For the first time, I saw what the rest of the world might have seen when they looked at them. Chemistry that couldn't be faked. No matter how much we both denied it.

Even when I was upset and kept her at arm's length in the last month, she had found a way to get past all my restraints and reach my heart.

Madison was my kids' nanny. Why did I have to keep reminding myself of that?

She was also almost ten years younger than me.

All pieces of evidence that proved that I should never harbor a crush on her.

This couldn't be serious. I had to get over it before it jeopardized the tour—and my stupid heart.

"I think we're done," I said, once we finished prepping all of tonight's food, wiping my forehead using the crook of my elbow. "Thanks for your help. I don't know how I would've gotten it done all by myself in time."

She said nothing, but a warm grin spread across her face, and it made me feel like a teenager all over again. When I had a crush on Anastasia Sullivan in high school and couldn't breathe each time we crossed paths in the hallways. Or when she looked at me and my heart threatened to rupture from my chest.

———

A little while later, Justine came over and wrapped her tiny arms around my thigh. "Daddy, can we do a dance *partly*?"

I looked at my phone. We had a little over one hour before our guests arrived. "Sure." I played a song on my phone.

She wrinkled her tiny face. "No, Daddy. Dance *partly*. With dance."

I drummed my fingers on the countertop. "That's not what we're doing?"

She shook her head with way too much zest. "We need to make a dance floor. And twirl around."

Madison and Mikaella joined us, my little girl beaming.

"What were you girls up to?" I asked.

"Girl chat, Daddy. About girl stuff."

I lifted my hands in surrender. "Fine. Don't tell me more."

Justine pulled at my T-shirt, and I looked down at her. "Yes, baby. The dance party, I totally forgot about that."

"Music, Daddy."

I put another song on.

"No. This is not good."

I was perplexed. What did I do wrong?

Madison fetched her own device and typed something. A catchy pop song played, and the girls started dancing. "See? Wasn't hard," she said with a wink.

We both burst into a fit of laughter.

"Gosh, it's awful. Please, tell me they don't make you listen to this sh—to this all day long."

Her grin widened. "Nope. It's exclusive to dance parties."

Mikaella came to get her, and Madison spun on her feet, laughing so hard with my daughters it swelled a part of my heart I thought had died two years ago. She looked so at home with us. As if she'd been here all along. I watched them, unable to avert my gaze, entranced by the happiness pouring out from them.

Justine neared me. "Daddy, wanna dance with me?"

I scrunched up my nose. "You want me to dance?"

She bobbed her head. "Yes. With me."

I rolled my shoulders back and breathed out. "In this case, how can I refuse a princess?"

I scooped her up into my arms and nuzzled her neck, my feet moving in some kind of dance steps.

Justine wriggled until I lowered her to her feet and wound her small fingers around mine, leading me by swaying her hips.

Soon, I got propelled into the joy emanating from the room.

"Look at you," Madison said. "Dancing. Like you were born to. I should've guessed the girls would be better at convincing you."

"Hey, I danced with you, no? You dared me, so I couldn't refuse." I shrugged, and we both dissolved into laughter.

My mind went back to the night in the country bar, and for a heartbeat, I wished we could rewind to that moment. Where everything seemed simpler. When I didn't foster a crush on the woman I wasn't allowed to fantasize about.

"Daddy, you danced with Maddie?" Mikaella exclaimed, catching up on our conversation. "When?" She turned toward her nanny. "Maddie, did you dance with Daddy?"

Madison's eyes searched mine and silently asked me to confirm or deny.

"You know what, sweet pea? I did. We ended up at the same place one night, and Madison taught me how to line dance. She was pretty awesome at it."

"Show me," my daughter pleaded.

"Yes, Daddy, do the *lintdance*," Justine agreed.

"Line dance," I echoed. "Maybe some other time."

"No. Do it. Please," Justine pleaded, batting her eyelashes.

How did she always manage to make me change my mind with those? The last time I tried, I'd had a few drinks. They'd injected me with enough liquid courage to ignore the eyes on us...on me. But now, sober and painfully aware of the woman in the room, breathing the same air, my chest tightened, and a wave of uneasiness crashed over me.

"Not sure I recall the steps." A warm feeling spiraled in

my stomach, tightening my insides, and my simple black T-shirt and tan cargo shorts felt hot on my skin.

"Daddy, dance," Mikaella said, tugging at my hands.

Madison played a song on her phone, snickering behind her hand.

"You think it's funny?" I asked, waggling my brows.

She pinched her lips together and gave me a head shake. "Nope. Not at all."

"Too bad, because if I'm doing this, you're doing it with me."

"Yes, dance with Daddy, Maddie," the girls cheered.

Her laughter multiplied, and her gaze darted between the three of us. I silently begged her to help me and find a way out of this. "Fine, cowboy," Madison teased. "Man up and follow me." The dark flush on her neck spread to her cheeks. She looked adorable as she positioned herself in front of me.

As if we'd rehearsed this dance many times before, we got in step. I focused on every movement of her legs, trying not to trip over my own feet.

The girls came standing next to me and did their best to imitate us. At some point, Madison pressed pause, taking time to teach us the right steps to follow. "Ready, you guys?" she asked.

The girls jumped and clapped their hands.

"Play it, woman," I said, unable to resist the contagious energy.

For the next half-hour, the four of us line-danced, and my daughters picked up the steps easily.

Madison halted to observe them, stars shining in her sea-green irises.

I watched her watching my children. A foreign sensation invaded me. I could barely breathe. All my senses were attuned to her. Her happiness brightened the entire room.

The whole fucking universe. I was desperate to stand in the glow she projected all around her.

She pursed her pink lips, and I quickly cast my gaze downward, forcing my mind to shut out any inappropriate thoughts.

The song ended, and we both were so engrossed in the girls twirling around that we missed when it changed to a ballad. A ballad I had written when I was eighteen—that now played in my house.

The air around us grew heavy, crackling with electric energy we couldn't escape.

Madison swayed her hips to the melody. Mikaella beckoned me with a finger. When I bent to level my face with hers, she whispered in my ear, "Maddie loves this song."

"She does?" We cocked our heads to watch her, now dancing with Justine in her arms. "She told you that?"

"Yes. She always sings it when it plays on her phone."

"Oh." *Ohhh.*

"You should ask her to dance with you."

I frowned. "Not sure it's a good idea."

She rested her fists on her hips. "Daddy, don't be a baby. Man up."

"Sweet pea, where did you learn to talk like this?"

"Maddie said it to you earlier when you were scared to dance, and you did as she told you. And Uncle Riley told someone to man up over the phone the other day. It worked because the man did what he said and stopped arguing."

I blinked. "How do you know that?"

"Because. He. Told. Me." She challenged me with her don't-be-stubborn look. "Now go. Maddie loves to dance. She always dances with us. She never dances with you."

Before I could find the courage in me to ask her, my daughter went to her. "Daddy wants to dance with you. Come on, Justine, you can dance with me now."

Madison's lips parted, and her fleeting gaze zoomed in on me. I was so bad at this. Why did I let my six-year-old drag me into this? Madison waited for me to do or say something. Anything. I wiped my moist hands on my shorts. Before I had the urge to shove my hands into my pockets and pretend none of this ever happened, I held out my hand under my children's watchful eyes. "Dance with me?"

Madison ate the gap between us and linked her hands to mine. "Okay," she whispered, breathless.

I shaped my free hand to the curve of her hip while hers came to rest on my shoulder. Fireworks erupted inside me. I got dizzy. I shut my eyes, trying to calm the storm ravaging my insides. The citrus blend of her perfume permeated my nose. Time stood still. I became aware of every beating of her heart as the pad of my thumb rested on the pulse point of her wrist. Each of our mingled breaths sent shivers through me. My mouth felt dry as desire raged its battle within me. I moistened my lips with a swipe of my tongue, and her gaze followed its movement. A quiver started in hers. We got engrossed in each other, and subtle signs of our longing fought to reveal themselves. I tried to look away but couldn't. I was mesmerized by the allure of her feminine scent and irresistible charms—the one I shouldn't let consume me, yet secretly yearned to.

Madison's lips moved to the lyrics, and I was a dead man. She knew the words to *my* song. We were dancing to *my* melody. "The One." I had written it one night after I'd gone on a date with a girl who turned out to be not what I expected. I remembered it as if it were yesterday. I'd returned home, bummed, thinking I would never know what true love was all about. The one all my country music idols sang about. For hours, I'd daydreamed about how it would be to find the perfect woman to share my life with. In a way, I believed I had stayed married to Lisa because failing at love was something unthinkable to me, and for a while, I had let myself believe we were *it*. That she would be the one woman I'd spend my life with.

Having Madison in my arms right now felt like nothing I'd ever experienced before. I had no idea what the tingles in my palms meant. Or why my heart felt like it could run away from my chest at any time.

I got lost in the green pools of her eyes.

If I weren't careful, I'd never be able to escape their magnetism.

I swallowed, but the dryness had now reached my throat.

Someone had cast a spell on me. This was the only explanation for how I felt.

All my cells vibrated.

Justine pushed herself between us, breaking the moment. "Daddy, there's someone at the door. They're asking for you."

I stepped back, trying to escape whatever enchantment had descended upon us.

For how long had we been so spellbound by each other that we had lost track of time?

I detached myself from Madison and brushed her upper arm with my fingertips, unable to find the right words to tell her how I felt—or what our connection meant to me. And to think I'd made millions of dollars as a songwriter. Yeah, the irony wasn't lost on me.

We exchanged one last glance. She blinked, and it

broke the remnant slivers of rapture that had taken us prisoners.

"Coming," I called out loud to whoever stood on my front porch.

Chapter 14
Sam

"**M**addie, Maddie, I wanna show you something. Come," Mikaella called out.

Carter, Madison, and I were sitting at the table on the back deck, enjoying a drink while my friend told us all about the latest developments at his foundation. Madison listened to him with laser-focused attention, the teacher in her clearly relishing the stories about the children he helped. She asked dozens of questions, and I simply watched her, amazed by how captivated she was by the way Carter and his wife, April, were helping kids through their art programs.

Madison pushed back her chair and rose to her feet, ready to follow my daughter who was pointing toward something in one corner of the backyard.

"You don't have to," I told her, bringing the bottle of beer to my lips. "I'm sure the girls can survive a few hours without including you in their shenanigans."

Since my friends had arrived, Madison and I had done a pretty good job so far of staying away from each other.

Before we sat with Carter and he entertained us with his stories, I'd caught her multiple times looking my way in a manner she never had before, and that shouldn't be allowed. And each time, a new whirlwind rose within me—one I prayed wouldn't sweep me off my feet.

She let a shy smile slip through. "It's fine, Sam. Really."

From my perch on the back deck, I watched her walk away. No matter what I did, my gaze kept finding her. Her charm was magnetic.

Madison's lips curled into the kind of smile that could shatter me when Mikaella joined her and tugged at her hand. That same smile could easily make me believe in love again if it were ever directed at me.

I perused the space around me. Riley was busy with Georgia—Carter's daughter—and Justine, chasing butterflies. April, Aisha Jones, and Devon were mixing drinks in the kitchen inside. Tennessee, Carter and April's son, was napping in the guest room inside. The baby monitor they'd brought was set on the table between us.

"Are you fucking her?" my friend asked out of the blue once Madison was out of ear's reach.

I blinked, my attention snapping to him. "What?"

He pressed his hands together, propping his elbows on the table, leaning closer, and lowering his voice. "You heard me. Stevens, are you banging the nanny?"

"No." I cringed. "What makes you think so? She's like twenty, man."

"You're eating her up with your eyes. If you think you're being subtle, you're failing big time. You look like a lost puppy drooling in front of a bone."

I clenched my hands, my tone turning colder. "Stop. Nothing is going on between us. Don't start rumors."

Carter lifted his hands in front of him. "I'm not, but you should see yourself. You're in love, Stevens. I know it because I went through the same denial phase with April." His eyes drifted to his wife through the large window, laughing with Devon and Aisha, tucking strands of her pink hair behind her ears. "She was driving me nuts. I was acting like an ass, as she likes to remind me sometimes. Truth? I was scared. Savannah Prince did a number on me, man. I believed I wasn't good enough for April at first. Anyway, if one person can understand the battle of will going on in your head, it's me. Look at us now."

I ran a hand over my face as knots, big sturdy ones, strangled my stomach. "It-it's not the same thing. She's my employee, and she's…she's like a decade younger than me. We're not at the same stage of our lives. There are kids involved…*my* kids. It's enough to kill my impulses. Everything would be wrong if we got together. Can you imagine? It'd be a total clusterfuck."

Carter lifted his glass of water and clinked my bottle. "So, you thought about it."

I murdered him with my eyes.

"Whatever. If you say so… You can man up, give it a chance to see if she mirrored your feelings, or be miserable. Hard choice." He let out a heartfelt chuckle. "Mm-hmm. Yep. Tough decision."

What's with everyone and that man-up expression today?

"She's a kid." Poor defense, but that was the only one I had.

"Stop. You can't be serious now. She's a grown woman who's all smitten with you. That much is clear from where I sit. She flushes when you two stand too close, and you're acting like a stupid teenager with a crush, sneaking glances her way every chance you get."

"You speak nonsense," I said, my defensiveness doing nothing to deter his suspicion.

"Yeah, sure I am." Carter watched me with a barely-contained smirk.

"Fine. We might have had a moment this afternoon. It's gone now. Over. I won't make a move. Our relationship must stay professional. If I indulge in the attraction and it fails, it will mess everything up. My daughters depend on her. I can't jeopardize that. I-I can't be a selfish prick. Nope… Not this time. They have suffered enough already."

"Whoa, you're stronger than I thought…or just dumber. Anyway, I'd like to be on the road with you and see how you resist her when you are spending six months cramped on a tour bus together. Yeah, I'd pay big money to see *that* unfold. Is it too late to cast you in a reality series about your big comeback?"

"Shut up," I said as Riley joined us.

"What are you guys talking about? Are you okay, Stevens? Your face is all red. You look like you're about to explode," he said.

"Don't worry about his face, Ry," Carter said. "I think it's his heart that's struggling. Maybe, at his age, he should reduce his stress level. Watch out for his blood pressure… or start eating a plant-based diet. Take my example, man. I should be your muse. Your inspiration to aim for bigger and better." Carter winked at me and stood to pick up his daughter from our manager's arms. "I'll go and put this one down for a nap with her baby brother," he said, rocking his half-asleep little girl in his arms. The father's role suited him perfectly.

"Yeah, you do that," I said, chugging the rest of my beer.

"And think about the reality TV series offer while I'm gone," Carter replied.

"What is this all about?" Riley asked. "Stevens, it's true you don't seem so fine."

"I'm good," I protested with a shake of my head.

"Then what was that about a reality TV show? I'm confused right now."

I sighed. "Carter is speaking shit. You know how he is, pushing my buttons. I won't—"

Carter walked inside, his shit-eating grin now reaching both ears when he looked our way. Yeah, I bet he was having the time of his life watching the control of my misplaced attraction dissolve before his eyes.

"Hey, Sam. There's someone at the door," Aisha announced, interrupting us when she poked her head out the back door. "Should I get it?"

"No," I said. "I will. Thanks."

"Who's missing?" Riley asked.

I shrugged. "No idea. Everyone is already here."

I perused my surroundings. My eyes found Madison, still busy with the girls near their castle, followed by Devon, Aisha, and April exiting the house to join Riley as I made my way in.

A funny taste filled my mouth when I opened the front door and found Jacob standing there, a bottle of whiskey and a pack of beers in his arms.

"Hey, man. I thought Maddie said you left for Chattanooga already."

"Yeah, well, change of plans. I'm here now."

"Huh, come on in. Make yourself at home. Everyone is outside." From our two previous encounters, I could tell Jacob was in love with Madison—this much was obvious. My stomach clenched at the thought that we were drawn to the same woman. "Maddie is in the backyard. Huh…somewhere." I gestured to the back door with a hand.

"Thanks. Where should I put this?"

"Here," I said as we crossed the kitchen.

Jacob dropped the booze on the island.

"I'll start the barbecue later. For now, there are snacks outside. You can also hit the bar to make yourself a drink. If you miss anything, ask me. Or ask Maddie. She's familiar with everything in this house."

He grabbed a beer from the pack he brought, and I led him outside. All my friends were now seated at the table around the back deck. April was in Carter's lap, a hand splayed across his chest, laughing at something he said. They stared at each other as if nothing in the world existed but them. A sting of envy stabbed my chest, and the lyrics of "The One" replayed in my head. I'd always been a sucker for love.

My attention traveled to Devon and Aisha, deep in a conversation about Aisha's next album.

"You actually never told us where this man of yours was tonight?" Devon asked her.

"His sister. In Michigan. He had some activities planned with his nephews."

Gavin Moore, Aisha's boyfriend, an art therapist with kids on the autism spectrum, worked with Carter and April at their foundation to give kids access to art programs. Their love story was the inspiration behind many of her hit songs.

Further to our right, Riley was busy on his phone. Nothing unusual since the guy never took a day off.

From the end of the backyard, Madison spotted us. Her gaze traveled back and forth between me and her…

huh…boyfriend? I really couldn't tell the status of their relationship.

She neared the house just as Justine called out, "Jacob," before I could introduce him to my friends.

"Hey you," he said, tapping the tip of my baby's nose with his finger as we reached them, stepping off the deck onto the lawn.

Madison cleared her throat. "Jake…you came? I thought you left early this morning for the convention." Okay, so she hadn't expected him to show up. Hmm…interesting.

He sipped his beer and offered her a shrug. "I went. It felt wrong to be there without you, so I came back. We'll drive there tomorrow morning. Together."

Madison stood still, clearly taken aback. "You what?" she asked when she found her voice back. "You went and came back? For me?"

"Yep. Thought I'd surprise you."

"I love *surpirises*," Justine screamed. "Do you have *surpirises* for me too?"

Jacob shook his head. "Sorry, princess. Next time I'll figure something out."

My baby clapped her hands, oblivious to the tense air surrounding us.

I opened my arms, waiting for her to leap into them. "Baby, let's go and see if anyone needs anything."

"Bye, Jacob." She waved at him as we climbed back the four steps leading to the deck where most of my guests were seated.

While I poured fresh drinks and my little one passed around a veggie platter, my eyes stayed on Madison and Jacob. From where I stood, I could tell they were arguing about something. Madison folded her arms over her chest, looking hurt. Jacob blanketed her in his embrace. Her whole demeanor told me she didn't agree with whatever he was saying.

The caring side of me, the one believing Madison and I had become friends, longed to intervene. The sad curl of her lips made me feel queasy inside. It got my blood pumping in my veins.

Jacob skimmed her cheek with his thumb, and her easy smile returned.

My heartbeat eased, my whole body relaxing now that she didn't seem so concerned anymore.

"Who's that?" Carter asked as I sat in the empty chair next to Aisha.

A strange sound escaped my throat as I popped open another beer. I should have opted for something stronger— whiskey…or maybe tequila—since I wouldn't hear the end of it.

"Jacob. Madison's *friend*."

Carter's eyes flared, and he choked on a bite of food. "You mean boyfriend?"

"Not that I know of."

"Stevens, you're kidding, right? Tell me you are. Earlier you—"

I shrugged. What was the point?

"Fuck, the nanny is banging a rock star?"

I sighed. "He's a chemist…or biologist, or something related to that field. I don't give a fuck, so I don't know." My gaze followed them as Jacob, dressed in all black with motorcycle boots on, leaned forward to kiss Madison's cheek, my daughters now bombarding him with a hundred questions. This time, she didn't pull away.

"Everything makes sense now," Carter said, following my line of sight. He tsk-tsked. "So much sense."

I said nothing and downed half my beer in one gulp.

I'd need all the liquid courage I could get to go through the rest of the day.

The kids ate first, and we all gathered around the table as April stepped out of the house, carrying the cupcakes Madison had baked—each topped with far too many lit candles. If I had to guess, I would say she put thirty there. I lifted my daughters into my arms as my friends crooned the birthday song to me.

"Happy birthday, Daddy," Mikaella said, perched on my lap as she kissed my cheek. "Whoa. It's a lot of candles," she exclaimed.

"Yep. I'm turning into an old man, sweet pea," I added with a wink.

"Can I blow the *crandles* with you?" Justine asked, with her arms looped tightly around my neck.

My lips spread wide into a grin. "Sure. Candles, baby. Let's do this. The three of us."

They both cheered.

"Are you ready?"

They nodded.

"On three. One, two, three."

With the two most important people in my life held close in my arms, I celebrated turning a year older.

While the kids sat to eat dessert, I took the time to thank each one of my friends. Months ago, I would've never thought I'd celebrate my milestone birthday surrounded by people I loved. Funny how life turned out sometimes.

I shook Jacob's hand, and when I reached Madison, I kissed her cheek. It was the first time I'd allowed myself to get that close to her. Her loud intake of air when my lips connected with her skin vibrated through me. I schooled my features, trying to dissipate the agitation rising inside me.

Hours later, after the kids had gone to bed, exhausted but with delighted faces and sugary smiles on, we all sat back around the table to eat.

The night was warm, pink and violet stripes painting the clear summer sky.

I relaxed as we enjoyed great food and greater wine.

"April, I just wanted to tell you I'm a big fan," Jacob said, clinking his glass with hers.

My friend cupped her heart, a soft blush tinting her cheeks. "Thanks. Wow, it means a lot."

"Told you, Fairy, you're amazing," Carter said, dropping a kiss on the side of her head, pride radiating from him.

"I was sad when you announced you'd be writing mostly music from now on," Jacob continued.

"I'll try to keep writing novels, but only one title a year or every two years. We'll see."

They continued their discussion while I zoned out and focused my attention on my plate, doing my best not to watch the nanny sitting across from me or notice the charged air ping-ponging between us. Or perhaps it was just the late hour, the booze, and my imagination playing tricks on me.

"So, Jacob. What do you do for a living?" Devon asked next.

Madison, sitting on his left, lifted her eyes and locked them on mine. A small tilt appeared at the corner of her lips.

It stole all the air from my lungs, and I coughed, the bite of baked potato in my mouth tumbling down my throat and choking me.

How could I be so affected by just a hint of a sign from her aimed at me?

This time, we fixated on each other from across the table, neither of us able to break eye contact.

Her face turned scarlet, and she twisted in her seat.

My body tingled, and my heart banged against my ribcage.

My senses shifted to hers. My food tasted weird, and my nostrils caught the fading whiffs of her perfume. I wasn't so hungry anymore. Madison's lips parted, as if to mouth something meant only for me, but Jacob demanded her attention, leaning closer and whispering in her ear.

She nodded, and I averted my eyes.

Jacob's gaze captured mine. His eyebrows twitched. Not in the mood for a pissing contest over who had the bigger dick, I looked away and asked Aisha about her last European tour. There. Better. Safer. My pulse calmed, and the ties crushing my organs released.

"Guys, we should do this more often. Now that Stevens has joined the family officially, after years of fighting against it, I want all of us to stay close. You're all precious to me, so let's spend more time together. Let's make it a regular occurrence. Also, thanks, everyone, for being here with us tonight to celebrate our host hitting a new decade." Standing, Riley angled his upper body to address Madison and Jacob. "You guys, it's great to have you here with us tonight. And Jacob, thank you for being selfless and letting Madison join this grumpy fellow," he said, pointing at me, "on tour. None of this would be possible without her. She's one hell of a woman. The missing puzzle piece to this whole adventure." He zoomed in on me. "All y'all, raise your glass to Sam turning thirty. Happy birthday, Stevens."

We all cheered.

Madison eyed me from her side of the table over the rim of her glass, the column of her throat rippling as she swallowed. Why did even her throat have to be appealing?

Pressing both hands to the top of the table, she moved to her feet. "I'll go inside. Huh…to check on the kids. I'll be right back."

I discarded my napkin on the table. "Wait, I'll come with you."

We needed to have a chat—to clear the air—before it caught fire and burned everyone standing too close, us included. I had to be the mature one here and kill whatever sparks were sizzling between us.

Jacob jumped to his feet before I could stand up. "No man, it's your party. Stay here. I'll go with her. I think we can manage." He flashed me a don't-you-dare half-smirk before following Madison inside, his hand pressed to the small of her back.

His possessiveness rubbed me the wrong way, even though I had no grounds to be upset.

I pushed my plate away, definitely not hungry anymore.

Chapter 15
Madison

"The guy's in love with you. Are you blind? Is this some prank you two are playing on me, and you're both in on it?"

"What are you talking about?" I asked.

Jacob harrumphed. "Okay, you're smart, but you can't be so clueless."

"You're wrong. Sam doesn't love me. Not this way. I…I would know."

"You're kidding, right? You can't be that oblivious. You spend all your time at his place. You're young, hot, sweet. Why wouldn't he want to bang you? To make you his? Any man in his right mind would want to. I'm telling you. I know I'm one hundred percent right. He's fucking gone for you. That much was evident tonight. He never stared anywhere but at you. The. Entire. Fucking. Time. I. Was There. Get prescription glasses, Maddie. Your sight is cloudy."

I unbuckled my seatbelt and turned my upper body in his direction. We were parked on the side of the road, less than a mile from Sam's house. Jacob had offered to drive me home since I'd had a few drinks, and we planned to pick up my car in the morning. When we'd left Sam's house, tensions ran high between Jacob and me, and it took about five minutes before he parked the car and exploded, unable to keep his wrath to himself any longer. The streetlights cast a golden glow inside the car, softening his otherwise hardened features. Yet I couldn't miss the deep lines fanning from his eyes and the weariness etched across his face.

"Okay, this is getting out of hand," I said in a gentle voice, taking a big inhale to avoid adding fuel to his anger. Instead, I reached for his hand, squeezing his fingers. "My sight isn't defective. And I already wear glasses when I read. Listen, Sam is not into me. Stop projecting. Anyway, who cares? I'm here with you. Because I wanna be."

Jacob dragged his free hand over his face. "Are you serious? I fucking care. A lot. Because we talked about being together. I-I'm in love with you, for God's sake. If you haven't noticed by now, you're really blind." He yanked his hand away and punched the steering wheel with both fists. "This whole situation is a joke. I can't believe I didn't realize it sooner. And here I thought…here I thought I was intelligent. Clearly, not enough. Sam Stevens surpasses me. He invited us over tonight just to rub in my face how much of an idiot I've been, by openly eye-fucking my girlfriend the entire time."

"Jacob, stop. Right now. You are being ridiculous because nothing is going on between Sam and me. I would never lead you on. You and I agreed from the start we weren't going to date until I came back. You're the one asking to change the rules. I'm trying here. I really am. You know me….and my heart. But the thing is, I know myself too. If we get involved before the tour, I won't be able to go. When I love, I love something fierce, and it's hard for me not to feel intense emotions. That's why we set that rule. To keep our hearts safe while I'm gone. Until we decide if being together is still what we yearn for months away from now. If being apart is impossible and we gotta move forward… Together."

"That's the problem, Maddie. I don't think I know you as much as I thought I did. Not anymore at least… You enabled his behavior. You locked eyes with him. Countless fucking times. Do you realize that being someone's girlfriend usually comes with an unspoken rule of exclusivity?" He exhaled, closing his eyes.

A ball of nerves settled in my chest, bouncing around and affecting the rhythm of my heart.

Jacob inhaled, opened his eyes, and fixed them back on my face. Every word that spilled from his mouth was tinged with hurt."Why did you even invite me to go with you? Or maybe you knew all along I'd be in Chattanooga, and you thought you could play his game and that I wouldn't witness it. If that's the case, I'm sorry I ruined your plans. Even Carter Hills noticed. I was the butt of the joke. At first, I thought I was being paranoid, so I waited to see if it would stop…but it never did. Yeah, the joke is on me."

"Do you hear yourself right now? I'm not a master conspirator. I'm the girl who does everything not to fall for her best friend while trying to keep the peace between all parties."

"Well, best friends are honest with each other."

"Can we talk about it without getting into a fight?"

"Another guy hit on you, in my face, for hours, and I should be all right with that? I swear, at first, I thought I was seeing things I conjured in my mind. When his fingers traced your arms before we left, I saw red. Fire-engine blinding red. You're lucky I don't make scenes in public or that I'm not a puncher because he would have earned at least a shiner."

"He's not in love with me. Stop being possessive—it's not a good look on you. God, I hate this side of you. And stop calling me your girlfriend like you have some claim over me. It just makes everything messier." Was I trying to convince myself right now or Jacob? Could he be right after all?

He blinked as if I had spoken another language, and a fortified wall appeared around him. He rubbed the spot between his eyebrows, strands of his hair falling over his forehead. He looked so handsome—and in pain—all because of me, for a forbidden crush I had no intention of pursuing.

I extended my arm in a tentative gesture to hold his hand and melt the iciness that kept us apart, but he leaned back, shaking his head, a twist of disgust shaping his lips.

Cursing under his breath, he blocked me out as he looked away, tugging at the roots of his hair while he stared out of the window.

"Jake. Don't shut me out. Please. The night we met, you said you liked my adventure-seeking personality." I inched closer and splayed a palm between his tense shoulders. He relaxed at the contact. "I can't believe you're questioning my motives. You gotta respect my wishes."

His breathing accelerated, and he turned until we faced each other, a mask of hurt covering his visage. He studied me with glossy, bloodshot eyes. Then he lifted his hand, reaching for my cheek. His knuckles skimmed the skin under my eyes, and his thumb traced my lips. I shivered under the intimate touch.

"It matters. It fucking matters to me…so much."

Tears now flowed down my face.

Jacob pulled me to him and rested his forehead against mine, his hand molding to my nape. His ragged breathing mixed with mine. "Maddie, I'll ask this question once. Tell me the truth."

I braced myself for the words about to come out of his mouth. He swallowed and leaned back, a grave look carved on his face. "Do you love him? Are you in love with Sam Stevens?"

I gasped. What Sam and I shared, or what I imagined we shared, meant nothing. Nothing. How many times would I need to repeat it to believe it myself?

"Answer me, Maddie. Here and now. Be honest with me. That's all I'm asking. Are you attracted to him? And. Do. You. Love. Him?"

I gulped a large intake of air. "I-I don't... I...I don't know." I glanced down, unable to meet his eyes. "It's just a stupid crush, okay? Or at least, it was."

Something invisible clamped around my heart. Was it shame or the dead weight of the lies I was feeding myself right now? Sam and I had shared a moment earlier today when we danced. I'd felt it. Even if I tried, I couldn't convince myself otherwise. But still, it was a dead end. Those feelings should be kept locked as far as possible.

"Anyway, I won't do anything about it. Our friendship is important to me. It means a lot, and I won't spoil it." I inhaled a shaky breath, desperate to explain myself. "He's my boss. Crossing this line would have consequences. I'm happy when I'm with you. We're so much alike, you and I. You're my best friend, Jake. For now, it has to stay this way. I'm sorry I should've told you. I realize it now."

Jacob pulled away, but I refused to release him. "Fucking friend zone. Maddie, no smart guy wants to be stuck there. Trust me."

"Don't push me out," I begged, my voice colored with despair. The streams down my cheeks intensified. No way could I shut the dam once it broke. "I'm sorry I'm breaking your heart. I love you, but I'm not ready for you...for us to be together like that." My voice was strained, and my sobs drowned my words. "Can we just go back to where we were...for now?"

He shook his head, his fingers laced behind his neck, distress bleeding from his entire being. "Maddie, I know your heart. I can tell you love me. That's the problem. You wear your heart on your sleeve, or your emotions on your face, and you can't bring yourself to hurt those you care about. It's just not in your DNA. But the thing is, you can't love us both...or be attracted to both of us. At one point, you're gonna have to choose. This moment is right now. It's either me or him. If it's me, you resign. You can't be around him if you want us to work out and have a true shot at a lasting future together. One day or another, one of you won't be able to fight this. I'm not risking our relationship for something that can be prevented."

"You're doubting me?"

"No, it's other men I don't trust. I'm a guy, and you're...huh...you're you."

"What does that even mean?"

"Maddie, you're exceptional. One of a kind. A diamond in a sea of rubies. If the guy is intelligent—and I suspect he is—he'll realize your worth sooner or later. Good luck resisting him when that day comes, especially if you already have feelings for him. If you can't decide, I'll let you walk away. I will not be your consolation prize, your second choice...the one you settle for. If you hope for us to last, it should be me—only me—all the way. It shouldn't be a hard decision to make."

"But I can't... The girls... They count on me. I...I

promised. I can't just leave. It's more complicated than this. It's not just about me…or you…or us. What about the tour? What will happen to the tour if I'm not there?"

"Come on, Maddie. The guy is filthy rich in case you haven't noticed. I'm sure he can find another nanny to watch over his kids. He's not desperate."

A cocktail of emotions mixed inside me. More prickling tears overflowed my eyes, as if tiny needles were piercing the backs of my eyeballs.

"No," my voice cracked. "You can't ask me to choose. Not now. I can't leave the girls… It-it's not fair to them. They…they trust me. I'm all…I'm all they've got. You know my story. You know how bad I've been hurt when I was their age. How…how my parents failed me…for years. They're… Jake, they're just kids. They don't deserve to be let down. Not if I can prevent it."

He shook his head, edged closer, and grabbed my upper arms. "I'm not saying you're not good at your job, Maddie. Or that those kids aren't adorable and that you can't bring them peace. What I'm saying is that Sam Stevens has the means to find a replacement to care for his daughters. He's not without resources. You'll find another family. I know how much you suffered, and I wouldn't wish the same on anyone else—but this isn't about you. *They are not you.* You can't be responsible for the choices their own parents made, and for their own mother walking away." He exhaled before continuing, "Don't go back there. Please. I love you, but I…I won't beg for your love. Being together must be what you really desire too."

A curtain of tears blinded me. "Ohmygod, this is an impossible situation. I-I can't walk away. Mika and Justine mean the world to me. I'm not quitting on them… I just can't. Their mother has already done that. I-I've been there. You're the only person I've ever confided in about my past. I never…I never told anyone else. I trust *you*. Why can't you understand?"

Jacob recoiled, throwing his arms over his head. "Fuck, Maddie, you're not their mother. It's not your responsibility to fill in for her. They aren't yours… It-it's just a job. You can't compare their situation to yours. It's not even remotely the same."

I pressed the heels of my hands over my streaming eyes. "I…I can't. I won't abandon them. Wh-what do we do then?"

"If you're going back to his house, then we're done. I also can't be your friend anymore… I-I can't be *just* your friend. I want more. I'm longing for more. Even though you're not ready for me, I am. I *am* ready for you…for us." He turned around, not letting me see the storm of emotions running through his gaze.

Silence fell between us, heavy and unyielding. It stretched on, neither of us daring to speak.

"You should go," Jacob said after what appeared like hours.

"But—"

"Now." Chills ran through me at the finality in his voice. "If you were sure about us and if you were willing to give us a chance, you wouldn't take this long to come up with a definitive answer."

"No, I don't wanna go. I'm choosing *you*, but I'm not resigning. We both have dreams. You're one of the most important people in my life."

"That's the problem. I shouldn't just be one of the most important people in your life… I should be the number one. If the situation were reversed, would you let me work for a woman who's madly in love with me?"

I said nothing.

Jacob shook his head. "See? You've made your choice.

Your silence speaks volumes. I just hope it's the right decision—for all of us."

"Stop. I didn't choose anything. You forced these decisions on me. I don't want us to break up. There are two of us in this relationship."

"You can't break up something that doesn't exist, Maddie." Jacob's voice was stripped of all fight.

"And you, you can't decide by yourself what's good for both of us. I have a voice, and I'm using it. What we have, it's precious." My voice weakened. "I'm not letting you go without a fight."

"Well, that's the thing. No way am I waiting while you spend all your time on a tour bus with him. It's not fair to me. You can't ask me to wait for you… We both know I'll be the one with the broken heart in the end."

I scanned the space around me. From driving around town for hours just for the heck of it, to grabbing takeout and confiding about our lives—and our dreams—under the stars, Jacob's car had always been a safe place for us. After tonight, though, it would forever be tainted by a fight I wasn't sure I could win.

My world was crumbling, and I had no idea how to prevent the downfall. Until now, I thought I had everything figured out.

The worst? Sam wasn't in love with me. Jacob was speaking nonsense. I would die of shame if my boss ever found out I'd been harboring a one-sided crush on him. The man had baggage, and with the tour and the new direction his life was taking, a girlfriend was clearly nowhere near the top of his list.

"What do we do now?" I asked Jacob, forcing the words out. "Can we sleep on it and talk about it tomorrow?"

"No." His decisive answer shook me to my core. "Do

whatever you wish, Maddie. We're over. Our friendship isn't salvageable. It would hurt too much to have you without truly having you. Maybe someday we can be friends, but right now, it's asking too much of me."

His eyes darkened, and his lips formed a thin line. This time, the walls he built around himself were high, sturdy, and unyielding.

I stayed still.

"I'll call you a cab to go pick up your car from his place. Wait here until it arrives. I'll go for a walk."

I opened the passenger door. "Stay. I'll walk back to his home." I wiped my tears with the back of my hand.

"Maddie, no. It's unsafe. I can drive you back."

"No. I'm sorry about everything."

Before the door slammed after me, I heard his last words. "Me too. Goodbye, Maddie. I hope you find what you're looking for with him."

Alone, broken, and in the middle of a neighborhood I didn't recognize, I followed the instructions on my phone's GPS, not even bothering to hide from my sorrows.

Chapter 16
Madison

I didn't remember the hour-long walk from Jacob's parked car to Sam's house. A foggy cloud had enveloped my mind, my thoughts a jumbled mess inside my head.

A vehicle I didn't recognize slowed down beside me. "Miss? Are you okay? You look lost. Want me to call someone?" the driver, a man in his late forties, offered.

I blinked, rebooting my confused brain. "Huh, no… I-I'm fine," I said, giving him what I hoped looked like a ghost of a smile.

"You sure? You look sad. I bet someone is worried about you."

"I…I can assure you they are not. Anyway, I'm here." I pointed to Sam's long driveway, lined with tall trees on both sides. The house was barely visible from the street. An open forged-iron black gate between stacked-stone pillars bordered the road. I had no clue if he ever used it or if it just served as a decor element because, since the first time I'd come over, Sam had never closed the gate or talked about closing it. "I've arrived at my destination." I flipped my phone so he could read the screen. "See? Even my phone agrees."

"Okay. Have a safe night then." He rolled his window back up and drove away. For a while, I contemplated his taillights as he disappeared into the night.

When I reached my car, my hands were trembling, and I couldn't fish the keys out from my purse. Sobs rocked my body, and I was unable to think clearly. With my back pressed against the steel frame, I slid down to the pavement, dropping my head between my knees.

Tonight, I had lost the best friend I'd ever had—the one person I trusted enough to share every horrible detail of my childhood with, who brought me peace, and made me smile just by being himself.

My broken friendship with Jacob had left a void in my chest that I wasn't sure I'd be able to repair one day. My fingers itched to call him, to tell him our argument was a big misunderstanding, and that I chose him, and would resign to be with him. But I couldn't coax myself to say the words he yearned to hear out loud. Because it would be a lie. A terrible lie.

Time passed.

Jacob and I had left the party at eleven. Then we fought for what appeared to be hours. Right now, I had no idea how late it was.

Darkness descended upon me.

My demons clung to my skin, sucking all the good and hope in me.

I lost my best friend. Just the thought of it sent fresh sobs and tremors through me. I couldn't imagine a life without him in it. His accusing words replayed in my head on a loop, and I had no idea whether what he'd accused Sam of was true or not.

The broken pieces of my heart punctured my chest.

I hurt. My body hurt. And my soul hurt too.

I woke up when two strong arms lifted me up and brought me inside. His scent assaulted me first. Then came the protective embrace of his arms as he carried me.

Sam sat me on the couch, the living room lit by a single lamp in the corner, its golden glow making him appear almost mythic as he stood before me. A figment of my imagination.

Without a word, he crouched down, pushed my hair away from my eyes, and stared at me, concern swimming in his irises. Our gazes fixed on each other for a long moment. He rested his hands on either side of me, and his eyes swept the length of my body as if to make sure I had no visible wounds.

"Since you're not telling me shit, I'm gonna ask. Are you all right, and did someone hurt you?"

I shook my head.

When did my vocal cords stop working?

Even though I tried, no word passed the seam of my lips. Sandpaper lined my throat. A drum fest had taken up residence inside my head. My heart could barely pump blood, bleeding from every crack and tear.

"Where's Jacob?" Why was he saying his name like that? As if it were a disease.

I shrugged.

Sam's eyes rounded. "Come on, Maddie. Help a guy out here. Where is he? Did he leave without you? I thought he was driving you home… He said he'd make sure you get there safely."

I shook my head, glancing down, fidgeting with the bracelet around my left wrist.

"Why are you here? At this hour?" He paused, and when I didn't reply, he asked, "By yourself? Are you sure you're fine?"

I nodded. Moisture returned to my mouth, and I swallowed, shaking my head from side to side. "Ja-Jacob… Huh… Jacob and I… We had a fight." Why was my voice not sounding like mine? "It was bad…very bad…and he left." I buried my face in my hands as a fresh batch of sobs rocked my body. My shoulders heaved. Jacob had left. I would never see him again. The thought shattered me. I already missed him. How would I survive a life where he wasn't a part of it?

"When? Why? I knew you two were close."

"He…he was my best friend."

"Did that punk do something to you?"

I sighed. "He's not…he's not a punk. We love each other." A sarcastic laugh escaped me as I spoke the words aloud. "It's not enough. The timing isn't right."

"You've lost me. I'm confused. Can you be more specific?"

"It's complicated. Anyway, I walked and… My car was here so…" Hot tears ravaged the back of my eyes, and I turned my head to avoid looking at Sam, so he couldn't see the truth. It did nothing to lighten the weight of his stare on me.

"Maddie, you can stay here tonight. Don't cry, okay? I feel powerless when you do." His voice was soft and soothing. Comforting and familiar.

My ache amplified. It burned a hole through my chest.

Sam got up and paced the room before me. "Tell me what I can do. I'm pretty good with broken hearts. I swear, I should get a Master's degree in heartbreak." His humor vanished the moment the last word left his lips. "Or… huh…we can watch a movie, something super depressing, and cry together. I'm a sucker for dramatic, *someone will die at the end*, romance stories."

I dried my tears, and a small smile peeked through my devastated state. "You are?"

"Yeah. Don't tell anyone, though. It's not good for my rep."

I pretended to zip my lips with my fingers. "I won't tell a soul."

"You're in?" he asked.

"Sure. I'd like that. Thank you."

"Let me get some snacks and a blanket. Make yourself at home. I'll be right back."

I blew out a long breath and let the couch swallow me.

In the last few months, the Stevenses' house had become a second home to me—or a third if I counted Jacob's place. More tears welled up in my eyes at the thought of losing him, but this time I wiped them away quickly.

Sam returned and sat beside me, spreading the blanket over us. He placed a bowl of popcorn between our thighs and put on the most tear-jerking movie I'd ever seen.

"Ohmyfreakinggod, this is so depressing," I managed to say, my words lost in tears, halfway through the movie. "How's crying over *their* lost love supposed to help me with *my* heartbreak?"

Sam sniffled and shrugged. "No idea. I-I told you I had a talent for choosing heart-wrenching movies. There's more to me than playing the guitar and enjoying dares."

This side of him called to me, just like it had the last time we had spent quality moments together—building that greenhouse where the girls and I had planted flowers and seeds. Every time I faced him without the broody front, the annoyance, the armor he hid behind, I felt we could connect on a deeper level if we gave it a chance.

Since the night at the country bar, this was the most real version of Sam Stevens I'd witnessed. Other than when he played with his daughters. A part of me always relished the easygoing side of his personality. The human not shying away from his flaws and emotions.

"I'm…I'm not denying that you are. You earned your title, fair and square." I scooted out of the blanket and pressed pause on the remote. "Water? I've gotta rehydrate."

I stood and made my way to the kitchen, needing a few minutes alone. The more I got engrossed in the movie, the more I pushed my own feelings aside. For now, it would have to do. Until I could face them and deal with them, instead of pretending they didn't exist. On my own time. Away from my boss's inquisitive gaze.

Sam's voice carried through the house. "Bring something stronger. There's a bottle of vodka in the freezer. Riley left it there earlier."

I stopped by the bathroom and washed my tear-stricken face. Better. I still looked like a mess, but a less afflicted one.

I grabbed two bottles of water and placed two shot glasses in the front pocket of my hoodie. My eyes lingered on the tub of mint-chocolate ice cream as I opened the freezer to fetch the vodka. A leftover treat on the countertop also called my name, and I snatched it too.

I carried all my precious heartbreak cargo back to the living room.

"Wow, did you raid the pantry? What do we have here?" Sam asked as I took my place back by his side, sitting cross-legged on the couch.

I winced. "Hope it's okay… The ice cream was begging me to take care of it."

He let out a warm chuckle that seemed to warm some

of the broken pieces of me. "Sure. I love how your mind works. Vodka and mint-chocolate ice cream should be an interesting mix."

"I have something for you first. Close your eyes."

He angled his upper body toward me and frowned, but he obliged.

"Gimme your hand." I put the chocolate cupcake in his open palm. "You can look now. Happy birthday," I said when he did.

"It's past midnight. It's not my birthday anymore."

I shrugged. "Let's just pretend it still is."

Facing me fully, he brought the sugary treat to my lips. "Want a bite? Chocolate is good for the soul. The woman who baked it told me that once."

He was quoting me. What I had said to him when I first started working for him, in response to his question about why I was always baking.

I took a big chunk, relishing the frosting coating my tongue. "Delicious," I said with a mouthful. "Whoever she is, she has great tastes."

Sam took a bite and gave me the last one. "She does." His thumb grazed my lips.

I gasped as the space between us grew charged, the air warm and electric.

"You had a little frosting there," he murmured before bringing the dollop of icing to his mouth and licking his finger clean.

"Th-thanks." To keep awkwardness from creeping in and ruining the moment, I opened the ice cream tub, and armed with spoons and facing each other, we attacked the milky treat.

Sam pressed play on the remote and poured us two shot glasses of iced vodka, offering me one before raising his own. "To heartbreaks."

"Yeah. To heartbreaks," I echoed. "And messy relationships."

The liquid burned the lining of my throat as I chugged it. I blinked. My stomach churned, and I grimaced, trying to keep it down.

"Guess liquor isn't your poison of choice."

I shook my head, my hand pressed against my lips.

"Don't worry, it gets better after the third one… maybe. At least, I think it did when I was younger."

We both chuckled.

"Let's test that theory." I held out my hand, ready for another shot.

Sam poured two more shots and slid one toward me.

Tilting my head back, I guzzled the vodka in one gulp, the taste lingering on my tongue.

"Second one isn't better?" Sam asked.

"Nah. Let's get the third one out of the way." We downed another shot each. "It doesn't taste better, but the burn is more enjoyable…sorta. Crap, we're missing all the movie."

"Madison Prescott, you can swear. Who would have thought?"

I shrugged. "Sometimes. Don't get used to it, though. This side of me rarely makes an appearance, and alcohol is usually to blame."

We sank back onto the couch, shoulders brushing, spoons digging into the melting ice cream, my mind swimming in vodka-soaked bliss.

I wasn't sad anymore—just content.

At one point, Sam took the tub out of my reach.

"Hey," I protested. "I need this. I'm the one with the broken heart, remember?"

"I know, but I'm the rightful owner of this delicious snack, so it kinda balances out."

I sighed. "One point for you. Can I at least have one last bite? Just to etch the taste into my memory."

He lifted an eyebrow. "Is this even a thing, or are you fucking with me?"

"For me, it's real." I pressed my hand over my heart. "When something is too good—or too beautiful—I try to burn the feeling into my mind so I can remember it forever." I offered his a half-shrug. "My sister says it's weird."

"It is, but it's also super sweet. I dig it."

I used this moment of distraction to jump over him and dip my spoon into the almost-empty tub like a thirsty girl in the desert who hadn't seen rain in months.

As I brought the spoon to my mouth, I realized my boobs were in his face. His throat undulated, and I pressed my lips together, struggling to maintain my composure and not get flustered.

"Huh…oops." Panic swirled inside me. *Think fast, Maddie.* I tried to shift back in my seat, but the spoon betrayed me, tipping and dumping melted ice cream onto his crotch. I froze. Heat flared in my chest. "Ohmygod… I'm so sorry." My hand shot down to wipe it off before my brain could catch up with my actions.

Sam's very stiff and thick erection vibrated under my touch.

We both went motionless. I was pretty sure the Earth stopped rotating too.

What was I thinking? Gosh, what was I doing? *Retreat. Retreat. Retreat.* My brain screamed the message, but my hand stayed there, glued to his manhood as if it had a mind of its own.

"I didn't…huh…I-I wasn't… It-it's not what you thick… What you *think*. With an *N*. It's not what you *think*. It was just a…a reflex? I…gosh…I didn't mean to rub it off." Kill. Me. Now. "Oh God. Now anything I say sounds awful. At least I'm not dripping wet like that time in your backyard, and this time, you're not at risk of sliding right into me… My puddle. Oh no. Sorry, it sounds terrible. Huh…you know what I mean."

Shut up, Maddie. For once, just zip it.

Our gazes met and fused together. My heart lurched into my throat, and I grew light-headed. Did I stop breathing? My head felt too fuzzy to think rationally. Sam's stare shifted between my eyes and my mouth. We stayed frozen, and I had no idea for how long. Seconds felt like hours.

After a moment, some clarity returned to my numb brain, and I pulled my hand away, slouching back into my end of the couch. I pressed my palms against my face in mortification.

Without a word, Sam poured us two more shots. We gulped them down, both of us desperate to erase the last few minutes from our memories—at least I was—and to return to safer territory.

Thanks to my mishap, my body was now attuned to his proximity, even without trying. His scent. His breathing. The heat radiating from him. I could feel it all, in high definition, enveloping me.

I refused to put too much thought into our little…huh… I had no word to describe what had just happened. Our collision? My head, not functioning at full capacity, couldn't come up with a better word.

Sam stretched his arms across the backrest, casually scooting closer to me, his proximity impossible to ignore.

My heart banged in my chest. All I wanted was to lean in. My head—the part still capable of logic—pleaded with me to move away. The tug-of-war between what I craved and what I should do ended in a draw. As if my body knew I needed someone else—or something else—to take the lead, the alcohol hit my brain and took control.

I turned my upper body toward Sam, my heart thundering in my chest like a wild symphony. He closed the gap between us, and I shut my eyes. The tension between us, now almost palpable, felt like it could catch fire at any moment. My brain disappeared, leaving my heart in charge.

Our lips collided in a breathless kiss.

My mouth opened to welcome his tongue inside. Nothing about it was slow or delicate. No, it was pure carnal need. An urgency, a survival necessity.

I didn't recognize myself. My body responded to Sam as if he controlled it, in a primal, instinctive way.

"We shouldn't… It-it's wrong… So, so wrong." His words were barely audible as his tongue pressed deeper into my mouth.

My head spun, and a series of yelps passed my lips. How could any of this be wrong when it felt so right?

"Maddie, you taste like something I could easily get addicted to. Fuck. What are we doing?"

I shrugged. I had no idea. All I knew was that I was done being afraid. I was burning up. Tugging at the hem of my hoodie, I yanked it off, tossing it to the floor, leaving only a thin cotton shirt clinging to my skin.

"I haven't kissed anyone in two years. I'm…I'm like a virgin all over again. I-I can't stop… You're gorgeous… bewitching."

His words sizzled through me. I wanted more…so much more.

He cupped the back of my head with his hand, deepening the kiss. "How can it feel so right?"

At least we were in agreement about that.

"Shut up and kiss me," I begged, moving to my knees to straddle him. I arched my back as he nibbled the skin of my throat, his teeth grazing me like I was the most decadent chocolate he could indulge in all night.

Tingles. Ache. Heat. They all pooled in my lower belly.

He traced my spine with his fingertips, sending a shiver rippling through my body.

"You're too good, and too young, for me. I'll burn in hell for this." Sam kneaded one of my breasts over my shirt, brushing over my hard nipple, and I became putty in his hand. Gripping the back of his T-shirt at the nape, he pulled it over his head, revealing his sculpted chest.

I watched him in awe, unable to tear my eyes away from the sight of him.

He grabbed a fistful of my hair, guiding my mouth back to his.

"Age is just a number. It means nothing." I leaned back, gasping for fresh air after he'd stolen every molecule of oxygen from me.

His muscular hands slipped under my shirt, familiarizing themselves with my heated skin.

My head spun faster.

My breath hitched in my throat.

The room lit up in a full spectrum of colors.

"Fuck, Maddie. I've never wanted anyone the way I crave you. It's agony having you around every day, knowing I can't do anything about it. You're the only one who gets me… No one else does. Everything about you appeals to me...all of me."

I sank into the kiss, letting everything else fade away. My fingertips dug into his scalp as I pulled him closer, unwilling to process his words just yet.

Could tonight just be about physical pleasure, without all the complications? My brain scrambled to catch up, my thoughts tumbling over each other. I wasn't that girl—the one who could have a no-strings-attached, one-night stand without expecting something more. Yet, this felt too perfect to ruin by overthinking what it meant.

Sam held me against his chest before gently lowering me onto my back, his strong frame hovering over me. His eyes locked onto mine, a raw, thirsty desire radiating from every inch of him.

"I'll have my way—"

"*Daaaddy? Daaaddy? Daaaaaaaddy?* The monster is back. It's under the bed." Justine's heart-wrenching cries echoed from her bedroom upstairs, freezing the blood in my veins.

The intoxicating tension between us cooled in an instant. The promise he was about to make faded into nothingness. We broke apart abruptly.

He pulled the T-shirt I handed him over his head. "I'm sorry. I have to go to her." He flashed me a small, mischievous smile, his gaze sliding over my aroused body, hunger still burning in his eyes.

We both breathed hard.

I bet my face was as flushed as his, and no doubt he could see my diamond-hard nipples pressing through the thin cotton of my shirt.

"Stay here. Don't move. I'll be right back."

He disappeared upstairs, and the gears in my mind sluggishly started turning again, each thought dragging behind the last.

I traced the length of my lips with a finger, not sure if I had dreamed the last hour of my life. What did we do? What did *I* do? Making out with my boss was all kinds of wrong. We'd violated so many rules with that kiss. We had crossed so many boundaries.

In seconds, I sobered up—well, not really, but enough to recognize my wrongdoing. The images of what we'd just done swam in my mind. Rousing. How could I ever look him in the eye again? How could I look at myself?

I slumped onto the couch, burying my face in the crook of my elbow.

I had to go. To leave. To get the hell out of here.

Hours ago, I had told Jacob I'd never act on my crush, and I meant it. Now I had complicated everything.

Before I could move, Sam came back, his hands stuffed into his pockets, his head hanging forward.

"Nightmares. They come and go." He raked his fingers through his hair, looking away for a fraction of a second.

"Is she okay?"

His attention returned to me, and his shoulders dropped. "Yeah. She will be. She's asleep now." He inched closer, his gaze searching mine.

I pressed my cheeks. They burned scorching hot under my palms.

"Maddie. Listen. We… *I*… It was a bad idea. We can't do this." He flicked his hands between us. "We can't risk the tour. It's important to me. To the girls. To Riley. And I hope to you too. We can't be together. It will fuck everything up. It's just… Sex complicates things. We got lost in the heat of the moment. Are we cool?"

I shook my head. Then I nodded. Because everything he said rang true, but I didn't know if I should agree or not, the question blurry in my boozy brain.

"You…you sure we're fine?"

Oh, now I understood the question. "Yeah, we are."

He scratched the skin at the back of his neck. "Good. Huh…I guess. We should go to bed. It's almost four in the morning."

I nodded, not sure what to add. Then reality hit me. "Huh, Sam? I can't drive home."

"Come," he said. "You can crash in the guest room."

We stood in the doorway, inches apart.

Sam twirled a strand of my hair around his finger.

Shivers ran along my back, reaching my toes, and sent tingly goose bumps to my skull.

"Everything you might need is in the en-suite bathroom or the closet. Stay as long as you want to. You're… you're part of this family."

I bowed my head, trying to escape the magnetism of his gaze.

"Good night, Maddie."

"Night."

My heart plunged ten stories down inside my chest.

My shoulders slumped, and I whirled around, desperate to hide the deception I was sure was written all over my face.

"Maddie?"

I turned around and risked a glance at him, bracing myself, ready to swallow every word that was about to leave his mouth.

Sam leaned forward and caught my lips between his for a nanosecond, igniting a new spark within me. "I'm sorry." He turned around and left me there, needy and more lost than I'd been in a very long time.

I woke up, unsure if the crappy feeling inside me was from a hangover or just a major lack of sleep, and a weight across my chest. My head pounded. My eyelids weighed tons. My tongue stuck to the roof of my mouth. And my heart ached in my chest.

"Daddy, are you up?" Justine asked, straddling my torso, prying my eyelids open with her tiny, prickly fingers.

"Baby, stop. Daddy needs his rest."

"And *I* need to eat. I want *bracon*. A mountain of *bracon*. And eggs," she said, clearly more rested than I was. "Do you want *bracon*, Daddy? Like a big mountain?" She giggled, opening her arms wide.

"Ten more minutes," I begged, closing my eyes.

Images of last night flashed behind my eyelids.

Vodka. Ice cream. Madison touching my dick. Her smile. The twinkles in her eyes. The taste of her. Her hands on me. My hands on her. Her boobs. Her neck. The bolt of desire throbbing through my entire self almost to the breaking point.

My dick woke up faster than I did as my pulse raced and the memories of what we did toasted my body until it combusted with unattained release.

Madison. The sweetness of her lips. The hardness of her nipples. The caresses of her hands.

Fuck, Maddie. She must still be asleep downstairs.

All traces of sleep vanished as I sprang to a ninety-degree angle, setting my giggling daughter down beside me on a pillow. I was so not ready to answer my children's million questions that were sure to follow if they saw Madison had spent the night.

How could I break her out of here before the girls noticed she had slept in our guest room?

Fully awake, I was now a man on a mission. An extraction mission.

"Justine, wake up Mika and get dressed. We'll go eat breakfast somewhere."

My baby girl's enthusiasm reverberated within my bedroom walls, and she hurried to her own room. "Mika, Mika, wake up. We're going to eat *bracon* at the *rest-the-torrent.*"

I shook my head. How could she come up with new words for everything?

Dressed in a pair of dark jeans and a plain white T-shirt, I tiptoed downstairs before my daughters had time to join me. I combed my hair with my fingers, trying to tame the locks I knew must have pointed in all directions.

In front of the guest bedroom, I firmed my back and took a deep breath in. I could do this. No reason to make things awkward between us. Last night, Madison and I had fun, but this was it. Nothing more. We could slide back into our roles today. We had to.

Much of what she had said last night turned out to be a foggy memory hours later. Some parts, though, were still vivid, like a movie playing in my head—on a loop. Damn it. I almost fucked my children's twenty-one-year-old nanny. On my couch. And in the heat of things, I'd had no remorse whatsoever. It had just felt like the most natural next step in our relationship. *Relationship?* I bit my own tongue to evade the alternate reality I'd stumbled into since last night. *Work relationship.* I bet I had confused my body and mind quite good last night. It was all on me, though. I was the father. The responsible adult. I should've stopped the kiss at the first brush of our lips.

My dick swelled at the memory of yielding to the temptation I'd been battling for weeks. A warm buzz infiltrated my blood.

I stretched my neck to the side, cracked my knuckles, and took another deep breath in.

The door opened before I could find the courage to knock.

Madison appeared, looking rested. Did she have some special youth power I didn't possess anymore? The words I'd rehearsed vanished. Every single one of them.

With less than a foot between us, we stood still, heaviness tinting the air as we lost ourselves in each other's gaze. It confirmed that I hadn't dreamed of the yearning we'd shared hours ago.

Her bed hair not only made her look younger in the morning light, but it also gave her an irresistible just-been-fucked vibe. Everything I had a boner for. My erection pushed against the zipper of my jeans at the sight of her. She pursed her pink lips. Dirty thoughts flashed before my eyes at the prospect of everything she could do with those plump wonders. Heat, a scorching inflammable fever, coursed along my spine. My balls tightened. My pulse sped up, and my airways struggled to carry oxygen to my brain.

All the images of things we'd never experienced, but I couldn't stop fantasizing about, had front-row seats in my mind.

This was bad. Before I could assess how screwed I was, I chased the reflection away and focused on the girl standing in front of me, looking vulnerable and so damn gorgeous.

"Hey," I said once I found my voice and blood started flushing my brain again.

"Hey."

"Sleep well?"

"Yes."

Why were we unable to make complete sentences?

"Good." *Enough with the one-word replies.* "Listen, the girls and I are heading out. I'd invite you to join us, but I don't want things to be weird, and it's your day off."

"It's okay." Her gentle tone sent shivers through me. "I gotta get home anyway and figure stuff out." Her eyes glazed over, and she looked away.

My palm molded to her cheek before I had time to assess my actions. "About last night—"

We both breathed hard, and I let go of her.

"Don't worry, Sam. I'm sure we'll be able to put this behind us and move forward. I was emotional, and we drank a lot. Let's not let it affect our working relationship, okay?"

Yes, *working relationship*. At least we both agreed.

I nodded. I fucking nodded, though all I craved to say was that it wasn't a mistake and that I wanted to finish whatever we had started. And kiss her senseless. But Madison was right. We had to get over it.

"Why don't you sleep in? I'm sure you can use the rest.

We'll talk later." My eyes traced down her body, each curve pushing the flimsy boundaries of my willpower. I grabbed her hand and traced her knuckles with the pad of my thumb. "You can stay here tonight if you don't feel like going home. I mean it."

Her breathing accelerated, and she jerked her hand away.

"Sorry." I shoved my hands into my pockets to avoid touching her again.

"Thanks, but I'll be fine. I'll get back on my feet." She wiped a lone tear rolling down her cheek. One I'd like to steal away so she wouldn't cry ever again.

"We'll be out of here in ten minutes. Sleep in or make your exit. Whatever you choose, please let me know you're okay later."

She hung her head low. "I will."

"I'm sorry about Jacob and you. I can't understand why he wouldn't wanna be friends with you anymore." She looked past me as I added. "Should I be worried?"

"No. Please don't be. It's on me. We didn't agree… He said what we had wasn't salvageable… I'll…I'll get better. What other choice do I have?"

"Don't drown in your pain. Whatever went down between you two, I'm sure it'll get better."

"It won't. Thanks for caring."

Madison never delivered short answers lacking conviction, and this conversation was the sign she wasn't being herself.

I leaned forward, hating the distance between us, but jerked back just in time—before I could do something stupid. Again. Like hugging her or comforting her. With my mouth. And my manhood. Buried deep inside her. Hammering the pain away. "We'll catch up later. Call me if you need anything."

"Sure. Thanks."

"Daddy, we're ready. Where are you?" Mikaella asked, her feet stomping down the stairs and closing in on us.

"I'm here." I gave Madison an apologetic smile as she closed the door in my face. And every door to my heart.

"Ready, Daddy," Justine said, running after her sister, dressed in a teal princess gown with colorful gems stitched to the bodice.

I lifted them both in my arms. "You girls look like queens. Let me grab my stuff, and we can go."

My attention stayed fixed on the closed door for what felt like infinite seconds.

"Can Maddie come with us? Her car is in the driveway. Daddy, have you seen her?" Mikaella asked. "Is she here? Maddie? *Maaaddie?*"

My heart bled in my chest cavity.

I had to grow a thick skin, and quick. "She isn't here. I think she left her car in the driveway last night. We'll call her later to know if she needs help to pick it up, okay?"

"Can we ask her to come with us?" Justine asked. "She loves *bracon*."

Mikaella folded her arms over her chest and pouted. "I want Maddie to come with us too. You're not *grinchy* when she's there. She can ride with us. Can we call her already?"

My heart leaped in my throat. "Another time, girls. Now let's go. I'm sure there will be a line to enter House of Pancakes, and I'm starving."

The week went by fast. Between rehearsals, radio interviews, and all the promotional appearances Riley had scheduled for my big return, I didn't have time to think about the other night. Until I came home, and Madison looked at me with those eyes of hers that could steal my breath away. And my heart. The ones that could turn me into a slave if she asked me to. The ones that reminded me of *the* kiss.

The ones that still displayed the sadness I'd pay big money to heal.

As long as I kept busy, I had no time to wonder about *what-ifs*, broken dreams, or impossible endings.

With her.

In all the time we spent around each other, we never spoke of that kiss again, both of us choosing to classify it in the *mistakes not to be revisited* file.

With each passing day, the weight of my loneliness sank in a little more every night when I went to bed. Alone.

Solitude had never felt this heavy before.

Then darkness settled around me, and I had to use all my inner strength to resist the object of my sinful temptation. Jerking myself off thinking about her was a feeble consolation prize, and felt all shades of wrong.

"Girls, tonight we're celebrating," I said as I joined them in the backyard where they were running after cottontails. Every now and then, the rabbits invaded our backyard to the girls' greatest pleasure.

"Why?" Mikaella asked, coming closer.

Justine was still chasing the poor animals around, chuckling and waving her arms.

"My album is done."

My daughter jumped into my arms. "Can we listen to it, Daddy?"

I shook my head. "We can play it, but it won't be the final version. Not yet at least. Now there will be people making it even better."

"Like music magicians?"

"Yeah, like that."

I caught a smile on Madison's lips when my focus landed on her. "Congrats, Sam. I can't wait to hear it too."

"Thanks," I said, bringing my attention back to my eldest daughter. "Let's dress nice and go out. To that restaurant you and Justine like so much with the aquarium wall and slushies."

My girl's eyes flared, and she wiggled in my arms until I set her down on her feet.

"Justine. Justine, Daddy said—"

"They're really proud of you, you know?" Madison added from beside me as my gaze followed the two bundles of joy dancing around, the cottontails now forgotten.

My heart filled to the brim with pride and love at their infectious display of happiness.

The girls came barreling toward us. "Can Maddie come?" Justine asked.

I shrugged, avoiding Madison's eyes. "Sure. If she wants to."

Justine hugged Madison's knees and looked up at her. "Please come with us." She made her sad puppy-dog face, which she'd mastered to perfection, eliciting a giggle from me. Mikaella joined in, and soon both my daughters were begging her to join us.

"I don't have anything good enough to wear, girls. I'm sure your daddy wants to celebrate with you two. We could bake a treat next time I'm here and celebrate together then."

Justine's lower lip shuddered. "Maddie, why don't you come to the *aquarellium* with us?"

"Please," Mikaella pleaded, now on her knees. "Say yes. Pretty please."

"Girls… I… Ohmygod, you're torturing me." Madison's amusement laced her voice.

My daughters looked at me with their big eyes, and I

shook my head before kneeling down as well. With my hands folded in a prayer-like gesture under my chin, I batted my eyelashes at her. "Please."

Madison burst into a fit of laughter, wiping the tears pooling in the corners of her eyes.

It was the first time in a week that her smile seemed genuine. The sight warmed my heart.

"You guys are impossible. How can I resist? Can I go home to shower and change first?"

I jumped to my feet, her smile tugging at my heartstrings, unable to resist her pull. Why did I enjoy being tortured by her this much? Or was I just completely gone for her? Fuck, we'd agreed to keep our distance. Begging Madison to join us was far from being my smartest idea. I pinched the bridge of my nose and sighed.

I kept my focus on my daughters, trying to block out the woman standing next to me for a few seconds. "Girls, go on. Dress to impress, okay? But wash your hands first."

Once they disappeared inside, I spun to face the woman I'd longed to steal another kiss from and who was testing all my self-restraints.

"Sam, I won't come. This celebration is between your daughters and you. Just tell them I'm sick or something."

I lifted a finger to silence her protest, cutting her off before she could add anything else. "Stop. Don't. I told you already. You're part of this family now. The girls are right. It's a family celebration, so you're welcome to join us."

"But—"

"No buts. Not tonight. It's a big day for me. And we're friends, or I like to believe we are."

Madison cast a glance down and nodded. "Friends. Yeah, sure. I still have to go home to change."

I tipped her chin up with my finger and locked our

eyes. "Go get ready, and we'll pick you up in about an hour. How does it sound?"

"Perfect," she said in a breathless whisper.

The four of us sat in a semicircle in a dark wooden booth at the back of the restaurant. Soft country music played from the speakers. Madison and I sat side by side, a girl on each side, giving them the end spots since they kept standing up to admire the twelve-foot-tall aquarium wall on our left. They were both dressed in matching peach-colored summer rompers and white sandals. The joy pouring out from them was contagious tonight.

They had chosen my outfit: black trousers and a raisin-colored long-sleeve button-up shirt, which I wore with the sleeves rolled up at my elbows. At first, I hesitated, thinking I might be overdressed, but right now, sitting next to Madison, I thanked my daughters mentally for convincing me to indulge—and to put aftershave after I'd first resisted.

From beside her, I did my best to be subtle, stealing quick sideways glances as I drank in the sight of her. Wearing a navy-blue belted dress with a layered hem, tied around her neck, she looked both sophisticated and sexy. It offered a full view of her delicate shoulders. When I picked her up earlier and saw she had forfeited heels tonight and chosen cowboy boots instead, a slice of my heart had bloomed. I had failed at reeling my smile in. We were so much more alike that it hurt to think I couldn't have her the way I dreamed of at night.

The loose, silky curls of her hair cascaded over her back, and all I wished for was to wrap them around my fingers.

Her pink-painted lips curved when her eyes found mine, and I was gone for her all over again.

The server returned to our table with a bottle of

expensive wine and two glasses. My non-official date covered hers with a hand. "Not for me, thank you."

"You're not driving. We're here to celebrate, you sure?"

"Okay… Maybe just one. I won't let you drink by yourself."

We exchanged a glance, and the server filled half her glass.

I raised mine. "Cheers. To the album, the tour, and for everything you've done for the girls and me in the last few months. I wouldn't be here today without you. I don't tell you often enough, but I'm grateful."

Madison sucked in a small intake of air, and I felt hot all over. She blushed, the faint flush impossible to resist. "Sam, I'm just doing my job," she said, breaking the fragile silence that had settled and taken us hostage. "That's all."

I shook my head. "You're doing much more than that." She followed my gaze as it landed on the girls, laughing as they watched the fish."You've brought us back from the dead. We've come alive since you walked into our home." I sipped my wine, letting the silence stretch between us.

"Do you…do you ever feel like everything around you is spinning at a dizzying speed and you can't stop the motion?" she asked after a long minute, the alcohol loosening her tongue and shattering the glass box she'd been hiding behind all week.

"Is this how you feel?"

Moisture welled up in her eyes. "Yes. No. I-I miss him. Growing up, I didn't have a lot of friends. I never had a best friend before Jacob. It was the first time I'd let someone else in completely, and I'm not sure how to deal with the loss. He's shut me out completely."

I placed my hand on hers and gave it a squeeze. "Losing someone you care about isn't easy. I'm the best example. It took me too fucking long to realize my wife's leaving was a blessing. I was so angry, so hurt, that I didn't take the time to connect with the real underlying emotions. In my opinion, getting closure is important. I never had that. Thus, I'll always wonder why she ran away. I'm okay with the fact, but a part of me would like to know the reason…if there's one. Or else I'll always wonder."

"I'm sorry she did that to you. You guys didn't deserve to be hurt like that."

"Nobody does. I'm sorry your friendship with Jacob blew up. I could tell you two liked each other very much."

"Well, it wasn't enough."

The girls sat back when the waiter brought our food, and I released Madison's hand.

"Thanks, Sam. For listening to me."

I returned the curl of her lips. Perhaps all wasn't lost, and Madison's and my friendship could survive the other night's mishap.

"Can I ask you for your input?" I asked when we got to our main course.

"Always," Madison said, her previous emotional over-load cleared now.

I transferred a few lobster ravioli to her plate when she shared pieces of her pork medallions with Justine after she refused to eat her chicken tenders because they were not shaped like dinosaurs.

"You don't have to," Madison said.

"You're kidding, right? Plus, you gotta try it."

She returned my easy smile. "Thanks." She took a bite, and I got hypnotized by the expressions crossing her face as she savored the flavors. A moan left her lips as her eyes closed in mouthgasm. "Okay, you're right. It's delicious." She took another bite, and I forced my focus to remain on my own plate. "What did you want to ask me?"

"Oh, yeah. I almost forgot." I turned my phone on and

thumbed through the emails Riley had sent me earlier. "Album cover. I have four options to choose from. I have very distinct opinions about them and hesitate between two."

"You want my impression?" She rested a hand over her heart. "I'm touched."

"I always love having your input. You're straightforward. I respect that about you."

"Show me." I slid my device into her proffered palm.

"Shhh. Don't tell me anything." She placed a finger over her painted lips. "Don't influence me."

I rolled my lips over my teeth and focused my attention on my daughters instead.

"I'm ready," Madison announced after five long minutes, scooting closer to me and setting the phone on the table between us. "Option one. The design is nice. I love the color scheme. But we don't see you. I feel that with a comeback, your album cover should feature you front and center."

I nodded. So far it made sense.

"Option two. The close-up shot works. There's something in your eyes. It screams strength and vulnerability all at once. I love the black and white concept with a few strokes of color."

My pulse kicked up. It was like Madison had been reading my inner thoughts.

"Option three. The shot is nice. But somehow, with your back to the camera and that guitar strapped over your shoulder, it spells *goodbye* and not *watch out, I'm back*. And option four, I love the profile picture. I'm just not sure about the font choice, though. Overall, I believe number two represents who you are better. The last option misses the message your eyes convey." She met my gaze. "How did I do?"

I sat there, my jaw hanging open, speechless.

Madison wriggled in her seat. "So? Say something."

"First, you nailed it. I was hesitant between options two and four. Your thoughts mirror mine. One hundred percent. Second, thank you. It's now settled." I shot Riley my final choice and put my phone down.

"Do you like doing photoshoots?" Madison asked, resuming her meal.

"Not really, but it's part of the job. The first one I did, I was so shy, I looked frightened in all the pictures. It took another session to finally get me to relax and enjoy the process."

"I wish I would've been there to witness it. Sam Stevens, *The Legend*, afraid of a camera lens."

I joined in as her body vibrated with laughter. "Go on. Make fun of me."

Madison's thumb and forefinger almost met. "Just a tiny bit."

We finished dinner, the conversation flowing easily between us. I was relieved that the queasiness simmering between us over the past week had finally melted away.

Madison pushed her empty plate aside. "That was delicious," she announced after wiping her mouth with a black square napkin.

Justine moved to sit on her lap, and Madison leaned back to help her up.

"You're tired, sweetie?" My baby girl nodded as Madison wrapped one arm around her, the other one caressing her hair.

Justine buried her head deeper in her chest. The same exact spot where I'd dreamed so many times I could bury my face too.

Mikaella, on my right, busied herself with coloring books.

"I have to ask you a question," my date—or the woman I hoped could officially be my date—said, as I refilled both our wine glasses. "How did you know I was in the driveway the other night? I'm curious." She brought the Merlot to her lips.

"I was taking the trash out when I saw you."

"You were taking the trash out in the middle of the night?"

I shrugged. "I didn't wanna wake up the next morning with stuff all over the house and backyard, so I figured I'd clean everything before going to bed." I took a sip. "You're lucky I did."

A darker hue crept along her cheeks.

"Anyway, I couldn't sleep. I had a certain someone on my mind—"

"Can we go now?" Mikaella asked, the distraction more than welcome, cutting our discussion, and my confession, short. "I'm tired."

I lifted her up in my arms. "Sure, sweet pea. Let me pay the check, and we'll be out of here."

The server hadn't even returned with my credit card when her body grew heavier in my grip.

Madison and I walked outside and waited for the valet to bring the SUV, each of us carrying a sleeping child. "You sure you're all right?" I asked. "I can carry both."

"I'm fine." She returned my smile.

Tonight, she looked even sexier with my daughter deep asleep in her arms.

Reality hit me. It wouldn't be fair to her to date a single father of two.

She was young and had her whole future ahead of her. She didn't need reasons to settle down at her age. That was exactly what would happen if we went out together. She'd skip precious years of her life, forced to become a mother figure before she was even ready for it.

Some knots loosened in my upper back. I blew out a long breath.

Even though tonight I got a peek at what a relationship with her would look like, Madison could never be mine. It was about time I came to terms with the idea.

Thirty minutes later, I parked in front of the two-story powder-blue townhouse she lived in. During the entire ride, we barely said a word, too absorbed in our own thoughts.

"Thanks for tonight," she said, her eyes glistening in the dark. "I had a great time."

"Thank you for joining us." My tongue itched to say much more, but I remembered I had no right to steal her youth from her. No matter how attracted I was to her. A relationship between us could never happen. "I'll see you on Monday."

Something resembling hurt flashed in her gaze. "Yeah. Sure. See you Monday morning," she echoed, shutting the door behind her.

I watched her as she entered her house, and even after she disappeared inside, I stayed parked there, wishing she would walk back out, say *fuck it*, and drive with me into the sunset.

She's not yours. She'll never be. Get over her, Stevens, I said to myself as I drove away. *Time to move on.* For real this time around.

I hugged the girls goodbye and left them to play in their castle while I joined Sam by the grill. He looked so damn handsome wearing a worn-out heather-gray tour shirt and black cargo shorts, his hair swept away from his forehead in a sexy I-don't-care kind of way that made my knees weak. I implored my heart to stay put as I inched closer. He offered me a beer, but I declined with a flick of my hand.

It'd been a week since the four of us went out to celebrate his album wrap-up, and we agreed to be friends. Yep, I'd been put in the infamous friend zone. The joke wasn't lost on me. Things between us had been sailing smoothly since. Agitation stirred in me every time we were close, and for that reason, without either of us saying a word, we had gotten good at keeping our distance whenever we were in the same space.

A few times, when he thought I wasn't aware, I caught Sam staring at me in a manner that should be forbidden, one that made me clench my thighs. Then he would look away, shaking his head, and the lust-filled moment would be broken. I knew because I did the same. I watched him from afar, recalling his callous fingers playing my body, the tenderness of his lips when they had feasted on mine. The memories of him always sent a new pool of heat billowing between my thighs. We were stuck in an impossible situation, and neither of us had any clue how to navigate the longing we felt but couldn't surrender to.

Then my brain would go back to Jacob. And the idea he wasn't in my life anymore transformed my lust into sadness. I missed him. A lot. Since the night I'd kissed Sam, I felt like a fraud and couldn't find it in me to call the one I used to consider my best friend. To check up on him. One night, I had sent him a text when I was feeling lost and vulnerable and cried myself to sleep at the idea our friendship was over—for real. He never replied. His cut was deeper than mine, so it'd take him much more time to be able to talk to me without shattering every time. I came to the conclusion that even though we both liked each other, the intensity of our feelings wasn't matching. I loved him, but I wasn't in love with him, like he was with me.

"You sure you don't wanna have dinner with us? There's plenty," Sam asked, his husky voice doing nasty things to my body without even touching it and setting every one of my nerve endings on fire.

These days, I was never in a hurry to go back home after work. Being alone, because Emily's and my schedule never matched, sent me into a spiral of sorrows. At the Stevenses', I had people who cared about me keeping me busy. Darkness stayed at bay while I was hanging out with them. So, even though I knew I shouldn't, I had accepted almost all their offers to stay over for dinner since the night we had celebrated the completion of his new album.

"Nah. I'm always sticking around. You guys deserve some family time. I should get going."

Sam's dark eyes bore into mine, and I sucked in a breath, looking at my feet, making a mental note to fix my nail polish sometime later. See? I could think about things other than my boss and my bruised heart when I put my mind to it.

"Are you still struggling?" he asked.

I nodded. In a moment of weakness, I had admitted to him I had a hard time fixing my heart after the loss of my best friend. "I'm getting there."

I spun around, but he gripped my wrist before I could step away. The way he always did that had been shattering my resistance from day one. A gasp parted my lips at the rough growl emanating from him, deep enough to rumble through me. Every particle filling the air smelled like him, a mix of musky and woodsy aftershave and something exclusively him. Gorgeous and forbidden. Sexy and dangerous.

"Wait—"

My eyes returned to his, but he added nothing else.

His throat worked, and I got hypnotized by the movement. A heat wave swirled through my body. "Are we okay? If there are remnants of weirdness between us, can we kill it now?" He paused. "For the girls' sake. And because I miss being friends with you."

Or because living on a bus for half a year together all the time will be impossible if we can't tame down the desire searing between us. We'll both be hormonal messes. Cranky. Unpredictable. Time-ticking lust bombs. And living in hell won't be good for anybody. But

I added nothing, I stood there and nodded because I feared if I opened my mouth, I'd say or do something I'd regret—like begging him to give us a chance, or kissing him in broad daylight, healing both our hearts in the process.

Sam cleared his throat. "So?"

I came back to my senses, burying all the naughty images swimming inside my head and locking them away. In an *open at your own risk* drawer.

"Yeah, sure. No problem." I plastered a smile on my face. "I'm all good."

He winked, and I almost died right there but refrained myself just before I slipped. "Awesome, then you'll have dinner with us. Because that's what friends do. I would be a bad one if I sent you home to be all by yourself. You look off today. I'm volunteering to cheer you up."

I burst out laughing at the situation. Sam Stevens, the country music superstar, single father to his two adorable daughters, looked so cute right now and resembled a kid as he begged me with a boyish grin. How did I end up in this situation? It still made no sense at all. "God, you're killing me. Okay. Fine."

He raised his hands. "Ha. I knew you wouldn't be able to resist my cooking." His cheerfulness died, and a shadow crossed his eyes.

My gaze trained on his lips as he sipped his beer. No. Not going there. We could do this—meaning be professional in our interactions.

"Any city you're excited to visit during the tour?"

I thanked him mentally for the change of topic and forced a curve to my lips as if everything was fine. "Yeah. I've never been anywhere but Tennessee and Kentucky. I can't wait to go to LA, New York, and visit Texas."

"I'll get a lot of days off…for family time. One of

the conditions when I agreed to move forward with Riley's big plan. I'll give you a tour of New York when we get there. I'm positive you'll love it. Let me know what would make you happy, and we'll book time for it."

"That's really generous of you. I'm looking forward having my own personal tour guide. I'll let you know when I decide."

"Awesome," he said, his focus back on the grill.

"Huh, I'll go inside and make a salad if that's okay with you."

"Sure. Suit yourself. You can also relax and just keep me company here since your workday is over. After all, we just agreed we could act like two civilized human beings when around each other."

"I… We should see other people," I blurted out, before I could process the impact of what I'd just said.

Sam watched me with a surprised expression that didn't scream *I'm overjoyed with this idea*, and I brought my hands to my cheeks to ease the burn.

"That's what you really—"

A loud cry from the opposite side of the backyard startled us both and put an end to the awkward conversation. It seemed we were always interrupted whenever we tried to have a heart-to-heart discussion. We turned our heads in sync.

Justine came running, her sweet toddler's face morphed into a fearful expression. "Daddy, Daddy. Mika. She fell. Crack. She cracked her arm."

The kitchen tong in Sam's hand hit the ground as he sprinted in the direction of the castle.

Meeting a crying Justine halfway across the backyard, I scooped her up into my arms, with the sole objective of comforting her and easing her heart.

Mikaella's painful shrieks and Justine's fear-induced cries colored the silence.

"Shhh, I'm here. Everything's gonna be okay. You hear me? Your daddy and I will make sure Mika is safe and sound."

My lips lingered on the top of her head as I rubbed her back gently, my squeeze on her almost bone-crushing.

Sam entered my peripheral vision, his oldest daughter in his arms, looking like they'd just escaped a crumbling building together. Beads of sweat now grazed his angled eyebrows, and his lips formed a thin line. With Justine still in my arms, clinging to me with all her strength, I rushed to him.

"Daddy says I may have broken my wrist," Mikaella stated, her voice trembling and fat tears running down her reddened cheeks. She chose to let go this time and not shy away from the pain and allowed us to see the fragile side of her, the one she usually hid from everyone else, including her daddy. Most times, she concealed her emotions, choosing to act out when she was angry or sad instead of just crying it out. Holding back her tears until she was in bed, far from everyone else's attention.

"Good news is you'll have a super cool cast if it's broken," I said, trying to infuse her with some hope after I kissed her forehead. "And it could have been your leg. So, now you'll still be able to play outside and run."

"What's the bad news?" she asked with a wet frown.

"Being hurt is no fun, but you'll see, it will get better really fast." Flashbacks of my younger self wearing a cast years ago made their way to my conscious mind. "Huh, I broke my wrist when I was little. My sister drew on it to make it more pretty. Nowadays, you get to choose great colors. They're like a trendy fashion accessory in my opinion. Not fun, but necessary, so you better make the best of it. You'll be able to choose almost any color of the rainbow. Isn't it cool?"

"Thank you," Sam whispered, some of the wrinkles around his eyes vanishing.

At that moment, I wished I was the one erasing all of them by kissing his own pain and worries away, filling his heart with the love and hope he deserved

"Any color?" Mikaella asked.

"Yes. I'll call Emily, my sister. She's working at the hospital today. She'll meet with us."

Sam stopped me with a hand on my shoulder. "I'll go. You stay here. With Justine. If it's okay with you. Or I can take both girls if you wanna go home."

"Don't be silly. I either come with you or stay here with Justine, but no way am I leaving until I'm sure Mika is fine."

"Fine. I won't argue with you." His grip on me released suddenly as if he'd just realized he was touching me, and his arm fell at his side. He brought his focus to Mikaella, and the droop of his shoulders confirmed that he was worried about his child.

"Hey, listen to me," I said. "Everything will be all right. I promise. Mika is going to be in good hands. Ems is the best. I swear."

Sam's hand returned to my upper arm, and I enveloped it with mine to keep it there, knowing he needed the reassurance. "Thanks. I'll keep you posted." He let go of me and rubbed the skin between his eyebrows. "We'll get going."

I nodded and started to walk away when Mikaella's fingers fisted my shirt from behind. I whirled around to look at her. "What is it?"

"Maddie? Don't go home, okay?" she pleaded, holding

her wrist against her chest, more tears building in her eyes. "Stay with us."

"I'm not going anywhere. I'll be here when you get back," I said. "Let me call my sister to make sure they're ready for you when you get to the ER." I kissed her forehead, and she released me.

Sam nodded, and with Justine hooked to my neck, I made my way inside, searching for my phone.

———

With a sleeping Justine beside me, I scrolled through my phone, searching for the special video I had to edit and send over, the sound of her steady breathing the only noise in the room. She had fallen asleep in my arms, and I was still lying beside her in her bed, hesitant to move in case she woke up. Sam had texted me half an hour ago, confirming Mikaella had indeed fractured her wrist. Luckily, it was a clean break, nothing serious, and she would be out of her cast in about five weeks. The memories of my own broken arm from years ago twisted something in my stomach—something I couldn't quite pinpoint. A chill ran through me.

The chime of an incoming text message startled me. Sam had sent me a picture of Mikaella sporting a black splint on her left arm.

SAM

Still a teenager. No way is she gonna wear a colorful cast when they put it on in two days. *sigh*

The confession brought a smile to my lips.

ME

> Black is badass. I love it *black heart emoji*

As I scrolled through my phone, searching for that video, my gaze rested on a picture of Jacob and me that we had taken when we went to a music festival downtown. With his arm around my shoulders, he looked at me as if I meant everything to him. Then I landed on a picture of us the night we had gone roller skating, dressed in flashy color outfits straight from the eighties.

My heart squeezed in my chest. Why had I told him about my crush on Sam that night? It destroyed us. We were happy. We fit together. I ruined everything by being too honest, my forbidden attraction for the man who had hired me not going anywhere.

I traced his smiling face with my fingertip. "I'm sorry. For everything. I love you. I still do. It wasn't fair to you that I also had feelings for someone else. I miss you. A lot."

A lump grew in my throat. An incoming message forced my mind back to the present.

EMILY

> Met that boss of yours. Holy moly, Maddie.

> He's one hands-on dad.

> And he's hotter in person. Geez, girl. No wonder J got jealous. Sorry. Anyway, his little girl will be brand new in no time.

ME

> Thanks, Ems. For taking care of her.

That man spoke highly of you. He respects you. That much is clear. And the girl couldn't stop gushing about you either. They are good people. You're lucky to have them. I feel better knowing this since you'll be on the road with them for a long time.

A new picture came through. Mikaella eating a burger and fries, proudly showing her splinted wrist, and another one of Sam and her, flashing their pearly whites at the camera.

My finger traced the contours of his face next. His smile resembled a red moon, rare but something you never wanna miss when it shone in the sky—or on you.

"How will I survive six months of this?" I asked out loud to myself. Or maybe to a sleeping Justine. I buried my head in the pillow and closed my eyes as I abandoned my phone on the mattress next to me. The back of my eyes prickled, and I sealed my lids, preventing a trickle.

Just when I was about to fall asleep, a tiny hand caressed my cheek. "Maddie, look. They couldn't put a cast now. I have to wait for two days." Mikaella said. "Emily said I can even play in the fountains with it or go swimming. Are you awake?"

I peeled my eyelids open one by one, only to find her face about two inches from mine, her smile contagious, and her eyes illuminating the entire room.

I moved to a seated position and checked her bandaged arm. "Are you in pain?"

She shook her head. "No. Daddy got me a burger, then some medicine, and now I'm good. And Emily gave me a lollipop."

I pulled her into my arms and kissed her temple. "I'm glad you're okay. Wanna get into bed?"

"Can you read to me? Daddy said it's okay if you're the one who tucks me in tonight."

"It will be my pleasure. Let's get you changed first."

"Maddie, you said you broke your wrist too. How did you do it?"

I sighed. "I fell. I don't remember all the specifics, but I remembered wearing a cast."

Once Mikaella slept peacefully, I made my way downstairs.

Sam had set up the island with two plates of the chicken and rice I'd put in the refrigerator earlier after feeding Justine.

My heart lurched in my throat as I took in the *it's not supposed to look romantic* display.

"Hey you," he greeted me. "Hungry?"

"Starving."

"Good. I had no idea if you had eaten earlier."

I shrugged. "Couldn't. My stomach was tied in one giant knot."

We sat side by side and attacked our food in silence. "So," Sam started. "I met your sister."

I nodded, focused on my food instead of losing myself in his gaze if I risked a glance his way. "Mika told me she loved her."

"She's a super-doctor. Did and said all the right things to make her feel comfortable."

"I'll tell her. She'll be happy to hear that."

"Maddie, why did you lie to me?"

Why did my name have to sound so lustful when it came from his mouth? My body pulsed when he addressed me. Ribbons of sexual tension tied themselves around us.

I shook my head to escape his spell. His words finally made their way to my brain.

"I lied?" I pointed to my chest and gave him a quizzical glare.

Sam dropped his knife and fork with a soft thud on the countertop and turned until he faced me. "About your living situation." His harsh tone surprised me.

The accusation floated between us. Even though charged particles filled the void around us.

"I—" Why did I feel I needed to explain myself? Where and how I lived wasn't his problem.

He continued before I could tell him to mind his own business. "You sleeping on a couch or an air mattress on your sister's bedroom floor is not okay. Am I not paying you enough to get your own place? You should have told me."

I buried my face in my hands, humiliation warming my skin. Tonight, I would kill my sister once she got home. She had no reason to tattle to my boss. This. Was. Not. Okay. Even though I knew she meant well.

"It's temporary. We're leaving soon. I didn't wanna rent a place and move in, only to move out right after. The new doctor, Emily's colleague, needed a place to stay. I offered my bedroom. It's no big deal."

"The guest bedroom. It's yours if you want it."

I averted my eyes and snorted. "Not sure you and I sleeping under the same roof is a good idea."

He rubbed the column of his throat and spoke in a whispered voice that rattled my core. "We'll be doing just that for six months. Better get used to it while we have enough room to breathe apart."

"I'm fine."

"Come on. Get rid of your pride. You don't have a bedroom, and I'm offering you one. What's the problem?"

I inhaled a jagged breath. "Stop. I said I'm fine.

There're a lot of things you don't know about me. Stop trying to fix everything."

I pushed my plate away, not hungry anymore.

Sam's tone gentled, and his hand covered mine. "Hey, hey, it's not that. I'm just trying to help, not implying anything. The offer is there if you decide otherwise."

"Yeah, well… I'm in no rush to test the waters. Don't wanna compromise your tour. I'm dedicated to my job. I'll always do it the best I can. In the meantime, let's not rock the boat."

"If you change your mind—"

I moved to my feet. "I won't. Thanks for dinner, but I should go."

I grabbed both plates, but Sam stopped me, stealing the dishes from my hands. "Let me. You're not our maid, Maddie. You're the girls' nanny. And my friend. I can do this."

"I just wanna help."

He inhaled. "I know." He scratched his jaw. "Don't be mad at me. I'm sorry if I overstepped. I don't like the idea of you not having your own space."

My anger died down. "I overreacted."

"Wanna talk about what you said earlier? About us seeing other people? Is that what you really want?"

I pinched my lips together as I debated what to say. "Listen. I don't know why I said it. It's not my business what you do in your personal time. I was out of line. Forget it."

Sam's focus drifted back and forth between my face and the floor to finally settle on my eyes.

"Go home. It's late. I'll see you in the morning."

Without another look in his direction, I grabbed my purse and phone along with my pride and stormed out. I only halted when I reached the front door. With a roll of my shoulders back, I paused and turned around. "Night, Sam."

"Night, Maddie." Facing the kitchen sink, his hands were clamped to the countertop and his head bent down. Even without seeing his expression, I could tell our situation weighed heavy on him too.

The friend in me wanted to go to him, but the saner part of me knew leaving was the smart thing to do.

After one last look in his direction, I hurried outside, closed the door behind me, and let go of all the air I'd been holding in.

Phone in hand, I hovered my fingers over Jacob's contact. Right now, I missed him more than ever. More than I should. More than I was allowed to. If he asked me to drop out from the tour, would I be able to? A weight pressed against my ribcage. The answer hadn't changed. Unless Sam ordered me to, I would never be able to leave Justine and Mikaella.

A new realization sent a cold spur along my spine. Would I ever be able to walk away from Sam? Just the thought of not seeing him every day suffocated me. There, my body provided me with the answer to the question I feared the most.

In order to never be told to leave, I had only one choice. Let go of my infatuation.

Just then, I made a promise to myself. No more crushing on the man who possessed my heart without even trying to. From now on, I would stay away as much as possible and would move on when my time was up. I wouldn't let my emotions rule my life. I lost Jacob against my will, but I wouldn't let what happened with Sam wreck me even more. I'd been on my own all my life. I could still do this. Be happy by myself. I didn't need a man to make me feel good about myself or brighten my days. I was more than enough.

I put my phone back in my purse, started the car, and pulled away, feeling optimistic that I could really be the professional I'd told Sam I was.

That night, the nightmares I hadn't experienced in years woke me up. Sweat pearled on my forehead, and I sat up.

Air struggled to reach my lungs. Why was I feeling like someone was pursuing me? Dark shadows still lingered around me.

I couldn't recall what they were about, but they brought up a wave of nausea. Hurrying to the bathroom, I emptied my stomach. Something about Mikaella's accident made me feel queasy. I returned to bed, hot tears burning the back of my eyes, as sleep claimed me, and I prayed for a restful night.

Chapter 19
Sam

Rehearsal had ended early, and I came home to Madison folding laundry on the kitchen table. "Mind if I give you a hand?" I asked.

She shrugged. "Make yourself at home."

We exchanged timid smiles at the wit. Since we argued two days ago, things had been more strained than usual between us, and I hated that we had grown apart over a disagreement about her living situation.

"Can we talk?" I asked while I filled two glasses with lemonade and fixed a veggie platter with dip.

Madison nodded and followed me to the back deck, opening the door for me.

After I placed our snacks on the small table between us, Madison stretched on a lounge chair, and I handed her a glass.

I cleared my throat. "Listen, I wanna talk to you about moving in here," I said once I sat down.

She straightened up and turned toward me, ready to bolt. "Sam, I already told you I'll—"

I moved one hand up to silence her protests. "It's not what you think. Before the tour, I'll be away often at night and sometimes for an entire set of nights because I have some warm-up shows scheduled after the album launch next weekend. I was thinking it'd be easier if you live here full time."

Her eyes rounded, and she sucked in a breath and stared at me as if I'd said something terrible.

"I-I'm not sure it's a good idea, you know, with everything."

I let out a heartfelt laugh. "At this point, I'm pretty sure we can sleep in the same house since we're leaving in just a few weeks. And, good news, our rooms aren't on the same floor. Safe distance."

She got flustered and glanced down. Pushing her hair over her shoulders, she shut her eyes, appearing to weigh the pros and cons. She scrunched up her face and lifted her fingers to massage her temples. I could see the gears of her brain working. How I wish she'd allow my input on the subject. It'd be easier if I could opine on whatever torture her mind.

When she re-opened her eyes, her gaze darted to mine. "You really think it's necessary?"

I swung my legs over the edge of the chair to face her. "Listen, I wouldn't ask if I didn't think it was the best idea for everyone involved. You included. We'll have sleepovers on the bus like we discussed. The girls will feel more at ease if they know that's how things are gonna be when we hit the road and get used to it. You'll still have your weekends off. I promise the girls and I will give you your space. I'll talk to them. We'll rework the schedule."

Madison pinched her lips and exhaled.

I gripped her wrist, rubbing the inside with my thumb, before she could find a reason to end this conversation.

"The night we talked about it… I-I didn't want to overstep. I'm sorry if I did. This tour will be a big adjustment for all of us, but mostly for the girls. If they're happy on the road and feel safe and secure, it will be easier for everyone. You and me, included."

She relaxed her stance. "Yeah, it's a lot of change for everyone." She paused. "Not that I'm not ready for this. I'll never be able to thank you enough for this opportunity. It's a *once in a lifetime* experience. I just don't want us to complicate things…you know."

"As your friend, I can assure you everything will be all right. Call it a gut feeling, but you and I, we're a great team. The girls are happier than they've been in years, and I am too. I get to do what I love, and it's all because you're doing an amazing job with them. And because being around you makes us wanna be better. There's this aura you project that's impossible to resist. Also, as I already told you, without you, this tour wouldn't be possible."

"Nah, you would have hired someone else."

"No. It had to be you. The girls love *you*, and they trust *you*. It's a match made in heaven as Riley once told me. I believe in destiny. This, us, is living proof. In many ways, you've become the heart of this family. I don't know how to explain it differently."

A pink flush bloomed on her cheeks. Madison always looked adorable when she was being shy. "Thanks."

We stayed like this for long minutes, basking in the enveloping silence.

"Do you trust me?" I asked.

"Yeah. I do." Her voice sounded like a whisper.

"Then everything will be all right."

"Will you be here when I wake up tomorrow morning?" Justine asked when I kissed the crown of her head. For the last twenty minutes, she'd been sitting on my bed while I got ready.

"Yes, baby. I'll be back later tonight."

"Daddy, you look pretty," she said with a snicker, cupping her mouth with both hands.

I curtsied. "Thank you very much, Princess Justine."

Her laughter doubled, then died down. "Daddy? What if Maddie leaves and you're not back yet?"

"Not a chance. She's living here now. Remember, we set up the guest bedroom last week, and she moved in this morning. She'll sleep downstairs, but she won't go to bed until I'm back. She promised. Don't worry, okay?"

Justine nodded, and I wiped the tears building in the corners of her eyes with my thumbs. I understood her fears. In the last two years, except for the night they spent at the hotel with my parents, we'd never spent a night apart. I just couldn't.

"Don't cry, baby. You'll be fine. You like Maddie, right?"

She bobbed her head faster. "I *lovvvve* her."

"See? Then it'll all work out. Kiss me one last time, because I really need to go. Uncle Riley is waiting for me."

"Love you, Daddy."

"Love you too, baby," I said, fastening my arms around my little girl's body and holding her close to my heart. "Let's go downstairs, okay?"

"Okay," she agreed as I picked her up.

We joined Mikaella and Madison in the dining room, working on a puzzle together.

"Hey, sweet pea. I'm leaving. Will you be okay?"

"Yeah. Fine. Bye."

She didn't even bother looking at me.

"Come on, girl. Can Daddy at least have a good luck hug?"

"I'll give you a good luck hug," my youngest daughter offered, securing her arms around my neck once again, then scrambling down.

Mikaella sighed and stood up to give me a half-hug. "Everybody will love your music, Daddy."

I leaned forward and kissed her cheek. "I love you."

"Me too. Can I go back to my puzzle now?"

So much for the display of enthusiasm.

I shook my head, unable to hide my smile. "Sure." I ruffled her hair as she sauntered away.

Madison moved to stand to follow me. "Sam, you'll be great. Go, do your thing. We'll be fine. I know it's a big deal tonight, so just focus on that."

"I usually come home no later than nine. Today, I'll be delayed. You sure you'll be okay?"

"Yes. Now go. Stop worrying. I've got everything under control. Riley doesn't seem like the type of guy who likes to wait." She pushed my shoulder so I'd get going.

I spun around and walked backward, lifting my hands in surrender in front of me. "Yeah, yeah. I'm going."

"Keep walking." The sparks in her eyes acted like an arrow to my heart.

Now that she'd moved in, even though I still believed it was for the best, we'd have to adjust to being around each other all the time, and also keep our relationship platonic and friendly.

The sight of Madison always brought me back to the night we'd crossed boundaries. The one I still dreamed about most nights when I lay in the darkness in the privacy of my own room.

The thought of having her so close and yet so far from me at the same time sent my heart into overdrive. It would kill me. Liar. The last thing I wanted was to die. There were so many pleasurable things I had yet to do to her. And it involved no murder. Just some weapons of choice, endless pleasure, cries of ecstasy, and breathless shouts of my name. *Keep dreaming, Stevens.*

It had taken a bit of convincing for Madison to agree to take over the guest bedroom, but a part of me relished knowing she was safe and sound, had her own space, and wouldn't have to sleep on an air mattress anymore. If Mikaella hadn't broken her wrist, I wouldn't have met Emily and learned about her living situation. Madison never mentioned she had forfeited her room so another doctor could move in with them. Her sister loved her, that much was clear, and I was happy she confided in me that night.

Anyway, if we could survive these remaining couple of weeks of living in close proximity, being all cramped up on a tour bus for six months wouldn't resemble torture anymore.

"You're right. As usual. I'll see you later."

I scanned the dining room one last time before leaving to attend my album launch party, my heart cartwheeling in my chest and my adrenaline at its peak. Something I never thought would happen again in this life.

———

"Glad you could make it," I told Carter as he met me in the backroom of Wild and Country, the bar Riley part-owned.

"You're kidding, right? Miss Sam Stevens's grand

comeback? Never. I told you already. I'm too much of a fan when it comes to you."

I let out a chuckle. Carter Hills was the definition of a country music superstar himself. He'd been at the top of the charts for a decade, first with his band, Carter Hills Band, then as a solo artist after they parted ways. He had stopped going on big world tours a while back, but still, every time he released a new song, it shot to the top and stayed there until the next one came out. He was the epitome of success in our business.

"Having jitters?"

"A little. It's weird being back. Feels like a dream. It's hard to explain."

"Yeah. Been there. After the band split, when I forfeited the idea of a solo career at first." He let out a breathy laugh. "You'll be all right. Ry can be pretty convincing when he puts his mind to something. Don't worry. Once you step on that stage again, it will feel like you never left," he said, clapping my shoulder. "The future is yours, Stevens. I've heard your new stuff. Some of it, at least. I'm telling you, *The Legend* is back."

"Thanks, man," I said as we both exited the room, and people rushed to pull me away.

Carter flashed me a knowing grin and shrugged before disappearing into the crowd.

Riley said a few words before I walked onstage, holding my guitar. The crowd cheered, and I blinked to keep my fizzy emotions at bay. I'd missed this so much. The music. The energy. The thrill. Every part of it.

The memory of Madison and me singing on a small stage a while back flashed before my eyes. I wished she could be here tonight to witness the fact that I was chasing my dreams once again.

For my own sake—and to keep my sanity intact—I blinked again and pushed the images of her away.

"Guys, thanks for coming tonight. It means a whole lot to me. For the longest time, I thought I'd never stand on a stage again. Thanks to Riley 'Stubborn' Burns—yeah, that should be his middle name—I'm back where I'm supposed to be. Thank you, man. For believing in me and saving me from myself. For being my friend when I got lost. And for kicking my ass when I was being ridiculous. Thanks for giving me the chance to show my kids to never settle for anything less than what they desire. I'll never be able to fully show you my appreciation, but I'll say this: You've made me believe in dreams again. You've made me believe in myself again." I scratched the skin between my eyebrows and cleared my throat as beads of emotion lodged in there. "*Echoes* is a collection of fourteen songs I wrote about the last two years of my life. All y'all, please be indulgent tonight. I'm kinda rusty," I added with a wink. Everyone laughed. And the tension in my upper back dissolved. I strapped the guitar around my neck and breathed out all my angst. "Here we go," I said, strumming the first chord of "Broken Heart."

Ecstasy coursed through my veins.

My heart bounced, lighter than it'd been in years.

Electricity tickled my spine.

I played for an hour, but it felt like ten minutes. I could've done this all night. Every night. Sing and play the guitar.

"Ohmygod, that was insane," Devon said when I met my friends near the crowded bar area some time later. "I can't believe I didn't remember how incredible you were onstage. Sam, you have a God-gifted talent. Yours was the first show I attended in my life years ago, and now I also got to witness your big return. Never hide your music for that long ever again."

I leaned forward to kiss her cheek. "Thanks, Dev. It means a lot to me."

I blew out a breath now that I was out of the spotlight and slowly realizing what had happened tonight. The work from the last few months had paid off and the tour hadn't even started yet.

"How are you doing?" She squeezed my forearm, bringing my attention back to the present.

"Great. Much better."

"And with Maddie?" she asked with a quirked brow and a soft smile.

"What about Maddie?" I asked, my voice stilted and all my muscles strained.

"I just wanted to know if she's ready for the big tour."

I relaxed a little.

"Is there something I'm missing here?" she asked.

I tensed back. This wasn't the time or the place to lose it, so I forced a gulp of air in. "No. We're fine. She's fine. The girls love her. I'm glad she agreed to this," I said, gesturing to the space around with my hand.

"Great, then." She winked, and confusion stirred inside me.

What did she mean by that? A music producer neared us, and I pushed the awkwardness of our talk away. For now.

Aisha and Gavin congratulated me next. Then April. And a bunch of people from the industry I hadn't seen in ages.

I left around midnight, the longing to be on my own strong. Most of my friends were going to Carter's place in town for an after-launch party, but I had declined. I still required some time to adjust to this new pace of life. Baby steps here. After all, I had been hibernating for a long time.

I was confident I'd get there. Eventually.

All night, my thoughts had been drifting to my girls. I missed them tonight. I wished they were a little bit older and that I could have shared this moment, my big return to the music scene, with them. Then my thoughts traveled to Madison. Again. I was sure she would've liked it tonight too. Every time we met with my friends, she fit right in, and they all loved her. This was a more appropriate scene for a twenty-one-year-old than staying at home with young kids.

Since when did her presence in our lives become complicated instead of facilitating my existence? I was off my game on so many levels these days. I sighed and climbed into my SUV after saying my goodbyes.

And now, even the idea of going home felt conflicting. Could we really make it work—the two of us living under the same roof—or was I feeding myself lies to feel better about our situation? I would find out soon enough. I didn't have it in me to face the truth just yet, and still, I couldn't hide either. Was convincing her to move in really the right thing to do? My feelings and thoughts were tangled together, and nothing seemed straightforward anymore. I couldn't decide the right course of action. God, what had I gotten myself into? Had I complicated our situation even more by convincing her to come live with us?

Chapter 20

Madison

Sam had left earlier for his album launch party, and here I was, baking cookies with his children in his kitchen when all I yearned for was to be by his side. Like, *by his side*. I didn't care if he was rich and famous or poor and unknown, I loved how I felt beside him. As much as I told myself this was a dead end, I still couldn't put my feelings aside. Walk away from them. Forget about them.

The other night, he had sung us one of his old songs while we roasted s'mores over a campfire in the backyard, and the entire time, his gaze had rested on me as if he was delivering those lyrics straight to my soul—with a purpose.

Most days, the mutual decision not to be together still upset me. My head knew it was for the best, but it didn't change the fact I'd fallen in love with my boss.

Jacob was right. For a moment, I felt selfish for not choosing him. For not choosing the man who was allowed to love me back, without restraint, without holding anything back.

"You all right?" Mikaella asked.

The girls were perched on kitchen stools on either side of me, perfecting their cookie decoration techniques with rainbow sprinkles and edible glitter.

"Yeah. Sure. Why?"

She snickered. "Because you're icing the countertop instead of the cookies."

"Oops. Got lost in my thoughts for a minute."

"You're funny," Justine said. "And your face is all red."

I blinked. *Yeah, having forbidden thoughts about your daddy can do that to me.*

Fantasizing about the girls' father while I was here caring for them was wrong.

Around seven-thirty, I put the girls to bed, and Justine fell into a deep slumber as I combed her hair with my fingers, humming one of Sam's songs.

"Do you know my mama?" Mikaella asked when I was about to tiptoe out of the room, thinking they were both deep asleep.

I froze in the doorway. The girl rarely opened up about her mother. With a step back, I returned to the bedroom and sat on the edge of her bed, taking her tiny hands between mine. "No, honey. I've never met her. I'm sure she's very beautiful."

She twisted her upper body to fish something out of her nightstand. A picture folded in two. She stared at it for a moment before handing it to me. It was a shot of her as a baby, nestled in her mother's arms, who smiled at the camera. I didn't have one of those. A wave of bittersweet regret swept through me. I owned no pictures of me as a baby. Or a toddler. Something my parents didn't think mattered when Emily and I were little. To them at least.

But it did to me. I possessed too many from my older years, but none of the tiny version of me.

"I was right. She's pretty. You look very much like her."

Mikaella scooted closer and rested her head on my lap.

My fingers tangled in her curls. "It's okay to miss her, you know. My mama lives in another state, and I miss her too. I'm lucky I have my big sister around, though. She's my best friend."

"Did your mama leave you too?" she asked, her eyes clouded with an array of emotions.

A sensation I hadn't revisited in years paralyzed me. It froze my bones. Memories of my childhood resurfaced. For Mikaella's sake, I kept that part to myself. We were much more alike than I'd have ever thought. As if in some ways, these girls were living my own story, but with a different twist.

I decided to go with a distinct answer to the question she'd asked. "I moved away to attend college. I've always wanted to live in Nashville since I was little and we came to visit one day. I love everything about this city."

"My daddy used to sing in the bars downtown. He showed Justine and me around one time."

"I know. Your daddy is a great man. You're lucky to have him as a father."

"Maddie, do you think she misses us? My mama?"

My heart fragmented in my chest. I breathed out, searching for the right words. How many times did I ask myself the same question over the years? "I'm sure she does."

"So why did she leave us? Why didn't she take us with her?"

I wound my arms around her, wanting her to feel loved as she opened her wounded heart to me for the very first time. She rested her head against my chest, her tiny fingers entwined with mine.

"Sometimes people do things we don't always understand. I'm sure she had her reasons." *Or is it something we tell ourselves to lighten the pain? And to heal the scars of rejection?*

"Like she didn't love us?"

The vise around my heart clinched a bit tighter. With time, I'd come to the conclusion that people treating others badly was too often a reflection of their own fears. It wasn't about us, the ones left behind, even though we were the ones forgotten, ignored, or hurting.

"No. I bet there's a special place in her heart for you two." How many times had my parents repeated those same exact words to Emily and me growing up? Too many to count.

"And Daddy?"

I offered her a timid smile. "And your daddy too."

"Maddie? Do you think she'll come back to get us one day?"

"I don't know, honey. I hope she realizes how amazing, smart, and beautiful you and Justine are and comes visit… when she's ready."

"In my heart, I know she will. She has to. One day, she'll come back, and we'll be a family again. I'm sure Daddy misses her too."

The idea of Sam going back to the woman who had shattered his heart acted like a punch to the gut.

The clamp in my chest crushed me completely, and it pressed against my already bleeding heart, the wounds from my past hurting again.

"Can I tell you a secret?" she asked.

"Sure."

"I don't remember her a lot. That's why I keep this picture here. So I don't forget her face, because when I close my eyes, I can't see her face anymore. I tell my brain to make her appear, but it doesn't always listen to me. When I cry at night, it's because I'm not sure if I really miss her... And I wanna miss her. She's my mama. I should miss her. I should want her back and remember her face. Do you think there's something wrong with me?"

"Oh, Mika," I said, "She lives in your heart, and even if your brain can't recall her, your heart does. It forever will."

She tilted her head back to stare into my eyes. "But... Do you think it's the same for her? Like she can't remember us? Or what we look like? Do you think she has a picture of Justine and me by the side of her bed to make sure she remembers our faces?"

I dried the silent tears rolling down her cheeks, then the ones cascading down mine. "Mika, she's your mama. Even though she doesn't see you, she'll never forget you two. Of that, I'm certain. You'll always occupy a place in her heart too even if she's not around or able to visit."

"Do you miss your mama some days?"

"I do." I also wondered about the *what-ifs* sometimes, and would probably for the rest of my life. "It's okay to question things."

Mikaella and I hugged, the silence comfortably wrapping our confessions. We both injected love into each other. Our lives were much more similar than anyone could ever realize. We connected on a deeper level, and tonight had just proved it.

"It's late. You should get some sleep."

"Maddie?"

"Yes."

"Will you stay with me until I'm asleep?"

"Yes, Mika. I will."

I lay beside her.

"And Maddie? Don't leave us, okay? Stay. Forever. Please."

"I won't go away, honey. You two are stuck with me for a while." *Until the end of the tour at least,* I told myself. One day, I would have to go. I'd be the one leaving them behind. Tears coated the back of my eyes. I pressed them shut, keeping the painful sobs about to wreck my body locked inside. Someday I would abandon these little girls. And their father. Mikaella's breathing steadied, and her grip around my finger loosened. Before I burst into ugly cries, I hurried downstairs. In the garage, I rummaged through the boxes I'd stacked there earlier when I moved my stuff from my sister's house.

Before I could find what I was looking for, I dropped to the concrete floor and buried my face in my palms. My shoulders heaved as I wept. I should leave. I should leave now before I couldn't find the courage to leave at all before it was too late and we all ended up with broken hearts. I hiccupped. It was already too late. My heart belonged here, and I had no clue how to extirpate it from this house without ruining it for the rest of its existence.

Once I calmed down, I grabbed the novel written by one of my favorite authors and made my way back inside.

Making a glass of sweet tea, I sat down, desperate for any distraction.

At ten, my phone rang. I jumped at the noise and picked it up with trembling fingers when Jacob's face appeared on the screen.

A tightness squeezed my gut. My hands turned moist. I hadn't heard from him since the night I'd walked away from his car. Both times I had texted him, he never replied. I had stopped, choosing to respect his healing process.

I hesitated before answering, but my curiosity won the

battle. Moving to my feet, I grabbed a blanket before curling back up in the comfortable chair in the den.

"Hey," I greeted.

"How are you?" The faint sound of his voice shook me up.

"Jake, I… We're… What's going on?"

My skin prickled. I missed him. The way he cared for me. His kisses. The glint in his eye when he was happy. Our discussions. The hours spent with him. Our friendship. Hearing his voice sent a rush of strange sensations through me, threatening to undo me even more than I already was.

"Maddie, come back. Come back to *meee*. I love you. I miss you so damn much. I tried. I really did. But I'm miserable when *youuu're* not in my life. Please—" His voice broke. Was he crying? "Come on. Say something. I should've never let *youuu* go."

"Are you drunk?"

"Fuck, Maddie. *Donnn't* start. I might have had one drink…or too many. Who cares? It's not…it's not the point."

"I was just asking. I miss you too," I said, fighting a new batch of tears.

"I'll come to get *youuu*. Tonight. Pack your stuff. We'll be happy together. I promise. *I'mmm* so in love with you that it hurts."

"Jake, you can't drive in this state."

Sobs broke free on the other end of the line. "Maddie, I'm a mess without *youuu*. What we had…what we had was real. Why did you choose him? Why did it have to be him? I love *youuu*, okay? From the moment I first saw you. It will always be you. *Cannn't* you see it? He'll never love you the way that I do."

"Jacob. Stop." I sucked in a hissing breath. "You were

right. I love him. I'm not supposed to, and it's wrong, but I can't help it." I closed my eyes. Maybe this was the closure I required to move on. For some reason, that I refused to overanalyze, speaking the words out did not scare me as much as I thought it would. "You and I, we were good together. Our friendship was real. You made me happy. And I love you. You were my best friend. I probably will always feel something for you, but I'm not in love *with* you. That's the difference."

"How am I supposed to… How am I supposed to be okay without *youuu*?"

"You will be. We both will be. Give it more time."

He snorted. "Sorry I bothered you." He hesitated for a beat. "Are *youuu* with him right now?"

I shook my head even though he couldn't see me. "No. He has his album launch tonight. I'm watching the girls."

"Are you *fuckkking* him?"

I inhaled through my mouth. "We're not together. It's…it's complicated."

A thick silence enveloped us.

"Can I…huh…save your number?" Jacob asked in a croaky voice. "I'm not ready for a world *youuu're* not a part of."

"Yeah. I'll always be there for you. Perhaps time and space will make it easier. I miss you too. Every day. I'm sorry about everything."

Neither of us said anything.

"All I wish is for you to be *happpy*," he said after a long beat.

"I am. Or I will be… You take care of *you*, okay?"

He coughed. "Night, Maddie."

Messy emotions clogged my airways.

I pressed my palm against my chest.

Every fiber of my being hurt.

"Jacob, I want you to be happy too. Night," I said, hanging up.

Did everyone deliberately choose tonight to play with my heartstrings? First Mikaella, now him. My tears resumed, and I let them flow, hoping they would flush away my pain. I still loved him. Even though he wasn't the one. And I wasn't *in love* with him.

Mikaella's words replayed in my mind. *One day, she'll come back, and we'll be a family again. I'm sure Daddy misses her too.* Deep inside, maybe Sam shared his daughter's hopes and dreams. Maybe his nights too were haunted by the *what-ifs*, what could have been if his ex-wife hadn't walked away.

After my vision cleared and my emotions dissipated, I returned to the novel in my hand, the desire to evade my own life stronger than ever.

Chapter 21
Sam

Lost in my thoughts, with the adrenaline still coursing through me, I pulled into my driveway and exhaled. It had yet to sink in that I had a new album out—that I was back onstage. I had actually done it. The oversized grin would stay anchored to my face for days, I could already tell. I had no idea how to erase it. Anyway, why would I want to get rid of it? Happiness suited me. I realized it when I'd looked in the mirror earlier.

I snickered to myself as I climbed out of my SUV.

The light in the hallway cast a golden glow in the mostly dark house as I entered from the garage door. There wasn't a sound inside. Something that almost never happened around here.

I tiptoed to the kitchen, then to the den, wondering if Madison was already asleep. I found her curled up in a pink fluffy blanket in her favorite chair, a novel in her hands and dark-framed glasses perched on her nose.

It was a new look on her, and she looked mesmerizing.

A lazy smile spread across my lips. I could watch her for hours, and the view would never get jaded.

As if she sensed she was being observed, she lifted her eyes from her book and met my gaze. "Oh, you're back. What time it is? I thought you'd be out all night."

I wrinkled my face. "Gotta re-learn how to do this. Late night. Crowded bars. How did it go?"

"Perfect. We had a great time. Sam, your daughters are wonderful. You're doing a fantastic job with them."

"Thanks," I said, pride slicing my words. Yeah, my kids were awesome. "Tired?"

Her eyes glistened in the dim light. "Not really. Mystery novels always keep me on edge. What about you?" Something sparkled in her eyes. Conflicted emotions passed through her sea-green irises.

The tip of my tongue burned to ask her if she was all right, but I had to continue minding my own business. Every time I got sucked into her life, I had a harder time walking away or staying indifferent afterward.

"No. I still have a performance high running through my bloodstream. I can't go to bed just yet. Champagne? Riley gifted me a bottle to celebrate the last time he came over, and tonight seems fitting. It's a big deal."

"I suppose it wouldn't be polite to refuse."

Madison jumped to her feet and neared me, discarding the blanket and her glasses. Dressed in an off-shoulder white cotton shirt and light-gray sweat shorts, she looked undeniably feminine, her presence exuding a newfound sensuousness. My eyes drank her in.

Tanned legs.

Perky breasts.

Long neck.

High cheekbones.

Slender chin.

Madison was not only amazing with children, but also had a warm laugh, a great personality, and was smart beyond words. On top of that, she was gorgeous. Many of the reasons why it was so hard for me to stay away. She possessed everything I was a sucker for. For a second, I remembered how it felt to kiss her. To touch her skin. To lose myself in the comfort she brought me. Even after all this time, the memory hadn't faded away. The replay of it had become my personal hell on Earth.

My eyes lingered on her chest for a split second, wondering if she was wearing a bra. I shook my head. *Repeat after me, Sam. The nanny is off-limits. The nanny is off-limits. The nanny is off-limits.*

She sat on a stool, and I snapped out of it.

With half a spin, I grabbed the bubbly alcohol from the fridge and two flutes. I popped the bottle open, and Madison clapped her hands before her.

"Ohmygod, you should be proud of yourself. I know the girls are. You've come a long way in the last few months. I've witnessed the change. You've earned the right to celebrate. Earlier, the girls and I baked congratulatory cookies. You'll get them in the morning."

I flashed her a smile as I poured two glasses and offered her one. We clinked our flutes.

"That's so nice of you, Maddie. I'm glad you're here. Really."

She mirrored my smile.

We sat beside each other at the kitchen island and drank in silence. I relaxed a tad, unbuttoning the top buttons of my shirt.

Madison cleared her throat. "Mika told me about her mama tonight. The parts she remembers at least."

I blinked, making sure I heard her right. My throat closed. I took another sip, trying to drown the queasiness simmering inside me. "She did?"

My daughter had never talked to anyone about her mama leaving us. Up until now, she had never discussed Lisa with Madison, and barely with her therapist. She usually just made up stories in her mind that her mother was on a trip and would come back eventually.

Madison bowed her head. "She told me Lisa would be back one day. She really believes it. Since I didn't know all the details, I had no idea what to tell her."

"Lisa left when Mika was four." The words flew out of my mouth before I could lock them inside.

"You don't have to tell me," Madison said, interrupting me.

I chugged the rest of my champagne and poured myself another glass.

"Sorry I brought the topic up. I'm putting a dent in your celebration."

"It's fine. I have to tell you eventually anyway. Better now than later." I pushed my emotions away. The thought of Lisa, even after all this time, re-opened the wound I'd been trying to heal for a very long time. Not that I missed her. No, I'd realized much earlier that our relationship was a product of my imagination, and nothing about it had been real for a while. But the hurt she had caused our children, that was unforgivable. And that no matter however much I tried, I'd never be able to justify their mother's actions to them. "Mika saw her mama walking away that night. She was there when Lisa left without an explanation." My composure cracked. "She didn't even kiss her own kids goodbye. Mika stood there, and Lisa left without having second thoughts. My little girl should've never had to witness that. It's not fair to her." My voice broke on the last word.

Madison squeezed my hand, her warm touch sending waves of lust through me. Her skin on mine was enough to kill my demons and heal my insecurities. I was so damn screwed when it came to her. All the progress I had made in the last couple of weeks to grow a wall around my heart when she was involved was crumbling, brick by brick.

I craved her as much as I knew I had no right to yearn for her.

"Life, when I was super young, wasn't easy. For the first few years of my childhood, Emily and I…" Her lips quivered, and her eyes took on a glossy sheen, barely suppressing the tears building in them. Vulnerability swamped her face, and her gaze fleeted away before returning to mine. "We were…neglected."

I straightened, the confession surprising me. "What? What do you mean, *you were neglected?*"

Madison shook her head as if to erase a memory. "Let's just say our mother wasn't a fit parent. Neither was our father. And we suffered…a lot. Then it got better. It's all good now. We're super-knitted the four of us."

"I'm sorry. It's not what being a parent means. No kid should feel like a burden."

"There are a lot of unfit parents out there. Let's just say I have some experience with being left behind," she said. "I'm sorry Mika had to witness her mama quitting on you guys." She swallowed and averted her eyes.

I flipped my hand over and threaded our fingers, the simple gesture meaningful to me and meant to soothe the pain I saw in her gaze.

My breaths evened.

The storm in me lessened.

Knots around my heart slackened.

Madison freed her hand, and I felt the withdrawal of her skin against mine. "Sorry. I didn't mean to overshare," she said, avoiding my eyes.

"It's okay. I'm aware you're just trying to be my friend." I swallowed the rock forming in my larynx. What was it about her touch that soothed me so much? Would any other woman's hands on me feel the same? I was so out of the game. "Did Justine give you any trouble at bedtime?" I asked, trying to put the weird moment behind us.

Madison's smile came back. It lightened her face, made her irises greener. "No. We listened to one of your new songs five times and sang along. Then she fell asleep within a minute. Mika and I talked for a bit, then she was out cold right after."

I tilted my head, meeting her eyes. "You sang one of my songs on your own?"

"Yeah. The girls and I often do that… Well, huh… sometimes…at bedtime."

A pink flush tinted her cheeks. I arched a brow, and Madison wrinkled her face.

I wished I could be the one erasing the crease etching her forehead with my lips. Instead, I ended up doing the same thing she had done a moment earlier—grabbing her hand in mine and giving it a squeeze. The warmth I'd felt rushed through me once again and twined around my vital organs. "Sorry," I said, pulling my hand back into my lap. "We should get some sleep. Devon and Riley will pick up the girls tomorrow morning, so you'll have the entire day to settle in."

"Okay. Great. Thanks." She busied herself, twirling the glass between her fingers.

I rose from my stool and turned around to look at the

object of my forbidden attraction one last time."Good night."

"Night, Sam."

An hour later, still wide awake, I lay in my bed, unable to chase sleep. My whole night replayed in my head. It had been surreal to be onstage again after a two-year hiatus. Every time the small crowd had cheered me on, it repaired the pieces of my heart and the shambles of my confidence back together.

I was born to be on a stage.

I was wrong when I'd pushed music away from my life for so long. Perhaps this break was all I needed to heal and get back to it with a stronger passion. My mind drifted to Madison sleeping downstairs. I shouldn't think about her. Not in that way. But somehow, I couldn't erase the images of her from my mind. The taste of her lips on mine. The feeling of the swell of her breasts under my palms. No matter how hard I tried to push it away, the memory always came back. In full force. Like a fucking boomerang.

Her legs, her ass in those shorts, her tits bouncing under her shirt when she laughed, her lips as she told me about her night. Having a woman too close to me when I'd been alone for two years was dangerous. Why didn't I figure this out sooner?

We already agreed we wouldn't go there. Why was my heart, and every cell of my body, not on board with the plan? Why was a piece of me still hoping things could be different between us?

The magnetism of Madison's smile always drew me in. Every time. From our first encounter. That night, in Riley's cousin's office, I hadn't been just mad because I thought she was too young to take care of my children. No, I'd freaked out at how much I was attracted to her. Big time. The moment I laid my eyes on her, it was like I was seeing a woman for the first time in forever. As if love had no bounds. No limits. As if she could shatter every wall I put around myself after Lisa quit on us only by smiling at me.

As if my entire body had recognized her as mine and she knew the secret combination to my happiness. The missing piece of the perfect puzzle that my heart was. The salvation of my soul.

After all this time, it still made no sense to me, but it did at the same time.

Madison was the means to my end, the treasure to my quest on this journey, and yet, I couldn't indulge in everything brewing between us. I was forced to keep her at a distance, to guard my heart against her. To push her away when all I yearned for was to love and protect her. With my whole being. Here, now, and for the rest of my life.

Or maybe my fantasies were doing all the talking.

My ignored-for-too-long hormones were acting out, demanding to be satiated.

As if he could read my mind, the lower part of me hardened in my boxer briefs.

Fucking traitor.

She's the nanny. She's the nanny. She's the nanny.

How many times would I have to repeat this until my penis got the message? Until he resigned and went back to its state of hibernation?

As the traitor he was, it pulsed and thickened instead of lying low.

With a sharp gulp of oxygen and promising myself to never go there ever again, I curled my fist around the hard part of me and pumped myself, enjoying the feeling and the anticipation of the high it would procure me.

The simple gesture didn't calm my screaming hormones. Instead, my dick pleaded for more, relishing the attention. Pushing all my troubling thoughts as far as possible, I worked myself faster. I couldn't stop. I would never be able to stop. I longed for more. A lot more. I wanted it all. The family, the love story, the career. The woman. Her lips, her ass, her tits, her mouth. Her heart.

Would she let me in if I knocked on her bedroom door? Inviting me in and pushing me onto her bed.

Would she kiss me back like she did that night? Like I was her only source of fresh air?

Would she take me into her mouth and make me forget that life before her had ever existed?

Would she let me taste her until all my senses were soothed? Devouring every morsel of her flesh until all that was left was the taste of her on my tongue?

Images of Madison in her red dress when I'd first met her swam in my head. Images of her curled in the chair tonight when I'd gotten home, sporting glasses, swirled around. The pink hue of her sinful lips. The crests of her hipbones. That little bracelet around her sexy ankle. When had I even become obsessed with ankles? The way she pushed her hair over her shoulder when we talked. Her enticing smile aimed at me—only me. The compassion in her eyes. The feel of her soft skin under the pads of my fingers when our hands joined. The way we connected, that appeared so easy, so natural. The sizzling chemistry we shared. Her ability to get me to open up about my past. And my fears. The glint in her gaze when she looked at me and thought I didn't notice. The smile she couldn't contain every time I showed joy and elation in her presence. Her laughter. Intoxicating and mesmerizing.

I stroked myself faster.

I felt the feather touch of her skin on mine again.

I heard the sound of her voice in my head. Her laughter. Her whispers.

No, I shouldn't think about her like that. She was living here. In my house. Taking care of my daughters.

She'd live on a tour bus with us. For months. I tried to put a stop to my imminent release but couldn't. The scent of her perfume filled my nostrils.

"Fuck," I grumbled.

I flipped the covers over, overheating in my bed.

The tip of my spine tingled.

This felt so good. Risky, but addictive.

My erection throbbed.

This was bad. But bad was hot. Bad was sexy. Bad was forbidden. Madison was forbidden. Our relationship was. Our friendship should be too. It put my sanity at risk.

Air rushed out of my mouth.

My toes curled.

I bit my biceps as I came, stronger than I had in a long time, swallowing the deep growls about to tumble out and fill the silence of the night.

My fantasies hadn't been this real in forever.

Breathless, I stayed there, my hand still around my grateful length, feeling the warmth of my release spilled across my stomach.

I inhaled. And exhaled. Trying to bring my pulse back to normal.

Impossible.

Madison occupied all my thoughts. Kissing her that night had been a rookie mistake. The flashbacks haunted my nights. Would I ever get relief from the ache?

My entire house smelled of her, her perfume permeating every corner. Right now, it was stronger. I could almost taste it. It enveloped me. It quieted the voices in my head.

I could feel her. In every room.

Her energy. Her cheerfulness.

I reclined, eyeing my mid-section covered with the aftermath of my orgasm.

A smile peeked out. Feeling alive had never felt so good. Almost too good. The real thing would ruin me. It would destroy me. In six months, I would be a free man.

Once I agreed with myself, and my traitorous dick, that this little mishap could never happen again, I cleaned myself up, rolled to my side, and closed my eyes, hoping sleep would come and turn my mind off for a few hours.

And deliver me from my own prison.

To be continued in **Rising Star**...
(book two in the *Lonesome Heart* duet)

emmanuellesnow.com/products/rising-star

ABOUT THE AUTHOR

Soulfully Beautiful Love Stories

USA Today Bestselling Author Emmanuelle Snow is an author of contemporary YA and women's fiction love stories, who gives life to strong characters who'll fight with all they have to reach their life goals and find their own happiness. She loves her characters to be relatable and realistic.

Emmanuelle is in love with love. Especially complicated, deep, and passionate feelings that make a relationship extraordinary and complex all at the same time.

In her spare time, when she's not writing or reading, she likes to go on road trips—with her four kids and her own soulmate—watch movies, paint, or do some DIY, always with a cup of green tea in her hand and listening to country music.

She splits her time between beautiful Canada and the small US towns she adores.

Find all of Emmanuelle's books here:

emmanuellesnow.com

———

Want to connect with Emmanuelle online?
YOU CAN FIND HER HERE:

Website
Author's bookstore and merch store

Snow's VIP newsletter
emmanuellesnow.com

Readers' VIP group Snow's Soulmates
facebook.com/groups/snowvip

amazon.com/author/emmanuellesnow

goodreads.com/emmanuellesnow

bookbub.com/authors/emmanuelle-snow

facebook.com/esnowauthor

instagram.com/snowemmanuelle

x.com/snowemmanuelle

pinterest.com/snowemmanuelle

tiktok.com/@snowemmanuelle

ALSO BY THE AUTHOR

CARTER HILLS BAND UNIVERSE

(suggested reading order)

Carter Hills Band series

False Promises

HEART SONG DUET

Blindsided

Forevermore

Whiskey Melody series

Sweet Agony

SECOND TEAR DUET

Cruel Destiny

Beautiful Salvation

BREATHLESS DUET

Wild Encounter

Brittle Scars

Upon A Star Series

Last Hope

Midnight Sparks

Love Song For Two Series

LONESOME HEART DUET

Fallen Legend

Rising Star

TWO OF US DUET

Snowbound

Wicked Love

MEDORA BEACH UNIVERSE

Wrecked series

Cast Away

Ride for a Fall

Touchdown series

Kickoff

Read them all

emmanuellesnow.com

All available on author's bookshop